I0675909

Shadows II

The Half Life

Graham Brown
and
Spencer J. Andrews

Stealth Books

Blue Lotus Publishing

The Half Life

ISBN: 978-1-939398-40-6

Cover design by Kit Foster

Also by Graham Brown & Spencer J. Andrews

Shadows of the Midnight Sun

The first instalment of the epic Shadows trilogy.

"…surges alone, effectively putting the reader on the raw edge of chaos…" – Webbweaver Reviews

The Gods of War

In 2137 the world is dying. Mars is humanity's only hope. But war has already found the red planet.

"…epic military science fiction at its gritty, page turning best." – Jeff Edwards, award winning author of _Sword of Shiva_

Prologue: The Dark Stone of Power

Arabian Peninsula, 1186 A.D.

The morning sky burned red as blood, as if a great fire raged in the heavens. Far below, on a long forgotten corner of the earth, a group of men on horseback thundered across the tawny sands of an enormous desert. They carried shields adorned with the Cross and a banner blessed by the church, but they were far removed from their appointed route, far from the Crusade in the Holy Land.

Richard of Wessex rode at the head of the procession atop a magnificent steed. Fifty had set out from the court, but only the most hardy had survived.

Richard's second, a man named Thaddeus, rode up to him. "The morning air is cool, but the sun will soon take its toll. We should find shelter and we should find it soon."

The small force had been riding at night to avoid the blistering heat of the day, but the prize and their destination loomed just over the horizon.

"Look around you," Richard said. "There's nowhere to rest, no shade for miles. Not until we reach the ruins. Even if there were some place to take cover, I wouldn't stop now. Not this close to our destination."

Thaddeus knew better than to argue. He knew Richard's mind well; he knew the obsession that drove his master. During their first journey to the Holy Land, Richard had become interested in the history of the ancients. In return for sparing the life of a Moorish historian, he'd been given an ancient scroll. The writing dated to an era when even the Pharaohs were just a whisper on the distant horizon of time. Its contents were written in a forgotten language and Richard spent nearly a year searching for someone who could read it.

In the end, he found a rabbi of the most ancient sect. After reading the parchment, the rabbi tried to destroy it. Only under the pain of torture did this teacher reveal its secrets. It described a weapon of unlimited power, a weapon even the angels of God feared, a weapon known as the Dark Star. This device had been hidden in a canyon beyond the reaches of man, centuries before Moses walked the Earth.

"The ruins had better be near," Thaddeus said. "We're running low on water. The horses will soon drop from the heat. We should have taken camels like those the nomads ride."

"Disgusting animals," Richard said.

"Disgusting, yes, but far more suited to this place," Thaddeus replied. "If we don't find the ruins soon—and water with them—the sun will bleach our bones for a thousand years to come."

Richard nodded. Privately he worried that Thaddeus might be right. He'd left the rabbi under guard with orders that he and his family should be protected until the knights returned, and killed after sufficient torture if they did not come back in six months' time. He'd considered this warning adequate protection against some trick, but the deeper his band went into the searing desert, the fewer of them survived and the more Richard wondered if the rabbi had sent them to their deaths despite the threat that loomed over him.

So far the journey had been arduous, worse even than predicted. The sun and the heat were conquered by moving at night. But there were no landmarks along the way. Only sand dunes that towered hundreds of feet above them and moved slowly but constantly as if they were alive. For three nights they'd been unable to see the stars that led them because of a dust storm. And for two days they'd hidden from a swarm of locusts so large it blotted out the sky. A dozen men and horses had died after drinking from a poisoned well. Others had vanished in the night as if swept away by the wind.

But eventually they'd reached a pristine oasis shaped like the tip of a spear. This landmark, promised by the scroll, pointed them in the final direction. Two days after that, they'd come to the dry lakebed, the heat on its surface shimmering like a mirage in the sun.

If they could finish the crossing, make it to the hidden temple and retrieve the weapon, they would return to the Holy Land carrying a power that none could resist. Not the other knights or the lords of Europe, not the Jews, or the Muslims. Not even Saladin himself would stand before them.

"Faster," Richard commanded. "Faster."

As the heat of the day grew, the small party left the flat sands of the dry lakebed and reached the base of a canyon where another spring flowed. A trickle of dark water ran through the canyon. Palm trees and flowering plants grew around it. The horses drank and men filled their canteens amid colors and smells vastly different than the dust and sweat of the desert.

They moved forward in the shade of the canyon walls. Near the far end of the box canyon at the foot of a great cliff, they found the crumbled ruins of what had once been a stronghold. There was no sign of occupants and no clue as to who'd built it. The trickle of water ran down the cliff behind it and past the foot of the ancient stone.

"Tie the horses here," Richard said. "We'll approach the gates on foot."

"Is that wise?" Thaddeus asked. "On foot we'll be vulnerable."

"A great power is hidden within," Richard said. "More than any army of men could ever command. If an adversary waits for us here, it will matter little if we ride or walk to our doom."

The horsemen dismounted, and when their movement stopped, not a sound could be heard, not even the buzz of a single insect. No attack came. No spears or arrows from on high.

"It seems we're alone," Thaddeus noted.

"Still we must be careful," Richard said. "Who knows what treachery lies behind these walls. Leave two men to guard the horses. The rest shall come with us."

Richard stepped to the door as Thaddeus relayed his orders. With a shove from his gauntlet-covered palms, he pushed the doors wide, allowing light to spill into the chamber for the first time in centuries.

In a moment they were walking with torches burning. Carvings on the wall seemed to hold ancient Hebrew writing along with other hieroglyphic symbols that seemed vaguely familiar, though neither Richard nor any of his men could place them.

"We should have brought the old rabbi along," Thaddeus lamented.

"He would not have survived the journey," Richard said.

"Will we?"

At the far end of the room, stone steps led downward in a narrowing tunnel.

"The steps are swept clean," Thaddeus noted.

Richard lowered his torch. "So they are. Perhaps this place is not abandoned after all." He pulled his sword from its sheath. "Be ready," he ordered. "Just in case."

At the base of the stairway lay a narrow room. The ceiling of the chamber was low and rocky. The air was stale.

"This must have been a mine at one point," Thaddeus said. "I wonder what they dug from here."

Richard had no answer and no interest in pondering the question. All his thoughts were focused on the prize. He strode forward, the musty smell of water swirling around him though there was none to be seen.

On the far side of the chamber, four tunnels branched off in different directions. If Richard was right, they'd delved into the heart of the mountain behind the structure."

"We have a choice," Richard noted.

"The rabbi said we would choose our own doom," Thaddeus said, "like Pharaoh, selecting the final plague of God's wrath."

Richard paused. Only God knew what waited for them down there. Traps at the least. Or perhaps the system was so vast and confusing that once entered no man would ever find his way out, like the Minotaur's labyrinth of Greek mythology.

"Do we spilt up?" Thaddeus asked.

Richard hesitated. There were so few of them and yet… "Yes. Divide up. Two into each tunnel," he said. "Thaddeus and I will search the far left tunnel. Do not be afraid. We wouldn't be here if it were not God's will."

The men nodded and slipped into the gaping mouths of each passageway. As the glow of their fires diminished, Richard hung his own torch on an iron hook that sprouted from the wall. "To mark our way back," he said.

He and Thaddeus entered the last tunnel. They encountered little on their journey until they'd traveled at least a hundred yards.

"Cover your torch," Richard said. "But don't put it out."

Cautiously, Thaddeus blocked the light of the torch with a cap. As their eyes adjusted to the darkness, a small pinpoint of light could be seen at the far end of the tunnel. It shone like a star in the night sky. Richard became aware of a feeling inside of him, a surge of energy that woke all of his senses. It drew him forward, and Thaddeus followed.

The hand carved tunnel became tighter and tighter as they approached the distant light. Richard was aware that they were now moving uphill. They passed through a small archway and entered a large chamber.

In the center, sat a golden chest. It was polished to a blinding glare. A pinpoint of light illuminated it from above—from a hole drilled through to the surface perhaps. The light seemed to play on it in a strange fashion, like the reflection from a mirror or from the surface of a pool. The walls around them were covered with carved hieroglyphs of a style Richard had never seen. "The language of the angels," he whispered in reverence.

Thaddeus was not listening. His eyes were fixed on the golden chest. "We shall be kings in our own right," he declared. He rushed forward, reached up, and pulled the heavy chest from its resting place.

"Wait!" Richard shouted.

The warning came too late. As soon as Thaddeus pulled the chest free, the sound of heavy stones moving was heard. A torrent of water came gushing into the chamber from sluices on all sides. The flood cut Thaddeus's legs out from under him and he fell back, the heavy chest pinning him to the ground.

Richard was also knocked backward, but he grabbed onto the archway and used it to brace himself. As the water level rose, a pair of heavy stone slabs began to close the portal behind them. For now, the water poured through the gap though its level was growing higher and higher. Once the two jaws met, the chamber would fill rapidly and both men would quickly drown.

Richard's first thought was to run, but something commanded him to stay. He pushed forward, battling against the swirling water. He reached for the chest and tried to lift it, but it was too heavy. *Perhaps it was solid gold as the old scroll had claimed.*

Beneath it Thaddeus struggled, but Richard had forgotten him. His mind thought only of the prize and his own glory. He pulled his dagger and tried to pry open the chest, but the blade snapped off like a piece of dead wood.

Time was running out. The water had reached Sir Richard's waist. The doors behind were halfway closed. He pulled his sword, raised it high, and with a mighty swing cut the lock from the front of the chest. It opened as if on command, and Richard grabbed the satchel that lay within.

Turning, he waded for the closing doors. Lunging at the last, he was swept through the gap by the force of the water now funneling between them. He went under and was thrust forward, pushed on by the torrent now pouring down the long tunnel. He tumbled like a man caught in the rapids of a wild river. Some corner of his mind realized the sloped tunnel was part of a drainage system for the trap. A way to use the trap and reset it once its victims had drowned. But having escaped the drowning chamber, the rushing water became Richard's mode of propulsion.

Down the incline he went, banging the walls and floor, carried on until he was spat out into the *'room of the choice'* where the four tunnels branched off. The water swirled deeply here, and Richard sank to the bottom, dragged down by the heavy chain mail he wore. He was saved only by the water level dropping as it poured through large drains on either side, disappearing into some deeper part of the mine.

Disoriented, half drowned and soaked to the bone, Richard still gripped the satchel with all his might. The flow of water was already decreasing. Once the doors at the far end came together, it dwindled to a trickle.

Spitting water and heaving violently, Richard tried to catch his breath. In between bouts of coughing, he shouted for his other knights. He yelled until his voice was hoarse, but all that came back was the echo of his own panicked words.

Finally, he saw a flicker of orange coming towards him from deep within one of the tunnels. It continued to approach and then suddenly was snuffed out. A scream that ended with a dull thud reached him.

At this, his nerves failed. He ran for the stairs and charged upward. He had to get out. Even if he was alone. He stumbled and fell and continued to climb with maximum haste. Finally, he reached the great room above and the light streaming though the rotted wooden doors.

He ran for them, shivering and winded, until he burst through the enormous doors and into the blinding sunshine once again. There, he collapsed down onto the warm sand.

Looking up, he froze, as if a cold wind had blown through him. The last of his knights, left behind to guard the horses, lay dead, their bodies shot through with arrows. Standing around them were fifty men shrouded in Bedouin garb, curved swords drawn, faces covered except for their eyes.

They did not move. They did not speak. They just stared at him.

Richard's hand went for his sword, but it was gone, used to gain the prize he now held in his hands.

He reached into the satchel and pulled the weapon out. It was a flail made of dark and strange material. Spikes on the end seemed to catch the light and extinguish it. And it appeared to cast a shadow as he swung it through the air.

The chain from the handle was heavy and thick, the grip cold steel, mated with ivory. It was covered in writing similar to what they'd found on the walls in the chamber.

The eyes of the Bedouin were drawn to it, and Richard felt his own mind turn toward the weapon. He could see his reflection in the dull shine of the spiked ball. It was beautiful, fearsome and it filled him with power and rage.

Sir Richard turned to his opponents ready to destroy them with this weapon, but the instant he moved three arrows struck him in the back surging through his chain mail and out through his chest.

He dropped to his knees, releasing the weapon in the process.

Fighting to draw oxygen into his punctured lungs, Sir Richard gazed upon the faces of his adversaries. He saw no hostility. Only a sternness that brought to mind a sense of duty and a trace of pity.

"You should have gone back when we poisoned the drinking well," the closest of them said. His skin was weathered like animal hide; his eyes were sunken but he was not old.

Richard could not respond. There was no breath to move his tongue. He lay there, his death an imminent certainty, his eyes on the trail of his own blood. But instead of soaking into the porous ground, the red liquid was trickling across the powdery sand. It traveled like quicksilver in an alchemist's tray, glistening bright red in the sun as it moved uphill, against the slope of the ground and toward the weapon from the subterranean cavern.

Despite his pain, Richard was mesmerized. He stretched his hand toward the translucent black rock at the end of the flail and watched as his blood was absorbed into the spiked weapon itself.

His mind whirled even as his eyes began to fail. "What darkness is this," he whispered.

The leader of the nomads threw a cloth over the weapon, covering it like one might cover a deadly snake. "Yes," he said. "What darkness indeed."

.

Chapter 1

A flicker of light glinted from the edge of a steel blade as it slashed through the night. Instead of its target the blade found a wall of stone, blasting splinters of the rock outward in a cascade of sparks that lit up the dark labyrinth.

The intended victim moved back with surprising agility. Surprising because the eyes peering from beneath the hooded cloak were jaundiced and yellow. The face was old and weathered, the shoulders weak and hunched.

Christian Hannover paused before continuing the attack. Drakos— the Snake—the King of the Undead—all but cowered before him. For a thousand years, Christian had feared him and, at times, fought him. For almost as long before that, Christian and Drakos, who now went by Drake, had been allies if not friends. At the very least they'd been travelers on the same path. A path, Christian reminded himself, that Drake had lured him onto.

Christian stepped forward, determined to finish the war. He brought the shimmering blade down toward Drake's skull, but missed once again. Drake slipped away, spinning and slamming an iron gate behind him. Christian crashed into the gate but it held tight. He was sealed in. Trapped.

Laughter echoed down the dark corridor, as if this had been Drake's plan all along.

But Christian was not without strength. With a mighty kick, he blasted the barred gate from its hinges and sent it flying across the stone floor. He charged down the tunnel only to have another gate slam and then another and one more.

Breaking through these, he continued on until the ground shifted and the stone walls moved together. Now he was caught in a box of granite.

Sickening laughter came again from the other side of the wall.

"When will you learn?" Drake mocked. "You will never defeat me. You have only the strength that I chose to give you. This, you cannot break me with."

"Don't fool yourself," Christian called back. "I have more strength than you guess. No wall you build can keep me out."

With a surge of adrenaline he could scarcely control, Christian slammed into the granite wall with his shoulder. Cracks appeared in the mortar and several of the stones moved. Dust puffed from the gaps like dragon's breath.

Seeing this, Drake's laughter died and Christian charged once more, crashing through the blocks, smashing them outward like a battering ram.

Drake stood in surprise. In awe. *In fear.* He turned, ran, and leapt over a chasm, dropping to a lower level of the dungeon and racing into one of the tunnels that led deeper into the catacombs.

Christian raced to the edge intending to follow.

"Wait," a voice called.

He stopped and turned. A woman in a shimmering gray dress was standing on another level. Light spilled from a door behind her.

"Elsa?"

Elsa was dead, long gone from this world. Was this another trick of Drake's to delay him? Or was she real?

"Why are you here?" he shouted.

"I'm here to help you," she said, calmly. "Follow me."

"You shouldn't be here. He'll harm you again."

"He can't hurt me anymore," she said.

"He'll use you against me," Christian shouted. "To break my will."

"Your will is your own," she corrected. "But you need to be shown the path. Follow me."

He was confused, furious. "I don't need your help anymore. I know the path. It leads to Drake and to the end of all this misery. Now leave!"

The light vanished and Elsa with it. Christian regretted it instantly. But he didn't hesitate. Not now. Not after all this time.

He leapt into the chasm, landed on the lower level and began to run. The tunnels divided and twisted back on themselves. Dead ends turned him around and burning torches blew out in rapid succession, as if a living wind had raced by them in the dark.

Christian continued forward, but at each turn he became more lost. He saw shadows in the dark. Priests. Angels. Demons. Enemies and friends and those who straddled both lines. He was losing Drake. Losing the race.

He charged forward, running faster and faster, until suddenly the ground was gone from beneath him and he was falling.

He fell through the darkness and woke up at his kitchen table with a visible jolt.

"Are you alright?" a kindly voice asked from across the table.

The words came from a frail looking woman in a wheelchair. Ida Washington, a Professor at Columbia University and Christian's only living friend. Ida's brown eyes exuded a warmth he could scarcely remember. Her skin was like caramel with a few freckles and age spots thrown in. Her black hair had the slightest touch of gray. And her spirit was unbreakable. At times he wished his own spirit was as strong.

"I think I was dreaming," he said.

She cocked her head to the side. "I thought you told me, *your kind* don't sleep?"

Your kind. What else could she call him? The Fallen. The Undead. The Nosferatu. Christian was one of lost souls who'd become trapped in the void between worlds, neither truly alive nor dead. Unfeeling in many ways, but driven on by the only emotions left to them: pain, envy and fear. They did not age, and though the few humans who knew of their existence sometimes called them immortal, that was a misnomer. They could die. In fact, most of them did, either at their own hand or the hand of the Church.

"We don't sleep," he said. "I'm not sure what just happened."

A wry grin curled across her face. "You don't have to pretend, Sonny. Students fall asleep in my class all the time. I try not to laugh when their heads clunk on the desktops. Apparently, I'm not the thrilling speaker I used to be."

Christian smiled; another thing *his kind* wasn't known to do. At least not with warmth and feeling. "It's the journal," he said, nodding toward an ancient book on the table in front of them. "It's putting me to sleep."

The *Journal of Hunters* had come into his possession through a priest he'd met in New Orleans. A man who'd been tasked with hunting both him and Drake and all those who had been taken under the curse of the *Fallen*. It told the secrets of the *Ignis Purgata*, the Holy Order of the Righteous Fire. It described what they understood, or thought they understood, about the Fallen.

It told of methods to hunt, trap and destroy. It contained prayers and rituals designed to keep the powerful minds of the Nosferatu from overtaking those who attacked them. It held the text of letters written by Drake begging forgiveness for the evil he'd done. And it explained the rejection of his plea. *Forgiveness was not for demons, but only for human kind.*

And yet, the most interesting part of the ancient journal suggested that the issue was not yet settled.

A prophecy had come to the church—from a demon no less. It told of an angel that would bring forgiveness. If the angel was successful, the curse would end and the *Fallen* would no longer suffer in the dark, nor plague society as they did. But it was not a prophecy with a clear outcome. At all points in the writing the future could divide. Success or failure. Life or death. Healing or pain. All were in the offering it seemed. Those involved would have to fight for one outcome or another.

A month prior, that prophecy had begun to unfold, heralded by the arrival of supernova in the night sky that some had called the Midnight Sun.

Many of the Fallen had been drawn together in the city of New Orleans, including Drake and his most trusted lieutenants who wished to destroy the angel before it could reach its full strength. The hunters of the *Ignis Purgata* came as well, to kill all the Nosferatu they could find. Christian was there too, searching for this angel and caught in the middle.

The stage had been set for a clash that would change the future one way or another. But as fate would have it: things turned out differently than anyone expected: no angel had appeared. Elsa had been killed in its place and Christian had nearly managed to destroy Drake and his Brethren. Though Drake had escaped badly wounded.

"The prophecy is false," Christian said.

"And you know this…how?" Ida asked. "Just because you can't see something, doesn't mean it's not real."

"You don't understand," he said. "I would feel it. I would feel a change. The only change I felt was with Elsa. And once Drake killed her, the light was gone. If there was an angel it was her, and she's dead now."

"Then why did the old priest give this book to you?"

"Because he wanted me to destroy Drake," Christian said confidently. "That's how this ends. It's always been how this has to end. The curse came from Drake. The *Ignis Purgata* hunted him because he's the head of the snake. If he's killed, the rest of the Fallen will either die or be released."

"Spoken like a man," she muttered under her breath.

"What's that supposed to mean?"

"You might be cursed and trapped in the void, but you're still thinking with a particularly male point of view. *Have to fight fire with fire*", she said in a mocking, man-like voice. "*The only way to fix things is to destroy them.*"

He could hardly believe it, but he almost enjoyed when she made fun of him. It made existence somewhat more bearable. It didn't change the truth, though. "And how do you see it?" he asked.

"The prophecy says forgiveness would arrive when shadows are seen beneath the Midnight Sun," she began. "You've seen that. A once in a lifetime experience. Even your lifetime."

"Actually," he said. "There was a supernova in 1064. The Chinese saw it."

"Was it like this one?" she shot back.

Not even close, he thought. The 1064 supernova was a just a bright star in the sky. The more recent one lit up the night like a dozen full moons.

"It says, *the angel is born blind and weak*," she continued, reading from notes she'd taken. "Perhaps it's a child, like Christ, in a manger somewhere. Do you think you'd feel the power of such a being?"

Christian considered this. Despite his name and the intricate way in which the Fallen were bound up with the crucifixion of the one Christian's believed to be the Son of God, he was wary of religious answers and history. He'd grown up in the Roman Empire when Jupiter and other gods of the pantheon were worshipped. He'd seen Christianity rise and replace them, seen wars and brutality from every sect and religion on earth ever since. Nothing changed.

He was about to say something snide, when a stern look from Ida told him that would be going too far. She went to church every Wednesday, Friday and twice on Sunday. She believed. She was waiting for a glorious body, healed from the paralysis she lived in and unbroken in the Christian version of heaven.

"Don't you sass me," she warned.

"I didn't say anything."

"But you were thinking it," she said. "If you were my child I'd wash your mouth out with soap."

"You're very strict," he said, almost laughing.

"My point is," she continued, "you might not need to destroy. Perhaps you can save others instead, by helping this angel. By guiding it."

"I'm telling you, Ida, it doesn't exist."

She sighed. "You're sure of that?"

"When you've lived without mercy as long as I have, you learn not to buy it cheap," he said.

She sat back and folded her arms. "Hmmm," she said, sounding disappointed. "So tell me how *you* see it. Why did the leader of a holy order, charged with your destruction, hand you two of their most sacred relics?"

Christian was ready for this. He'd been thinking about this question for a long while, wondering why Simon had trusted him.

"The hunters of the Church have cornered Drake at least twenty times over the last thousand years," he said. "None of them survived; most were cut to pieces, some were even turned to darkness and made into vampires who toiled at his side. I think Simon realized that *no human* can stand before Drake. I think he knew from our clash in Cologne that Drake and I are enemies, so he cast his lot with me. His own men killed him for it. They murdered him in the church for believing I could help. After a show of faith like that, I will not let him down."

"So you're going after Drake?"

"I have to," he said. "Now, while he's still weak and reeling from whatever Elsa placed on that stone blade."

"Going alone then?" she said, eyebrows up.

"I can't exactly take you with me."

"I wasn't referring to me," she said. "I was talking about what Simon wrote on the last page."

She flipped the journal open to the last written page where a bookmark had been placed. Christian didn't need to look. He knew what it said.

Ida spoke the words: "*You're our only hope. But you are not alone, my midnight son.*"

Christian remained still. This passage baffled him. In fact the whole journal was like the labyrinth in his nightmare. It seemed contradictory and confusing. It seemed to suggest one thing and then another, looping back on itself and offering multiple paths, none of which were clear.

Maybe if half the journal hadn't been drafted in various codes and from different hands it would have made more sense. Ninety men had led the *Ignis Purgata*, including Simon. All of them had written something. Half of them had used ciphers and puzzles to hide their real thoughts.

"Truth is," he said. "The journal hasn't helped at all. It's only delayed me, like Elsa in my dream. While we sit here trying to extract some implication from these cryptic pages, Drake is getting further and further away."

"So you don't wonder about that passage?" she asked.

Of course he wondered. *Did it mean there were others in the Church who thought as Simon did? Others who believed in the prophecy and might enlist Christian's help against Drake?* He doubted it. And after what happened to Simon, if there were any who thought his way, they'd have to be fools to reveal their true feelings.

"I don't know what Simon meant," Christian said. "I only know that I *am* alone. And I'm going forward alone. Everyone who's helped me, trusted me or loved me has been killed in this war."

"Not everyone," she pointed out.

"I worry about you every day, Ida. And while you're part of this now, I won't risk anyone else. I'm going to find Drake and destroy him on my own. And then—finally—this will end."

"So you think you can take him?" she asked.

"I wounded him in the swamp. I could feel it. He was burning inside. Burning with an icy fire. He's weaker now than he's ever been. If I find him before he regains his strength, I can finish this. I know I can."

Ida nodded and closed the book and looked at him with a scowl of disappointment. "So you don't want my help," she said. "You don't care for my cooking –which sort of makes sense, since you don't eat—and you're not interested in what this journal might really have to say. Which makes me wonder why you even brought me over here in the first place?"

There were several reasons. One was to protect her. If Drake became aware of Ida, he might have sent someone to harm her. Though Christian sensed that hadn't happened.

"I do need your help," he said. "I need you to go to Washington to find the woman I saved. The FBI Agent I turned."

"Ah," Ida said. "Agent Pfeiffer."

In the swamps after the battle, Christian had come across two members of the FBI. One of Drake's disciples had attacked them savagely. The male agent was dead. But Kate Pfeiffer was still alive, though she was rapidly bleeding to death. She begged for help and for a chance to see her son again.

In a moment of weakness he'd acted. He wasn't even sure the term 'saving' could be used, but he'd prevented her from dying by injecting her with the venom of the Fallen. The toxin had done its unholy work: healing her wounds but poisoning her soul. Now she was now dying in slow motion, and soon she'd begin to feel the lust for blood.

"I should have let her die," he said. "But I didn't. Now she's going to have to deal with the change. With the pain of the *fall* and everything that follows."

"Won't she just become like you?" Ida asked.

"It's not that simple," he said. "Even though she's tough, smart and has at least an inkling of what's happening, she still has no idea what's coming."

"You called it *the Half-Life*." Ida said.

Those who hadn't experienced *the Half-Life* could hardly fathom the transformation process. The depths of anguish snapped the minds of many long before the transformation was complete. As the color seemed to drain from the world around them and feelings of anger, rage and bitterness usurp all else, life took on a blackened, meaningless state, like a forest after a fire; silent and empty. Only life never came back unless it was stolen by draining the blood of others.

After they hit bottom, the clock starts ticking. Those that make it through six months usually survive in their new shells, but most die by their own hand in some dark space, broken and alone.

And among those who survived, the good suffered the worst. Truthfully, the ability to not feel, to be a sociopath in human form lent itself very well to the dark life of the Nosferatu. But for those who cared and loved and cherished, they either forswore the blood of others like Christian had and lived with the pain, or they did terrible things and suffered the guilt of the darkened soul, turning life into hell itself.

"It doesn't happen instantly," he explained. "It takes months for the mortal body to die, and the immortal to emerge. She won't understand it. She can't. And she won't survive without guidance."

"And just how am I supposed to help with that?" Ida said, rolling her eyes.

"Right now, she's probably in denial," he explained. "At some point, she'll stop fighting it and start to believe what I told her, however impossible it seems. When that happens, she'll seek me out. The change forces it on us. All who are turned search for their masters. I even sought Drake out seventeen hundred years ago. You'll tell her you know how to find me. At some point, that'll be the lifeline she needs."

Ida pondered this for a moment. "Is she going to be dangerous?"

"Only to herself."

"What about that thirst for blood thing?"

"It won't hit her for months."

Ida seemed less than thrilled. "Okay, Sonny," she said. "I'll do it for you. I have a feeling you're just getting me out of the way, but it's good to know you care. "

He did care. Although it seemed that everything he cared about in this world was quickly killed and taken from him. He feared Ida might be next, but with Drake wounded and on the run, this was his chance.

"You be careful," he said.

She pushed back from the table. "Between Drake, those churchmen who want you dead and being on the FBI's most wanted list, you might need to take that advice yourself."

Christian nodded, but it was only lip service. He didn't have time for caution. He needed to move forward and do it quickly. He'd seen no angel. No salvation in the swamps. No forgiveness for the Fallen. Now he'd try his own plan. And the chips would have to land where they may.

Chapter 2

West Africa

The night stars were brilliant in their luminescence, like diamonds on a sheet of black velvet. Staring up at them, Drakos could not help but be impressed by the celestial beauty and infinity of the heavens.

The thought struck him as odd. For two thousand years he'd been consumed with rage, anger, and malice. Why should he notice beauty now?

He decided his mind was playing tricks on him. Weary and wounded, poisoned by a witch who could see through time, he'd been changed somehow. Toppled momentarily from his perch as King of the Dark World. First the poison had taken his strength, and now his mind was following.

Damn that witch to hell, he thought.

Centuries ago the inquisition had tried to do just that, but Christian had interfered. Now all these years later, Drake had finished what they started. And though he'd killed her in the most brutal fashion, her tainted stone weapon had passed into Christian's hand. And thrown by that hand, it had punctured Drake's back just as he made his escape.

The pain was excruciating. It was spreading some kind of paralysis slowly throughout his body. What poison had she used? Palladium? Refined and powdered silver? Holy water? Could a witch half burned at the stake by the Inquisition even get her hands on holy water? He would never know. And truthfully it didn't matter. If he didn't find help soon, he would certainly die, consumed by the flames of perdition and cast into the fires of Hades as all his kind were in the end.

"No," he grunted, his hatred of her and Christian and all they stood for giving him power. "Damn them! No!"

The sudden curse startled those around him - servants both human and otherwise transporting their master in an armed caravan along a dirt road that led to a remote West African village. The small town was the home of his servant Kwese (who'd also fallen before Christian's blade). There Drake would find his last hope, a witch doctor named Zwana, whom Kwese had kept in his employment.

It was a strange tale, Drake recalled. Zwana was an evil man obsessed with pain and mutilation, but he had ways that could be of use. Ways of healing and destroying.

"What if Zwana refuses to help us?" one of Drake's servants asked.

At full strength Drake would have simply broken the witch doctor's mind and forced him to do it. But in his weakened state, Drake would have to be cautious.

"He will fear us," Drake said.

Drake could read his servants' minds. They felt fear already, caused by the sudden uncertainty of seeing their near-omnipotent master broken and weakened. One of them had already challenged him, perhaps too soon, for Drake still possessed the strength to destroy the beast, but the others were nervous. Their world had become murky and unhinged for the first time in centuries.

They feared other things beside Drake now. He could sense their nerves toward this witch doctor, their fear of the Church and above all their fear of Christian.

In the swamps of Louisiana, Christian had battled and shattered the Brethren, despite their combined strength. Kwese, Lagos and Xhou had been killed, Anya and Drake wounded.

They now feared Christian more than anything. They were afraid he would come for them. And truthfully, Drake feared this as well.

"You will focus on me," he said. "Your thoughts will stay locked with mine. Understand this, the witch doctor will heal me or he will die as painful a death as has ever occurred on the face of this Earth. Am I clear?"

Drake sensed their thoughts re-aligning. Their minds becoming one with his. Their master still ruled. It took most of his remaining strength, but he continued to rule.

The caravan pulled into a tiny village, a shantytown of huts and corrugated tin shacks. To Drake's surprise it looked deserted and desolate.

"It's abandoned," one of the Drones told him.

"No," Drake said. "Kwese's minions have fled, but this place is not empty. Two of you stay with me. The rest of you, search."

Drake's human servants walked from the Land Rovers, as did two of the Fallen. But the final two Drones remained beside their weakened master as he climbed from the SUV and stood painfully on his own.

These two would form the basis of his new guard. Akash was a teen from Bangladesh. Drake found the boy killing an older man when he was just a teenager. Akash's mind and psyche had already been damaged by the poverty and cruelty of the world he lived in. It was easy to turn him, to offer him something more. But until recently, Akash had been just a pawn. Now he was Drake's bodyguard. He could do little but fight and kill. But he did that well.

The other vampire with Drake was Tereza. She was intelligent and sophisticated. A socialite from a prominent family who never fit that mold. She desired excitement and danger and had run from her home at the age of twenty-three. To Drake she was a useful tool, one that could be trusted. He'd treated her well, giving her a clan and rights to a part of the Middle East centered on Istanbul. It brought her respect and power in the world of the Fallen. To her credit she used it wisely. But she was not as willful as Akash, not as strong or simple. She could sense Drake's weakness more acutely, and he could feel the fear creeping back into her mind.

Stay with me.

She looked at him and nodded.

Out past the tin shanties, the older section of the small village was made of thatched roof huts raised off the ground by stilts to keep the crawling insects out. Most of them seemed abandoned, left to ruin. No fires burned. No voices could be heard.

The place seemed as dead as Drake was about to be, but the longer Drake lingered, the more his mind cleared. Not only could he feel Zwana's presence, he could see the witch doctor in his mind's eye. His evil shone bright like a fire on a barren cliff.

"Give me my cane," he demanded.

Tereza handed him a cane. Drake took it and hobbled over to the most dilapidated hut of the village.

Follow.

The command was thought. Akash and Tereza heard it and fell in behind him, matching his pace until he stepped into the shack.

Darkness gave way to firelight as a match was thrown into a pile of kindling at the center of the hut. Smoke swirled up and out a small hole in the roof, while orange flames sent flickers of light dancing around the walls and across the ceiling.

In the corner sat a man whose face was dark as coal, but whose hands were bleached white.

"Zwana," Drake said.

"I am he," said the man.

"Then you know who I am," Drake replied. It was a statement more than a question.

"Kwese long ago put your image in my mind," Zwana admitted. "I must say, you're not as fearful as he made you out to be."

"You're not seeing me at my best," Drake insisted. "And besides, fear is a strange thing. Like a shadow, sometimes it's larger than that which makes it. Sometimes deceptively small. If you task me, I will show you fear like you've never imagined."

The witch doctor seemed unmoved, so Drake thought of the fire and then glared into Zwana's eyes. He saw Zwana's hands begin to shake and then one arm flicking back and forth as if he were trying to brush something off him. In Zwana's mind, the flames were crawling on his skin, burning him alive.

"Enough!" he shouted. "I know your tricks. But you need not perform them tonight."

Drake felt otherwise. In fact, he felt he must control and possess this man now or he would lack the strength to try again. He focused on Zwana's eyes, bright white in the darkness. Probing his mind, Drake discovered what had happened to the villagers.

"So you killed them," he said, seeing that Zwana had drugged the water and then gone from hut to hut slaughtering the human villagers.

Zwana tried to resist, thinking of the wall, of the floor, of the ants and even Kwese, but it was no use. Drake found the truth.

"And you ate them to survive, when the crops around you failed," Drake accused.

Zwana's body was locked, his jaw frozen. He could not have responded if he wanted to. But Drake saw his words. *Is that not what your kind does?*

"The scavengers kill and feed off humans to feel worthless emotions," Drake corrected. "They are like hyenas picking the bones of dead cattle. We are more than that. We are lions."

Drake was fairly certain he'd impressed Zwana enough. And, as he was almost ready to fall, he pursued it no further. "You will heal me," Drake ordered. "And I shall pay you handsomely for your services"

"I will not help you, demon from beyond the void," the Shaman said. "Unless you help me first."

Drake paused. "What do you wish?"

"That which Kwese would never grant me. More life. Your kind of life."

Kwese had never been willing to turn Zwana because he feared that the witch doctor's power combined with the abilities of the Nosferatu would make him more dangerous than most. An assessment Drake would agree with. "You wish to be one with the darkness? You know what awaits you if that's done?"

"I have seen my fate in the world after this," Zwana said. "There is great pain waiting for me anyway."

As he spoke, Zwana clutched at a gnarled stick beside him, one that was old and worn smooth in the two places where his hands fell, discolored with the years of oils from his palms. It seemed to Drake like a mirror of Zwana's soul, twisted and changed by his own proclivities.

"If you wish to live…" Zwana said calmly, "…you will grant me my price."

Drake stared and then slowly, almost nonchalantly, offered a nod of approval. "If you wish, it shall be given to you. I suspect you'll regret it, but that's your affair. First you will heal me."

"No," Zwana said, standing. "Once you have given me immortality, I will remove the poison. But not before."

"I have no time to wait on you," Drake demanded.

"The ritual is already set," Zwana insisted. "For I knew this day was coming."

Drake pondered his situation. He had no choice. He motioned for Akash to come forward. "Give the witch doctor his part of the deal."

"No!" shouted Zwana. "You! The King of the Nosferatu. You will grant my power, you whom all obey."

Drake moved closer toward Zwana. "You push your luck, wizard. What makes you think I won't kill you as soon as we've finished? What makes you think that while you're mired in the Half-Life I won't have my people destroy you?"

Fear replaced Zwana's arrogance. He went silent.

"Yes," Drake said easing back. "You know of the Half-Life. The pain of transformation. You have no power over me warlock. Only a chance to earn my respect."

Drake stared into Zwana's eyes, but could not find his thoughts. Perhaps it was his weakened condition, or perhaps Zwana's connection with the spirit world, but there was only swirling whispers and something…something hidden.

"What are you concealing from me?" Drake demanded.

"I have something you would value," Zwana said. But instead of focusing on Drake, the shaman's eyes went back to the fire - to the flames that danced between them, a refuge and a barrier all at the same time.

"Speak," Drake said.

"In my vision, I saw you coming here. I saw myself granting you life and… a gift…" Zwana whispered this as if in a trance. "A gift I must find for you," he added. "A weapon of unlimited power. One that will defeat your enemies and bring darkness to all the lands you own."

"I need no weapon you could find," Drake said, scoffing at the thought.

"It is said that this weapon can overcome the Church. It has the power to bring down the angels."

Drake inclined his ear ever so slightly. "What did you say?"

Zwana beamed with arrogance. "While you searched my mind I searched yours. You showed me too much *dark one*. You showed pain, but also fear. You are running from the one you created. And from something more terrible. An angel sent to undo all that you have built. A being so meek and mild you would not recognize it until it was upon you but in whose sight you could not stand."

"I have seen no such thing," Drake insisted.

"But you feel it," Zwana said. "You know it has come into the world."

Drake felt a sense of fury building inside him. For a thousand years he'd feared this angel. This abomination—by his perspective. The Midnight Sun announced its arrival, and Drake's attempt to lure it to the swamps of Louisiana and destroy it had failed utterly. He'd seen nothing, but he knew it was out there. He could sense it like whisper in the dark, like the ringing of silence in one's ears.

"Turn me," Zwana said. "Give me power and in return I will heal you. Give me great power and I will hunt your enemy, the one called

Christian. Give me ultimate power, power nearly to match your own, and I will lead you to a weapon that will make this angel bow before you."

Drake tried to determine if this could be true. It was frustrating trying to look into this mortal's mind. He made a quick decision. "I will grant your wish. If it turns out that your lips spew lies, I will destroy you. But if somehow your boast turns out to be valid, you will be rewarded like no other."

A grin stretched across Zwana's lips. And it seemed to Drake that perhaps fate had sent him here. Perhaps Christian and his witch Elsa had done Drake a favor. *Perhaps the debacle in the swamps of Louisiana was not the end, but actually the beginning.*

 "Now tell me this power you speak of," Drake asked. "How would I know this to be truth?"

"It comes from the book of truth," Zwana said.

"Book of truth?"

"For me," Zwana said, "there are many truths in the universe. But for you…you struggle against the one that Christians worship. You are cursed by their God. But before them came the Jews. And in the ancient days of the Jews—days they themselves would scarcely recognize—angels walked the earth. To test and punish, to heal and teach. Placed before these angels, men were powerless, all but one… one named Jacob."

Drake's mind followed the reference instantly. In his years of hiding, before he'd realized the power he possessed, he'd studied the Torah and the early writings of many Christians hoping to find a cure to the curse that had come upon him for scourging the one they called Christ.

Ironic, he thought that he, *the cursed one*, had seen scrolls and writings penned by the early Christians that no scholar of today knew about, that no church had ever seen. Teachings lost to the human world, remembered only by one they called a demon.

But the scripture Zwana referred to was older than that. Older than Dead Sea Scrolls and older than most in the Torah. It came from the book of Genesis and was well known. It stemmed from the earliest times of human civilization.

In a strange way it was one of Drake's favorites. For it told of Jacob, whose birthright was stolen by his brother Esau, much as Drake felt his life had been stolen by the Church.

Preparing after fourteen years of hiding to confront his brother Esau, Jacob expects to be killed. He sends his family and servants to a safe place across the river and camps alone on the far bank. That night he is visited by a being of great power.

"So Jacob was left alone," Drake said, quoting the scripture. "And a man wrestled with him till the dawn broke. When the man saw that he could not overpower Jacob, he touched the socket of Jacob's hip so that his hip was wrenched and painful. Then the man said, 'Let me go, for it is daybreak.' But Jacob replied, 'I will not let you go unless you bless me.'"

"So the being of power asked him," Zwana chimed in, 'What is your name?'"

"Yes," Drake said. "And when Jacob told him, the man said, 'Your name will no longer be Jacob, but Israel, because you have struggled with God and with humans and have overcome.'"

Drake's mind whirled, not only because he'd spent two thousand years struggling with God and man himself, but because he knew from context that Jacob had wrestled not with the Almighty God, but with an angel of God. More importantly, the text was clear—Jacob had overcome that angel, just as Drake needed to overcome the angel that would erase his own work of nearly twenty centuries.

"In a vision of torment I've seen how Jacob prevailed," Zwana said. "In his hand was a stone, a stone of power, it came not from this earth but had fallen from heaven. It draws the light and does not release it."

Drake considered this. "I've read no text where Jacob possessed a weapon."

"Would the ancient Jews speak of a weapon that could undo the work of angels, the work of their God?"

No, Drake thought, of course they wouldn't.

"They would hide it," Drake said. "Knowledge of such a weapon would be compartmentalized and destroyed. As would the weapon itself."

"Unless…" Zwana suggested.

"Unless, it could not be destroyed," Drake finished. "After all, if it was not of this earth…"

Zwana nodded and continued. "In my vision, the Hebrews cast this weapon into the hottest fire, but it would not melt. They crushed it under the densest stone, but it would not shatter. And so instead, it was hidden in a barren place, contained in a golden chest and draped in darkness so it could not poison the light."

"Do you know how to find this place?" asked Drake.

"My visions can lead you to it. But you will need to pay my price. I will be your most powerful servant, your champion, second only to you. And we will cast down the light in favor of the darkness, and our reign will have no end."

Drake considered the danger of the offer. With too much power Zwana would be a threat, but with too little, he would become suspicious.

"Do we have a covenant?" Zwana asked.

Drake had no choice. If such a weapon existed, if it was even a possibility, he had to risk it. He nodded at the witch doctor.

"Yes, Zwana, we do."

Chapter 3

Outskirts of New Orleans

A whip cracked in the dark of night, sounding like a gunshot. It startled Leroy Atherton, even though he knew it was coming. Ahead of him, in a barely lit section of an old warehouse a woman and a man were cornered by a group of four.

The whips of the four were coated with specks of palladium. The men who carried them also held crosses, but they were not members of any religious order. In fact, each of them had once been hunted by the Church.

"Be careful," the leader of the four cried out. "Don't look them in the eye. Remember what you've been through. The eye is window to the soul, and they will seek to turn ours back. To drag us back into the darkness."

"This is wrong," Leroy said quietly.

"We have to control them," a calm voice spoke beside him.

That voice came from Terrance Jackson, an old, wizened figure of a man. He was blind, his body sinewy and weathered like a high country tree; twisted by the wind, stripped of its leaves, but stronger than it looked and still holding to the earth with a tenacious grasp.

The Half Life

Terrance had once been a voodoo priest. He'd grappled with Drake and others of the Fallen. He'd seen across the void and back. Now he'd become Leroy's guide into the dark and twisted world that the unassuming man—the most unlikely of angels—was supposed to change.

"I don't know about this," Leroy replied. "If they don't come willingly, who am I—who are we—to force them?"

"You—and we—are here to save them," Terrance said without hesitation. "But unless you lost it somewhere, you didn't come with any instruction book. We have to be careful. This is how the church does it."

The four men with whips had once been members of the Fallen. They'd heard of a chance to be redeemed and sought Terrance out. Terrance had brought them to Leroy, and in a night of pain and redemption they had come back from the void, back into the light. They were young in the scheme of things, none had been lost for more than eight months.

Now they'd become a combination of disciples and a small army. They went into the dark to spread the word helping to round up others who might be redeemed, willingly or not.

The woman and man in the corner were clearly among the unwilling. But unable to escape the circle, they seemed ready to fight. The woman, pale and skinny, hissed and lunged at one of the disciples. A palladium whip drove her back while two other men stepped forward with crosses held high.

The Fallen experienced pain at the sight of the cross for reasons most of them would never know.

"This isn't right," Leroy repeated.

The figures in the corner began to cower.

"So what will you do?" Terrance asked.

Leroy was confused. Several times over the past month, Terrance had asked him this same question. Always at an odd time, always when Leroy was afraid, doubtful and having misgivings as he was now. He always answered the same way. "What do you think I should do?"

Terrance seemed disappointed, but put his hand on Leroy's forearm and squeezed. "Heal them."

Leroy knew his guide was looking for something more, but what more could he give? He was an unemployed electrician who knew nothing about religion, having spent his childhood as a Baptist in a family that didn't go to church except at Easter. What did he know about saving anyone? Let alone the twisted, tortured souls whose existence he wouldn't have believed in thirty days ago.

Two months ago he'd been in Compton, mourning the death of his son and plotting revenge on the murderer. After putting a gun to the teenage thug's head, Leroy had relented and stumbled back into a swirl of what seemed like madness and despair. He woke up in a hospital with doctors asking him strange questions. He had no answers.

"Heal them," Terrance said again. "It's what you're meant for."

Leroy placed Terrance's hand on a railing and began to move. The hissing and crying and cursing grew louder and the snap of the whips reminded him of horrible dreams, the kind that came and went and made no sense.

"Stop," he begged the disciples.

They looked at him.

"Please. I can't stand that sound."

With the disciples distracted, the male lunged forward, charging to break free. He tackled one of the disciples and plunged a hand with fingernails thick like claws into the man's stomach.

The whips fired and a sword-like blade was thrust into the attacker's back. The disciple wailed in pain and the creature of the night released a hideous scream that shook the rafters and shattered windows across the floor of the warehouse. It pulled away from Leroy's small army and staggered to the side, reaching around desperately trying to get the sword out of its back, but unable to grasp it.

As Leroy watched the demon fell to its knees, began to shudder and then burst into blue-white flame.

In seconds, the sprinklers above sensed the heat and began to blast full force. The fire alarm wailed and strobes began to flash.

In the midst of this, the female screamed and attacked as well. But one of the disciples caught her legs with the whip and tripped her up. He lunged forward and came down upon her, using the hilt of his whip as a bar to keep her teeth at bay. His partners joined him.

"Hurry," he shouted to Leroy. "We can't hold her!"

With his heart pounding and his mind filled with revulsion and fear, Leroy forced himself to step forward. He knelt beside the woman and put his hands on her face to stop her from thrashing around.

She went instantly still, as if some type of anesthesia had been pumped into her veins. She looked up at Leroy, her eyes were black, glossy and lifeless.

"I can give you peace," Leroy said.

The calmness faded. "Lies!" she hissed.

"I can," Leroy said back. "You must believe me. I can release you."

She thrashed violently, kicking one of the men so hard that he flew ten feet and hit the wall.

Leroy tried to hold her, tried to calm her, but it was no use. She whipped an arm free, grabbed the second disciple's throat and tried to rip his flesh open. Before she could, Terrance appeared and cast a handful of dust into her eyes.

She shook for a second and then began to shiver.

"A taste of life for you," Terrance said to the woman. "He offers you a banquet."

Leroy had no idea what Terrance had done. The voodoo priest was nothing if not a mystery. And quite frankly, for a guide, he was very poor at explaining things. But he was there in the nick of time, and whatever he'd thrown at the woman, she was breathing differently now. More like a scared kitten than a beast.

"Heal her," Terrance said once again.

Leroy hesitated. They were soaking in the downpour, but the burning figure was still ablaze ten feet away. The flashing lights and screeching alarm were disorienting.

"Hurry!" Terrance shouted. "Before this place burns to the ground with us inside it!"

"I offer you life," Leroy said to the woman. "I offer life like you once had. Filled with the tastes, and good smells and cold things to drink. Warmth for your body."

"Warmth," she repeated.

"Yes," he said, seizing on the word. "Heat, comfort, love."

"I'm so cold…" she said, "…so tired of being cold."

"You don't have to be."

Her head shook in shame. "I've done so many things," she said. "Bad things. I'll burn like my brother."

"No," Leroy insisted. "You can be healed and help me to heal others. You can live and be forgiven."

She looked around, her pale face streaked with water and half covered by stringy wet hair. For a moment, Leroy saw a hint of blue in her formerly lifeless eyes, a hint of color in her pale skin, brought on by whatever Terrance had done. They were pretty eyes, trembling eyes with speckles of green, but the color soon faded and disappeared.

"No!" she shouted throwing all of them off at once.

Leroy fell on his back and for a moment he thought he'd broken it. But the sensation came back quickly. He rolled and stood. The woman was running for the door when the dart of a cross bow pierced her back.

She fell as if she was diving to the floor and the blue flames of the *Ignatorum* erupted before she hit the ground. With the sprinklers now flooding the warehouse and the fire and police departments on their way, Leroy said the only thing that made any sense to him. "We'd better get out of here."

Terrance nodded and put his hand on Leroy as the surviving disciples gathered up their fallen comrade and the group made their way to the door.

By the time the fire department arrived they found nothing but a burning warehouse, as Leroy, Terrance, and the disciples were on a small boat motoring away in the darkness.

At the wheel was Terrance's wife, a sturdy and uncompromising woman of fifty, named Bella. Terrance stood beside her while Leroy sat in the back with the others.

"It's time for us to leave," Terrance said.

Bella didn't flinch. She just kept her hand on the wheel. "He's too weak for this."

"He was chosen," Terrance said. "You of all people know what that means."

She cut her eyes at him as if this was a low blow, but otherwise did not react. "So you'll be going too I assume?"

"After this debacle," Terrance said almost jokingly. "We can't stay here."

"Here, you have us," she said. "Here, you have powers to call on. Disciples. Spirits. Why leave that behind?"

He said nothing.

"I want an answer, Terrance."

"Because we must," was all he chose to say.

The Half Life

She stared at her husband the way all wives do when infuriated with their mates. A soft shake of the head showed her disgust and then she looked to the waters ahead.

As she turned, Leroy thought he saw a tear in her eye.

Nothing more was said, but Leroy knew what she was thinking; that his weakness would get them all killed by the Fallen; that helping him was a fool's errand and a waste of what little time Terrance had left on this Earth. He knew these thoughts were on her mind, because they were on his mind too.

Only Terrance disagreed, but maybe he was blind in more ways than one. He addressed Leroy, with the same calm voice he always used. "Talk to the man with the boat," he said. "Tell him we leave the day after tomorrow."

Chapter 4

The Mississippi River flowed with a quiet stillness that spoke volumes to Bella as she strolled along River Road. Terrance was at her side. The fire of the previous night was forgotten, the passion of the morning still in her mind. That, she'd hold onto forever.

Up ahead, an eighty foot trawler named the *Mercy III* was tied up to the dock. A thin trail of diesel smoke drifted from its stack as last minute supplies were being loaded aboard. On deck Bella saw Leroy talking with the captain. She wondered if that captain had any idea who he was speaking with.

"You're so quiet," Terrance said, massaging her hand. "Have you been looking into my future again? I told you not to look at my cards."

"I wouldn't do that." Bella snapped back. Though she had been, and they both knew it.

"Mmm hmm," he said. "You know they're not always right, especially concerning me."

She didn't mince words. "I don't need the cards to tell me I'll never see you again."

The conversation fell silent. A deafening silence, as loud as a freight train running through a small town. The gentle motions of his hand stopped. He ran his tongue across his lips and sucked at his teeth as he always did when deciding what to say.

Finally, he shrugged. "You're not getting rid of me that easily." It was a joke, but like a threadbare sheet, it really covered nothing.

"Terrance, listen to me," she said, trying to stop the slow walk that felt like a funeral procession.

"No, you listen," he said. "All this talk is not good. You're sending this stuff out into the universe. You know better than that. Besides New Orleans is my home, and I'll be coming back here. I guarantee it. Me and the mud. One and inseparable."

Bella tried to laugh and managed a fake smile. She also tried to change the tone in her voice. She remembered her mom sending their father to Vietnam with smiles and laughter. *You never send your man off to war worrying about you back home, Momma had told her. It's bad luck for them.*

"You and the mud," she said, licking her thumb and wiping a speck of dirt from his face, where he'd pulled up some weeds in the garden this morning. "I wish I could go with you," she added. "You know I'll miss you."

"I'll be back," he insisted. "Look in on Charles for me. I worry about that boy. He likes fun more than studying."

"Just like his grandfather."

"No doubt about that," he said.

They embraced, long and hard. "When should I expect you?"

"By the first moon of summer, I reckon."

"So in June."

"Yes," he said. "Easily by June."

The *Mercy III's* horn blew and Bella saw Leroy waving. She guided Terrance toward the fishing boat and gave him another kiss goodbye.

"You see," he said. "That's why I have to get back here, for that good old fashioned southern loving." He laughed. His laugh was deep, infectious and almost genuine, she thought.

With Leroy's help, Terrance climbed into the boat and held the rail as the bow and stern lines were cast off.

The trawler began drifting from the dockside and easing out into the channel. Looking at its dilapidated state Bella wondered if the weather-beaten vessel would even survive the journey to wherever they were going.

It turned downriver and shuddered anew, the engine chugging loudly. To Bella, it seemed like an old heart, beating heavily. It had energy and vigor, much like her husband's—stronger than it should be at his age, but nearing the end of its time.

She watched the boat until it vanished around one of the Mississippi's innumerable bends. Tears soon filled her eyes. She didn't quiver or sob, but the drops ran down her cheeks until she had to wipe them from her face.

She heard what Terrance had promised. She knew he planned to come back to her. He might even believe it, but she knew more than Terrance about his future.

The Half Life

"I wish it were different," she said, whispering in her husband's direction. "But the cards are never wrong, my dear."

Chapter 5

Washington D.C.

Kate Pfeiffer sat in a high backed chair in a spacious office deep within the J. Edger Hoover building in Washington, D.C. She sat ramrod straight. Chin up. Eyes forward. Her business suit was sharply tailored to her trim shape and impeccably pressed. She looked every inch the decorated agent her file described her to be, but her mind was a tempest of confusion and fear.

Despite plenty of sleep, her pallor was sickly, her skin pale, and her eyes glossy and vacant. Extra makeup and mascara concealed some of her condition. Colored contacts seemed to add life to her eyes, but Kate remained conscious of it, nervous that someone would notice.

The questions came toward her with dull monotony. Questions she'd already answered a hundred times in her own mind.

"What condition was Agent Massimo in when you shot the woman?"

"He was already dead, or mortally wounded. The woman had ripped out his trachea."

"Why were you and Agent Massimo operating without backup?"

"We were in pursuit of a suspect believed responsible for multiple homicides. We didn't want him to get away. Back up and an airborne sniper were on the way."

Her answers were clear, but the effort it was taking to concentrate was almost unbearable. Her mind was wandering. Her pupils constricted from the light spilling through the far window. *When had it ever been so blindingly bright in this room?*

She heard some mumbling and looked to the doorway. Someone was speaking on the other side, but the sound was incoherent.

"Agent Pfeiffer?"

She looked back toward the desk. Gene Serrano, the director of internal affairs, was staring at her.

"Did you not hear the question?" Serrano asked.

"Sorry," she said. "I was distracted by the noise."

"What noise?" He glanced around at the others on the panel beside him. "You could hear a pin drop in this room."

What the hell was he talking about? The murmuring was like a truck driving across gravel. "I'm sorry," she said again. "I have a terrible headache."

Serrano rolled his eyes and sat back, but another voice came to her aid, that of Kim Tan, director of the FBI.

"Cut her some slack, Gene. She's been thorough hell."

He was right about that. She'd been through hell and honestly, felt like she was still there. A month earlier, she and her partner, Billy Ray Massimo, had pursued a suspected killer into the backwaters of a swamp in Louisiana only to discover some kind of demented ritual taking place.

After a shootout, they'd lost the suspect but rescued a possible victim, only to have the victim —a woman named Vivian Dasher—turn on them and attack. Despite taking multiple rounds to vital parts of her body, Vivian managed to overpower Kate, take her to the ground and rip open a gash in her neck, lunging for Kate's throat with her teeth like some kind of wild animal.

Only Billy Ray's interference saved Kate. But he paid with his life. By the time Kate could get to her feet, Billy Ray's own jugular vein had been slashed and the woman was perched on top of him. It seemed as if she was gorging herself on his blood.

Kate emptied the rest of her magazine into the psychotic woman. A dozen bullets from point blank range. And still, the woman did not die instantly. She went into convulsions, shaking with muscle spasms until finally she went still.

"You fired twelve shots at the woman," Serrano said. "Can you explain why?"

Because the bitch wouldn't die, Kate thought, though she guessed that wouldn't be an acceptable answer.

"In my weakened condition I couldn't hold my weapon steady," she said. "I knew the woman had killed Billy Ray and—if I failed—she would certainly kill me and probably others."

Kim Tan seemed to like that answer. He should have, he'd coached it out of her days before.

Serrano looked at his notes. "Perhaps that was wise," he said. "They found eight of the shells you fired in the soil around her. You missed more than you hit."

Not possible, Kate thought. She'd seen the woman convulse with every squeeze of the trigger. She'd been less than five feet away.

"You must have been very weak," Serrano added.

"I was shaking from loss of blood."

"Yes," Serrano said, peering over his reading glasses at a note. "Two full pints. Enough to be fatal in most cases. Certainly enough to render any normal person unconscious. Which makes me wonder how, Agent Pfeiffer, how on this earth--," he added, removing his glasses for effect, "--did you end up fifty miles away calling us from a payphone with a badly done patch job on your neck?"

It was a trap she couldn't avoid no matter how craftily she answered the questions. There was no lie that could fit the situation, and the truth... If she told the truth they'd lock her up, not in jail but in a mental institution.

Her mind wandered back to the moment. The original suspect, a blond-haired man named Christian, reappeared and picked her up. She'd begged him to save her. He'd done something. It felt like poison in her veins, *it still did*, but somehow he'd healed her neck and taken her away.

She'd woken up in a boxcar on a moving train. He was there. She could feel him. He could hear her thoughts and she could hear his. He'd begged her to stay, but she flung the door open and jumped from the slow moving train. For reasons she couldn't explain, she knew he wouldn't follow.

As she ran away, she'd shouted to him: "Just leave me alone! I'll tell them you're dead!"

His reply appeared only in her mind. *I am dead, Kate. And so are you.*

"Agent Pfeiffer…" Serrano called out, "…we're waiting."

"I don't know," she said in a whisper. "I honestly don't remember."

"You don't remember?" Serrano repeated. He tossed his glasses down. "How's that going to sound when it gets out? How's it going to sound to Senator Massimo when he wants to know why his son's partner is alive, but his son is dead?"

"I don't know how it will sound," she said.

"It's going to sound like bull," Serrano shot back. "Which it is."

"Okay," Kim Tan said, standing up. "I think we've done enough for today."

To Serrano's frustration, the hearing was adjourned for the evening. Kate sat there waiting as everyone made their final notes and filed out. When the stenographer had packed up and departed, Kate was left alone. She was miserable, in pain, and even with the lights off and the shade pulled down it was too damned bright in that room.

She was strong woman, but she knew she was in trouble. Personally, professionally, emotionally; everything was falling apart. She needed rest but she couldn't sleep. And despite trying to block it out, despite trying to erase the notion from her mind, all she could think of was tracking down the blond-haired man and making him explain what the hell he'd done to her.

Chapter 6

Boston, Massachusetts

The rain fell steadily from a sky turned orange by Boston's city lights. It had been coming down for days and the streets of Boston were wet, the gutters flooded and the storm drains overflowing. Everywhere they went, cars, buses and trucks sprayed wakes of dirty water like boats speeding through the shallows.

From inside the first floor of a partially renovated office building, Christian Hannover listened as the patter of rain continued its soothing beat. He focused his gaze on the glass and steel tower across the boulevard. The building was owned by *Timeless Export - Import.* Vivian Dasher had worked there, prior to murdering an FBI agent in the Bayou and getting shot to hell by the agent's partner.

Vivian had been one of the Fallen. She was also one of Drake's minions. Christian figured that made this building one of Drake's strongholds and the best hope he had of catching up with his wounded enemy.

As he watched the city lights reflect off the building's glistening skin, Christian wondered how long Boston had been Drake's base of operation. The building was forty years old. Had Drake been there all that time? Hiding in his citadel as the cars drove by and the clients came and went without ever knowing what lurked inside?

Christian's own lair was just down I-95 in Manhattan and had been for the past sixty years. Perhaps Drake knew that and was trying to keep tabs on him, or perhaps this was just one big coincidence—the two princes of the night searching the world for each other over the centuries, but living only three hours away by car.

It didn't really matter, he thought. He was just musing. Finding a way to pass time. Trying not to wonder what he'd do if Drake had abandoned this lair for some other. He doubted he'd find Drake here, but he thought he'd find something. However, the longer he watched, the more concerned he became. Nothing out of the ordinary was happening across the street. No movement. No activity. But there was someone in there.

He glanced at his watch: four thirty. In less than an hour he'd have to hide from the light. He was considering an attempt at infiltration when a black limousine pulled up to the front of the building. A surge of energy coursed through him, not just because something was finally happening, but because he could sense the unmistakable energy wave of his kind.

The driver stepped out and waited by the passenger door. Through Christian's eyes the driver looked sub-human, bone and fangs and glossy black eyes. He was a Drone, stripped so completely of his humanity that to members of the Fallen, he was a hideous creature; though, to a human, he would look only sickly and perhaps slightly sinister.

The surprise to Christian was that this creature's presence would alter what he felt so strongly. Drones were powerful and hardy fighters but feeble minded. Their presence was felt more like a small insect buzzing around than a storm arriving.

"There must be another one," he whispered to himself.

It was too much to hope he'd find Drake, but something greater than the Drone was out there.

The feeling spiked as the front doors of the building opened and a woman dressed to the nines walked out in a hurried strut. She was a vampire and from the vibe she gave off, she was high atop the food chain.

Christian did what he could to draw his own energy down, to shroud himself in the surroundings, but she stopped on the sidewalk and stared in his direction for several long seconds before climbing into the back of the limousine.

In short order the door was shut, the Drone back in the driver's seat and the limo was moving again, traveling out into the pre-dawn traffic.

This was it. This was the chance he'd waited for all night. He needed information and this creature was the best chance to get it. He made his way across the half renovated room, passing paint-stained tarps and stacks of sheet rock. He arrived at a motorcycle, a dark blue CBR 750 that he'd stolen and driven up the stairs and inside the building.

Of all his sins, becoming a good thief was the only one he didn't regret.

As he donned his helmet, something flashed in his mind's eye, a brief sense of another tortured soul. He'd felt it before, but where?

He looked out through the plate glass window. A pale woman in a white Audi was staring back at him. Her face and hair were as ghostly as the car. It was Anya, one of Drake's four great lieutenants. The only one besides Drake to survive the battle in the swamps.

Christian wondered again how he'd failed to sense her. But then Anya possessed powers he and the other vampires did not. Even Drake couldn't open her mind. She stared at him, two plates of glass all that separated them. A window to her mind opened.

Follow me.

The words flashed in Christian's mind and then the window slammed shut.

Outside, the Audi's headlights came on, the engine whined and the car sped away from the curve.

Follow me. The exact words Elsa had spoken in the dream. Did it mean something, or was it a trap?

He throttled up the bike, kicked the front door open and drove down the steps and out into the rain. The back tire spun dangerously on the wet road as he turned. Considering the weather, a motorcycle might not have been the best choice of vehicles. Still he controlled the bike with an expert touch and quickly began closing on the Audi.

She was heading to the docks in South Boston. Many of the wharfs and older buildings there were abandoned; some had been empty for the past twenty years. Others were now warehouses and holding stations for off-loaded cargo.

As they got closer, he glanced upward. The sky was beginning to brighten, but if the clouds held it would be bearable.

The Audi moved onto the road fronting the docks and Christian followed, avoiding potholes and weaving around debris washed down by the rain.

The Audi pulled in, parking beneath an overhang. The limo was parked down the road beside another of the rusting warehouses.

Christian approached with care pulling up beside Anya. She was still as a statue, as pale as alabaster, her skin so white it seemed to glow. No doubt that she'd been a beautiful woman before her death and rebirth. Despite what Drake had done and what she'd been through, she was beautiful still.

Christian pulled in beside her and flipped up the visor of his helmet. Though he couldn't sense her thoughts, he projected his toward her. A warning. A threat. *If you move on me, I will destroy you this time.*

"I have no wish to die," she said aloud. "Once was enough, thank you."

He kept his senses on full alert. If she could mask herself it was possible she could mask the presence of others.

"I *am* masking another," she said, reading his mind. "You. For the moment I'm keeping you hidden. If I wasn't, she would sense you already. That's her skill."

"Who is she?"

"Her name is Evelyn. She's dangerous. Even to you."

"We'll see about that," he said. Christian was filled with confidence. He'd fought Drake and his legion. Fought them to within inches of complete victory. No mere underling would stand in his way, not any more successfully than the stone walls and iron gates had kept him from Drake in the vision.

"I suppose we will," Anya replied. She was so slight, so thin, he could think only of a knitting needle in the dark, catching the light when it hit just right.

"What do you want from me?" he asked.

This time she kept quiet as if she couldn't speak the words. But he heard them in his mind. *I want you to kill Drake.*

Christian was stunned. But then again, he'd sensed lust for power in all of the Brethren at one time, even for their master's position. It was the way of things. "So you can take his place?"

"My reasons are my own," she said. "But I assure you, they have nothing to do with power."

It was a moment the likes of which Christian could not recall. But Anya was unlike any of the others and, as he remembered, her attacks in the swamp had been almost predictable and easy to defend. Instead of fighting to the death, she ran when the chance came.

I want Drake destroyed. And like the old priest, I know that only you have the power to do it. It takes all my strength just to keep this thought as my own. But I can't overcome him. Not even injured as he is now.

"Where is he?"

"Evelyn knows."

"But you don't?"

"Drake no longer trusts me," she said. "He's stabling a new group of horses, in some ways a more dangerous group. They are..." she tilted her head, "unsound."

Christian considered that. Weakened and wounded, Drake would likely face challenges from within. A new group might be his only hope for holding onto power. Or one of them might try to swipe it from him.

"So this Evelyn is inside?" he asked. "Just waiting for me."

"On the fifth floor. She runs the business part of Drake's empire while he's off trying to save his own life."

"Then Drake is dying."

"As close to it as ever, but the effect is waning."

"Why don't you come with me?" he said. "I'm sure she's not alone in there."

"She's not. Many Drones are with her. But you'll have to go alone. If you fail, I'll need surprise on my side in order to have any hope of finishing what you've started. I will not show my hand."

He could understand that. "What do you hope to get out of this?"

"I'm a prisoner," she said turning to him. "What do you imagine I hope for?"

He understood. They were all prisoners.

She looked away. "You don't have much time. Evelyn will be heading to her crypt soon. And if these clouds clear away…"

Christian tried to see her thoughts but he couldn't break through her wall. How she could keep people out of her mind he didn't know, but the amount of pain needed to close the mind was tremendous. Whatever happened to her, he almost didn't want to know.

"It's a trap of course," Anya added. "Drake knew you'd come looking sooner or later."

He nodded. "I know."

"You're not worried about that are you?"

Christian shook his head. He was ready for a war, ready to take on all who stood in his way. He glanced at the horizon. Time was critical now. The clouds were thinning as the rains pushed out into the Atlantic Ocean.

He looked back at Anya and nodded. She nodded back to him.

Good luck.

Without another word, she put the car in gear and drove off.

Christian left the bike where it was and made his way down the road and into the building. Knowing there would be no element of surprise, he dashed up four flights of stairs. At the top of the fifth, Evelyn and her clan were waiting.

"Did you not think we'd sense your presence?" she asked.

He grinned, ready for the fight. "I didn't really care one way or the other. But I'll give you a choice. Tell me where Drake is and I'll let you live."

She began to laugh. "You really have no idea, do you?"

At that, two of the Drones rushed him, hitting him high and low and all three of them went flying down the first flight of stairs. Evelyn and the remaining Drone moved to the top of the staircase to watch.

Christian got to his feet quickly. One of the Drones stood almost as fast, but Christian kicked it down the next flight of stairs and through the wooden railing sending it to the bottom of the warehouse.

The other Drone went for Christian's throat, trying to rip it out. Christian blocked the attempt, and with a quick strike to the Drone's knee, broke its leg in two.

The third came rushing down the stairs gripping a sixteen-inch knife that might as well have been a short sword. Before Christian could react, two more Drones came bursting through the walls on either side of him. They wrapped themselves around him like constrictors, pinning his arms as the charging Drone lunged with the huge knife.

Christian turned, rotated and pulled back. The knife went into one of the Drones that was bear-hugging him and went right through, plunging an inch or two into the side of Christian's torso.

The pain was instant, but it only released more power. Christian threw the dying Drone off of him and fired a shot with his free hand, hitting the third Drone square in the chest and shattering every rib in the creature's body. It dropped to the floor, choking for breath.

Before he could celebrate, the final Drone wrapped its hand around Christian's windpipe and began to dig its claws in.

Christian focused on its feeble mind. *Let go.*

The pressure was released instantly. The Drone stepped back.

By now, the Drone who'd been stabbed was on the verge of death. In moments, its body would ignite and burn the place to the ground.

Christian stepped forward. He pulled the knife from the poor thing's side and looked at the surviving Drone.

Outside. Carry him.

"No!" Evelyn shouted. "I command you not to listen!"

It was no use. The Drone did as Christian ordered, and Christian began to climb the stairs once again, moving slowly, methodically.

Evelyn suddenly seemed fearful. She was calling for re-enforcements. Christian sensed other Drones rushing to join the fight. Five, ten, maybe twenty or more.

Summoning all his strength and channeling the rage and bitterness he felt, he issued a mental command.

Stay where you are!

The clattering of feet ceased. The approaching army halted and Evelyn began to quiver.

In pain from the puncture wound, but more determined than ever, Christian marched up the stairs. He could sense her fear. He could see it on her face. She was shaking. She retreated until her back hit the wall.

He reached the top step. "Am I so much worse than you expected?" he asked.

She said nothing. She was no match for him and they both knew it. She wouldn't even fight.

Looking around, he could see this was her crypt. All the windows were blacked out just like his loft. An army of her making protected her, but they'd been stopped in their tracks.

Most likely Drake had deceived her. It was his finest art. Had he told her of Christian's strength, she would have run. She would have fled or hidden herself or given in easily. He could sense her considering that now.

"The dawn has arrived," he said.

She knew this too. She had nowhere to go.

"I won't give Drake up," she insisted.

"I don't need your permission," he growled. "If you won't tell me, I'll just take it. And in exchange, I'll spare your life as I promised."

"I won't let you in." Evelyn said.

"You have no choice."

She opened her mouth to protest but Christian had already found a way in. He began to break down her mind even as she tried desperately to keep him at bay. She slid along the wall toward one of the blacked out windows. Christian stopped her and moved closer, staring into her eyes, forcing her to look at him.

There were images. Drake was landing on the oil platform in the stolen helicopter. He was wounded; he was crawling. Evelyn in a boat rescuing him. The light came up before he could get to shore. It made things worse. Burning skin, agonizing pain.

Poison. Poison on the witch's dagger. Damn her. Damn her to hell.

Evelyn slumped to the floor, covering her face. Christian picked her back up and knocked her arms aside.

Where? Where did you take him?

He saw an airport. A private jet. It took off into the night.

Where?!

He looked deeper, focused harder. And then he realized the awful truth: she didn't know.

Now!

Not his thought, but hers. He broke free of the connection and spun around just in time to see another figure charging with a blade in its hand. Not a Drone, but a human servant. One whose presence Christian couldn't sense.

The man hit him and swung his knife with an uppercut. Christian caught the man's wrist and stopped the blade an inch from his heart, but now the rest of the army was coming. Evelyn pulled her own knife and plunged it downward towards him; it sliced across his shoulder.

He threw the human off and was tackled by a charging Drone.

The two of them went crashing backward, out through the blackened window and into the burgeoning sunlight of a new day which stung as it tried to etch lines in their skin. They tumbled, dropping toward the dark waters of the harbor five stories below.

The last thing Christian saw was Evelyn in the broken window frame, stealing a glance and then peeling back from the glare of the day and vanishing in the shadows. An instant later, he and the Drone hit the surface and the world suddenly went dark.

Chapter 7

Brief seconds in the sunlight were like fire and noise to both Christian and the Drone. The cold waters of the bay quenched that fire and silenced the noise, but the battle continued. The impact had jarred both bodies and the two of them grappled, sinking to the muddy bottom. There, Christian wrestled with the creature until he pinned it up against the algae covered wall of the concrete pier.

Despite his own pain, he held the Drone tight, giving it no ability to move. It struggled, but it was no match for Christian's strength.

Staring up at the surface Christian he fought the urge to swim upward. Even the Fallen could drown. Fire, stabbing weapons, drowning: all of these could end a so-called immortal's life.

Christian had no intention of letting that happen. At least not to him. He turned back to the struggling beast in front of him. He released its arms, grabbed its head and twisted quickly, breaking its neck. The fourth way he knew to kill a member of the undead.

The Drone went limp. Air bubbles flowed from its mouth and nose. Christian pushed off the wall and began to swim away as fast as his wounded body could move, while remaining submerged.

The heat of the Drone's immolation could be felt. The sizzling sound it made was sickening to hear, but the light allowed Christian to see where he was going. He swam to a huge wooden pylon, like an oversized algae covered telephone pole. That put him beneath the overhanging dock, swimming upwards he surfaced in the darkest recess he could find.

He sucked at the air like any other man would, thankful for its life giving properties. But now what? He was trapped. Even the reflected light was enough to sting and weaken him.

He looked around. Across the channel, he saw a small inlet and a sewer grate. It had been a long time since he'd made his home in a sewer, but it would feel like heaven on Earth if he could get there.

He took a deep breath, dove under and began to swim. The light from the Drone's destruction began to fade. Christian felt as if he was going off course. He pressed on, continuing to kick even though every extension of his wounded leg was like being struck with a blacksmith's hammer.

By the time he could see the outline of the sewer tunnel, he was beginning to black out. Only fifty feet away, but it might as well have been fifty miles.

His legs became too weak to move; only his arms were working. He sank. He hit the bottom and pulled himself forward. Though he'd stayed underwater, the sunlight still reached him. He remembered how Drake looked on the oil platform: a helpless old man.

The Half Life

Without warning he banged his head into the concrete wall around the sewer tunnel. He surfaced in the shade beside the grate, caught his breath, and with one great pull yanked it open, breaking the old rusted lock. Quickly, silently, he climbed inside like a river rat coming home.

Fortunately, it was only a storm drain. Sewage was no longer allowed to run into the river untreated, but it was still filled with filth and sludge and the smell of decay and gasoline that had come from the streets with the runoff from the storm.

He crawled through a foot of water that ran on top of six inches of sludge. When he was deep enough into the tunnel that it was almost dark, he paused and pulled himself onto a narrow ledge.

He collapsed there as the dirty water flowed by him. He noticed that his legs had been charred by the Drone's fire. The lower half of his slacks had been burned off. His skin blackened and peeling.

It was the closest he had ever been to the Ignatorum. The closest he had ever been to his own death, he thought. A little higher and the knife would have hit his abdomen. Had he been more wounded, the Drone might have snapped his neck instead. Even if it hadn't been instant, he might have floated down with the current. Eventually the sun would have finished him, burning him to ashes and nothing else. No trace of his body would have remained. No sign that he'd ever graced this earth.

Ashes to ashes, dust to dust. Even for an immortal.

With his strength slowly returning, Christian stared into the abyss surrounding him. Trash floated by; discarded things no longer wanted, needed or even thought about. He felt a strange kinship with the refuse. He wondered if his existence and struggle even mattered. Maybe the world would have been better off had he never been born. Or maybe it would have been exactly the same. Depression enveloped him in the cold dark thoughts of the Nosferatu, the inner place where the curse settled deepest.

"No," he said aloud. He would not let his mind go there.

He pushed himself up against the old battered brickwork of the tunnel and readied himself for the next act. Taking a breath, he reached for the handle of the knife sticking out of his thigh. He gripped the blade's handle tightly, took another deep breath and then, with a slight twist and a pull, drew the blade out of his leg. As the blade ripped free a primeval scream exploded from within him. It echoed over and over again, deep into the far reaches of the tunnel.

It came back to him weaker and cowed, much like he was.

He tumbled over onto his side and just laid there in the muck. The wound would close and scar but never heal.

"What was I thinking?" he muttered to himself.

He'd decided to come right after Drake. He hadn't even found him and was now wounded just like Drake.

Maybe it was vanity to think he could destroy the King of the Fallen. Perhaps that's what Elsa—or his unconscious mind—was trying to tell him in the vision. Who was he to think he would accomplish anything beyond burning in the fires of hell, like all of *his kind* did?

Not all.

The thought flickered at him from nowhere, but it was valid. Not all the Fallen burned. James Hecht, who had more reason to suffer than most for the evil he'd done, hadn't caught fire and burned to ashes when Christian shot him in New Orleans.

Why didn't he burn? Christian wondered. The answer was obvious. For the same reason that bullet snapped his head back and blew out half his skull. He was human when he died. He'd consumed enough of the woman's blood to become human again.

As absurd as it sounded, Hecht had found the exception to the rule. If the church was right—and the flames of the Ignatorum were the beginning of hellfire and brimstone—then fate, it seemed, had something else in mind for Hecht.

He was dead as dead, but he hadn't burned.

Delirious from the pain and filled with thoughts of failure, Christian pondered the idea. An escape clause, an exit ramp from all the madness. He considered the possibilities. Seventeen hundred years of torment was a long time. As for any evil deeds he'd committed against his fellow man, he figured he'd paid for them and more. For the murder of his commander almost two millennia ago, the act that brought Drake into his life, that debt was now settled. Paid. Finished.

He stared at the blade in his hand and felt a calmness come over him. Could he do it? Could he really do it?

Now that I know the secret, yes. I could do it.

And yet the thought disgusted him. He was a soldier, a captain in the 14th Legion, leader of a thousand men. For them, for him, quitting on the field of battle would be the worst sin of all. And there was no doubt in his mind, he was still at war.

"You'd need to steal the life of another to make it work." These words floated towards him from somewhere in the darkness. "Isn't that where your guilt came from in the first place?"

The voice seemed to be coming from everywhere and nowhere. It echoed around him and then faded. And then, in the distance, a pinpoint of light began to grow. Not harsh like the daylight, but soft and flickering like a candle.

"Elsa?"

The light took shape and he saw the perfect image of his lost love. She stood there in all her beauty. A young woman, like he'd known her centuries before, dressed in white and grey. She was healed of all her scars, unmarked by the burns of the inquisition. She was beautiful.

"Don't be afraid," she said. "For I've come to bring you care, love, and hope in this dark hour."

"Twice you've visited me, now," Christian said. "How can I know if you're real?"

Like the other vision, she refused to answer this question.

"I know the thoughts of your troubled mind," she said. "I always knew. I know of the great pain that you're in. I know that you've glimpsed the secret. But you fail to grasp its importance. You wish the coldness of your life to be gone, you wish the anger and the pain and the regret to be sent beyond the void forever, but you have been chosen and you have a far greater purpose than your own comfort."

He could not stop staring, afraid that she might disappear. "What did you mean about the secret?"

"I told you before; your death can accomplish nothing. Only your life can heal this broken part of the world."

Christian stared as she floated in the air like mist. Light began to move around her. He thought of the prophecy. "Are you the Angel? Are you coming back?"

She remained silent as Christian crawled towards her.

"Please," he said. "Please, answer me."

"I'm not the angel," she said.

"Then who is?"

"One you won't meet until the end," she said. "But it's not for me to show you. What I must tell you is that time is running out. After all your lifetimes on this earth there is little sand left for you. Drake is healing and is searching for something of great power, something he cannot be allowed to possess. If he grasps this new weapon, his power will grow. His darkness will be stronger than the light."

"Great," Christian grunted sarcastically. "And I thought we were doing so well."

The image did not respond to his dark humor.

"What is he's looking for?"

"Do not give up," the image of Elsa whispered. "Follow me. And when your time comes, I'll be waiting for you on the other side."

The image started to fade and Christian lunged forward. "No. Don't go. Please! I don't know where to begin. I don't know where to start. I don't even understand what you're saying. You can't keep giving me these riddles."

He reached out for Elsa and his hand passed right through the fading image of her. He pulled back as the image vanished.

Trust and believe, for faith must be your only guide now.

The darkness of the underground world regained its foothold and the sound of the trickling water was all he heard. Darkness crept back into the brick and mortar and Christian could do nothing but stare into it.

He had no idea where to go next, but he knew more than anything that he needed help. He could think of only one place to get it.

Chapter 8

Washington D.C.

Steam billowed from the cup of coffee in Agent Pfeiffer's hand.

She took a sip. Though it was piping hot she could barely feel heat on her tongue. She dumped ten sugar packs into it but couldn't taste them. She walked from the metro with a pair of dark Ray Bans on, yet the morning light felt like needles in the eyes.

What the hell is happening to me?

She hustled into FBI headquarters and took the escalator down into the comforting darkness of the basement. She'd moved her office with permission of director Tan. She'd chosen the basement not just because there were no windows or natural light down there to burn her eyes, but because there were unsolved case files and a library of research materials that could be studied without anything showing up on a computer log. And because she was tired of the looks she got from other agents and staff as she walked the upper floors.

By now she was certain that Kim Tan and Serrano were watching her every move. But they were busy, and a computer-tracking bug was all she expected out of them.

Down in the dark, she drank the rest of the coffee and began pouring over files. She could hardly believe what she was finding. There were cases of humans drinking blood all over the place. Criminals believed to be on meth that attacked and chewed off flesh of their friends. Victims, human and animal, found drained of blood. There were cases in the United States, Europe, and South America.

Going back in time she found hundreds of similar stories. Some were obviously folklore. Others seemed to be legitimate reporting of strange facts. The case of Elizabeth Bathory shocked her beyond belief.

Bathory was a countess in Hungary who, between 1585 and 1610, tortured and murdered hundreds of young women. She was said to drink and even bathe in tubs filled with their blood, because she thought it made her more youthful and alive.

When she was finally arrested and imprisoned in a small room in her own castle, dozens of victims were freed from suffering a similar fate. A list with six hundred forty names was discovered, names of peasants and young nobles she'd tortured and killed.

"Madness," Kate thought. But maybe not untrue.

"What are you doing down here?"

Kate looked up from the reports to see the face of Ashley Blackburn, her new partner assigned by Kim Tan, who was nothing more than a spy sent to watch over her shoulder. A look of frustration crossed Kate's face. She quickly closed the database. *God only knows what they'd think or do if they knew she was looking into accounts of vampirism.*

"Just doing a little research."

"On what?"

"It's personal," Kate said.

"In the FBI database?"

"An old case, you wouldn't be interested."

"Let me take a look. You know a fresh pair of eyes can never hurt."

Kate shook her head. "That's okay, Ashley. I'm sure you have your own cases to solve. Why don't you let me help you with one of those?"

Ashley frowned. "We're not getting off on the right foot, are we?"

Hell no, they weren't.

"Ashley, I'll let you in on a little secret," she said. "I don't trust you. I know who you are and why you're suddenly assigned to me. Good for you, getting in with the brass as a snitch. But I'm not interested in helping you get a leg up on the FBI ladder."

Kate stared at Ashley waiting for some type of response or reaction. None came. She was good, Kate thought. In another lifetime they could have been partners, but not now. Not in this situation. All that mattered now was survival, pure and simple. She needed answers. She didn't need this woman getting in her way.

Finally the spy spoke up. "Look Kate, Director Tan gave me this position to help you. He knows you're lying. We all do. We just can't figure out why or about what. Let us help you. We know you're in a terrible spot."

Kate looked her new partner dead in the eyes trying to gauge her level of sincerity. Then, without warning, words came into Kate's mind. Whispers. *You psychotic little freak, I can't believe they've let you stay on active duty, let alone raise a child.*

Kate couldn't tell whether it was real or her imagination. Ashley's body language certainly didn't suggest she was thinking that.

"Excuse me," Kate said, standing and brushing past Ashley.

Kate made her way to the bathroom overwhelmed by everything that was happening. Her mind flashed to the cases she'd been going over, even more to the ancient history of the Blood Countess. The woman drinking blood from Billy Ray's neck popped into her mind: a thought she felt she'd purged from her memory. And then the image of her husband dead on the floor of their kitchen two years ago, blood all around him, but not enough to explain why he was so pale.

Somehow it was all connected. *All of it.* And the only person with answers was the blond man she'd seen in the swamps.

She needed to take a leave of absence. Needed to get away from all of this and find him if there was any hope to make sense of it.

"You alright in there?"

Oh my God, Ashley, leave me alone. Kate began splashing water on her face as Ashley came into the bathroom.

"Yes, I'm fine. Just a stomach bug, I think."

Ashley came up, washing her hands and checking her makeup.

Kate tuned her out immediately. Her only thought now was on finding this man and where to start. She didn't know who he was. Didn't know where he came from and yet, for some reason, she felt he was near. For some reason, she felt he was north, possibly New York City. Why she would think this she had no idea, but the thought was strong, powerful, and it kept coming back. That's where she'd start once this was over.

Kate grabbed a towel and dried her face. Then, staring into the mirror she was shocked. Her image was blurred. She reached out and wiped the mirror, but it was clean and dry.

Ashley turned to her. "You alright? You look like you've just seen a ghost."

Kate turned quickly. "Just stressed. Shall we go?"

Ashley smiled falsely, turned back to the mirror and then froze. Kate's image was blurred like a photo of a runner moving at high speed, but Ashley's reflection was sharp and clear.

"What wrong with the…?"

Without warning, the mirror shattered under the butt of Kate's Glock. Startled, Ashley turned to Kate, her mouth gapping open in shock. She saw only a blur as Kate's pistol smashed her temple and she went down like a sack of rice.

With quick efficiency, Kate dragged her into one of the stalls and cuffed her to the main pipe behind the toilet.

"You're not taking my son away from me! You hear me? No one's gonna take him away!"

Ashley started to come around, so Kate gave her a left jab to her temple knocking her out again. "Sweet dreams, partner."

Grabbing Ashley's phone, gun and wallet, Kate locked the stall from the inside and crawled out under the door. She straightened her clothes and walked out of the bathroom. She was now, or would be momentarily, a fugitive on the run.

The blond man. She would find him. She would make him talk. Force him to undo whatever he'd done to her. That was her only hope.

She made her way out of the building. The sunlight felt like sandpaper on her skin, but she pressed forward, rushing down the stairs and out onto the sidewalk. She passed dozens of people on the way. None of them took a second glance, until a voice shouted to her.

"Agent Pfeiffer!"

She looked out of instinct, spotting an African-American woman in a wheelchair whom she didn't know. "Agent Pfeiffer, I need to talk to you," the woman shouted, wheeling toward Kate.

Kate stared for a second and then she panicked and ran. She raced for the metro station, hearing the woman calling even as she rounded a turn and jumped onto the steep escalator that dove beneath the city streets. Unable to control her emotions she began pushing people out of the way in her haste to reach the bottom.

What had she done? Her career was over. If they caught her, they'd put her in prison or an institution somewhere.

She made it to the platform at slowed down. At least the darkness of the underground station relieved the pain of the sunlight. She tried to calm down but felt the paranoia of being followed. She was certain they were after her already. *Who was that woman? How did she know my name?*

She had to get out of Washington. The city was covered with security cameras and the FBI would review them all. They'd piece together what was happening. They'd build a task force and hunt her down. All she had was this one chance, one tiny window of opportunity before Ashely woke up and screamed for help. She couldn't go home, couldn't see Cal one last time, or collect him and take him with her. If she had any hope at all she had to leave now.

Mixing with the horde of commuters gave her a sense of invisibility, and as soon as the next train arrived, she climbed on board. The car slowly filled with people going about their daily business. No one was looking at her. But the train didn't move.

Come on. Let's go.... Let's go!

The Metro refused to budge and the doors stood wide and inviting. The other passengers around her began to shift on their feet. Even they felt something was off.

She was ready to bolt when the doors closed with a hiss. No one came busting through the crowd shouting out her name. No agents appeared on the platform making a last minute dash to catch the train as it sped away. She breathed a sigh of relief. She was safe for the moment. Maybe, just maybe, she had enough time to get away.

Chapter 9

West Africa

The King of the Undead lay in a pit of filth, submerged in slimy, fetid water filled with algae, bacteria and leeches. A thousand of them covered him; his arms, his legs, his chest, even his face. From the edge of the pit, almost nothing of Drake's bare skin could be seen.

Zwana insisted this was necessary, the most vital step of all, but covered in the blood-sucking creatures Drake felt weaker and weaker.

Only hatred spurred him on. *Christian. Elsa. The Church. Drake hated all of them. He would see them fall. One by one, he would bring them down. His will to live burned as bright as ever, and he would survive through this madness. He would find this weapon and destroy them one by one.*

With this in mind, he'd lay in the pit for hours each day. At night, Zwana would drag him out, pry the leeches off of him and force him to drink some kind of firewater.

The leeches draw the poison. Zwana continued to insist. The drink is to replenish your demon's blood.

"You see," Zwana said, looking a pile of the creatures, "the leeches are dead." Many appeared to be. Their color drained. Their slimy skin shriveled and dry.

"Like you, they take blood," Zwana added. "The poison of the witch was attacking your blood. Now it's gone."

Delirious and powerless, Drake focused on Tereza who stood close by. He placed one thought in her mind: *If this doesn't work, kill him.*

She nodded imperceptibly, her eyes drawn to a message on her satellite phone. "Perhaps this will strengthen you," she said. "Christian has been destroyed."

Drake narrowed his gaze but said nothing.

"According to Evelyn your plan worked perfectly," Tereza said. "Christian was so preoccupied with finding you that he never saw or sensed the attack coming. She watched him burn."

Drake wanted to believe it.

"The woman lies," Zwana said, chewing on one of the dead leeches, spitting its head back into the pit.

"Which woman?" Drake asked.

"The one farthest from you."

"And how would you know?"

"I see things," Zwana insisted. "As I saw your coming here, I also watched as your enemy fall into the waters. But he is not the one who burned. The woman lies to gain your favor."

In his cold, dead heart Drake knew Zwana was correct. His enemy could not be so easily destroyed. "What else do you see?"

"It is far distant," Zwana said. "But he will not come alone. He will stand at the head of an army."

Another of Drake's unspoken fears.

"You'll need your own army to fight him," Zwana said. "And you'll need it soon."

Christian had forsworn the turning of humans a long time ago. Would he really change his ways and build his own army of the Fallen? Drake didn't believe this and, if Zwana saw this, then Drake doubted his abilities. But there was something else…"Has Christian begun taking humans into the void?"

"There is one," Zwana said.

"One is hardly an army," Drake said. "Do you know if he will change more of them?"

Zwana stared at Drake as if wondering at his game.

"I am your master," Drake demanded. "You will speak when I command you to. And if you have the sight, you will share it with me."

Zwana looked off into the distance as if he was staring through time. "At the end, Christian will have only humans on his side," he said. "You will have an army of demons and the Dark Star in your hand. You will break him. You will break his body and his immortal power will be vanquished from this earth."

Funny, Drake thought, how a fortune teller who promised good things always seemed more reliable than one who foretold ill. Still, it made sense, Christian and his love of the humans. Of course he would rouse some to his side.

This Drake could accept and even look forward to, but there was one problem. The shattering of the Brethren had thrown his plans into disarray. In the absence of their masters, armies that had taken a millennium to build would devour themselves in weeks or months. There was no time to rebuild his organization. No time to turn enough new soldiers and train them to avoid the addiction of the blood. He was at a loss until a thought occurred to him. There was one place that remained untouched by Christian's meddling, one army of the Fallen that was still intact. *The Army of Seine. The foot-soldiers of Artimous.*

The name rang in Drake's heart with thoughts of betrayal and contempt, second only to Christian's. But now… now it offered hope.

"Continue the treatment," Drake ordered.

"Tomorrow," Zwana said.

"No," Drake demanded. "Now! I will be healed by morning, or you will suffer the consequences."

Zwana nodded. Reluctantly he helped Drake back into the pit and stirred the water allowing the surviving leaches swarm over Drake's body.

As they covered him, it dawned on Drake that roles in his great struggle had now been reversed. He was the hunted and Christian was now the hunter, perhaps even aligned with the Church if Zwana's vision was correct. But Drake now possessed what Christian had lost: an oracle, a seer of his own who could look into the future and foretell its myriad of wrinkles and folds.

Zwana would be his version of the witch who'd been at Christian's side for so long. With such foresight, he would surprise Christian. Appearing when and where his old friend least expected it, much as Elsa had surprised him in the swamp.

He would put a dagger in Christian's heart and take as much pleasure from the surprised look on his old enemy's face as he did in the ultimate victory it would give him.

Chapter 10

Vatican City, Italy

The curled parchment before them was more than a thousand years old. And still its mystery had not been solved.

It is said we shall become blind,

even as they begin to see.

Bishop Anton Messini read these words from the ancient parchment written in Greek. His aged hands trembled with the first stage of Parkinson's and his tired eyes strained to focus on the faded ink. He'd wanted to see the words for himself, to make sure they hadn't been misinterpreted or mistranslated by the scribes all those years ago.

"You still look upon the prophecy as if it moves you, Bishop."

The voice was firm and strong, everything Messini was not. It came from Henrick Vanderwall, the new *Primus,* the leader of the hunters of the *Ignis Purgata*: *Holy Order of the Righteous Fire*. His men were the Church's army in the battle with the Fallen. They walked the front lines. They fought and died facing the demons in the night.

Messini was their spiritual leader. Their commander in chief. He looked after their souls. But Henrick was their field general.

"Simon believed it," Messini whispered, thinking of the prophecy and his dead friend who had been the Primus for decades before Henrick. "Simon believed it enough to allow the demon to turn his mind against us. Just as John of Alexandria was taken in centuries ago."

He put the paper down, his hands now shaking with anger. "If I could, I'd burn this parchment. I would destroy it, erasing all record of this accursed prophecy from existence."

"Then why don't you?"

"You know very well why," Messini said bitterly. "It's not my place to decide."

"You could disavow it," Henrick suggested. "Make a pronouncement. The men would appreciate the clarity."

"Yes," Messini said. "I could."

"Then you should," Henrick insisted. "Immediately."

Messini cut his eyes at Henrick. "Be careful. You exceed your position with such demands."

"My apologies," Henrick said. "I'm only trying to…"

Messini waved at him as if the apology wasn't necessary. He turned and gazed out his office window. Soft clouds floated by, adrift on a slight breeze in a blue, Mediterranean sky. But the beauty of the day did not register. For the Bishop was living deep within his mind, contemplating the future. The further out he looked, the darker his thoughts became. He was troubled and confused. He was angry with his brother of so many years, Simon Lathach. Angry that he'd left the fight. Angry that he'd made such a foolish choice as to trust a demon.

Still, Messini thought, it was strange he should be angry. For he lived, and Simon Lathach was dead. Yet, he couldn't escape the feeling that his old friend had let him down. "Careless at the end," he whispered. "Reckless."

In truth, Simon's acts bordered on insanity. The thought of giving the Church's most prized possession to a demon. Why didn't Simon just listen to him and retire? He'd still be here, still be around to counsel him and help him in these difficult times. He'd still be alive to argue his points endlessly as he so loved to do.

Messini sighed to himself. In some ways the words of the parchment were already proving true. Without Simon to guide him, Bishop Messini felt blind. Until the end at least, Simon's judgment had never failed either of them. If the gift of discernment was truly bestowed from above, it had landed on Simon's shoulders squarely and doubly so, even if it failed him at the last.

He turned back to Henrick, who'd been injured in the fight with the demon. One bullet had hit him in the leg, but that wound had been easily repaired. A second shot had taken out his right eye and nicked his ocular bone, leaving an angled scar that streaked back up into Henrick's hair. A patch covered the missing eye.

"Not many leave the order without battle wounds," Messini said, putting his hand on Henrick's powerful shoulder. "But your wounds seem only to have made you harder, stronger and more determined."

"Thank you, Bishop. They have."

Messini nodded. Henrick was young and tough as nails. Well trained after years as Simon's second. He would do well as the new leader, but even so Messini would not allow him free reign. That had been his mistake with Simon.

Remembering that Henrick had arrived unannounced, he changed the subject. "What do you have for me?"

"Changes," Henrick said. "Beginning with this."

Henrick placed on the Bishop's nine-hundred-year-old desk what appeared to be a large rifle case.

Messini could guess what lay inside. He'd heard the rumors. Henrick intended to modernize the *Ignis Purgata*, to change the way they fought.

"My men will now use weapons crafted in this century not those designed in the distant past. They'll wear body armor. They'll carry guns."

"Guns cannot harm the demons, Henrick. You know that."

"This is no ordinary gun, Bishop." He opened the case and pulled out the most advanced rifle Bishop Messini had ever seen.

"What is this new machine you have?" the Bishop asked. "Is it a flame thrower of sorts?"

It was a good guess, for it had long been known that fire also killed the Fallen.

"No, your Excellence. This is a million watt, ultraviolet emitter. A rifle that fires light. I've had these in development for years and finally they're ready. They mimic the radiation of the Sun. If a demon gets caught in the beam from one of these, their powers are subdued almost instantly. Then the hunter can move in for the kill without fear of their great strength."

The Bishop was intrigued. "Is it safe to turn on? Can I see it working?"

"Yes to both," Henrick said. He donned a pair of unusually large sunglasses with lenses as black as night. He handed the Bishop a matching pair.

The Bishop put them on. The world became almost pitch dark.

"It's very difficult to see. How will you fight with these?"

"You'll see the whole room in a moment."

The Bishop heard the weapon powering up. It sounded like the wind rushing through a tunnel. An instant later the whole room lit up as if it were broad daylight. Within the aura of light was a circular beam of a slightly different shade, bluer in tint, more concentrated. A spot light, Messini thought, a focused beam within a beam.

As Henrick moved the rifle and the spotlight around the room, he explained. "We know the demons are unaffected by artificial light. This is due to both the general weakness of artificial light and its lack of an ultraviolet component. What you see before you remedies both of those concerns. The smaller light is a concentrated and focused beam of ultraviolet rays. A million watts of energy at its center."

Henrick switched off the gun. The room went dark instantly.

Bishop Messini removed his glasses. "Very impressive. What do you call this new creation of yours?"

"I call it the Nova Rifle."

A glimmer of hope returned to the Bishop's mind. Maybe technology would help win the war against the Nosferatu. Maybe they had been stuck in the seventeenth century for too long.

Unfortunately, the moment of hope was replaced by apprehension regarding the conversation that he and Henrick were about to have. "Please have a seat Henrick. We have much to discuss."

Henrick showed a slight look of disappointment as he placed the weapon back in its case, and sat down across from the Bishop.

"Henrick, you will lead these men, but you will report to me on a daily basis. Not ad hoc as Simon was allowed to do. Also, you must assure me that you will follow my orders to the letter."

"I'm confused your excellence. If I am to lead these men, I must decide the strategy for the destruction of the Fallen. I--"

"You are the leader, yes," Messini interrupted. "But from here on out you will take your orders from me. And your first order is to search for the angel referred to in this prophecy."

"So you do believe it," Henrick said accusingly.

"No," the Bishop said. "But unless it is proven untrue, then it is my duty—our duty—to protect this being from Drake and his kind."

"Wasted time," Henrick said. "Such a thing does not exist."

"We need to be certain," the Bishop said.

Henrick grew more furious with each passing second. The Bishop imagined his thoughts. *To be watched over like a schoolboy. To be given a task he disagreed with. These orders would test any man.*

"I beg of you," Henrick said. "Commission others to search for this false idol, others who believe it can be found."

"No," Messini said firmly. "They would be swayed as Simon was, but you... you alone would never give in to any demon's trick. You alone are suited for this task by your very disbelief. If others come to me and say, 'I have seen this thing; I have felt its power,' I must by prudence doubt them. But if you come to me with such a claim, I will know it's true."

Henrick stewed, unable to refute what was essentially a grand compliment.

"I beg of you, Bishop, give this task to others. My target should be the demon that killed Simon. The blond one who enters our churches and lives in blasphemy by calling himself Christian."

"For what purpose? Revenge? No one wants revenge on this demon more than I, but I refuse it. Vengeance is the providence of God. We have another purpose."

"Not revenge," Henrick insisted. "Protection. The blasphemer is a threat. Our greatest threat now. And then once he has been sent to Hell, I will find Drakos and dispatch him as well. And then—and only then—the curse shall be broken!"

"Do you think it will be that easy?" Messini asked. The question was rhetorical. "To destroy the King of the Fallen or even the one who almost killed you already? Don't let confidence blind you to the difficulty of the task."

"I'm not blind," Henrick said. He spoke angrily, perhaps because he was, in fact, half blind now, or perhaps because the words brought him back to the prophecy he disagreed with. "I move forward with eyes open. Throwing off Simon's myopic vision. That's why I bring you these new weapons and ideas."

Henrick's face was red with rage, and suddenly Messini saw what Simon had feared. Henrick was strong, but he had little self-control.

"*Simon's myopic vision*," the Bishop repeated sadly. "So quickly you speak ill of the dead. You, Henrick, are alive only because of him. He saved you years back and it seems you have resented him for it."

"It's not resentment; it's-"

"Enough," the Bishop said, cutting off all further conversation. "You will do as ordered, or I will rescind your appointment of command and remove you this instant."

Henrick fumed and for a second looked as if he would explode, but after a breath or two, he calmed himself enough to speak. "And if I find this angel," Henrick said with disgust in his voice, "then what? One by one we cleanse the filthy demons? Forgive them for all the lives they've stolen?"

"If God chooses to send them mercy, who are you to deny it?"

Henrick could not respond to this without denying his very faith and revealing himself as unfit to be in the order and, perhaps, the church itself. But the Bishop could sense it already; Henrick didn't want the demons to be forgiven, even if God did.

"His will, not ours," Messini reminded.

Henrick nodded slightly. His face still contorted.

"If there is no angel, you will not find one," Messini said. "But if one exists, not only will we be able to undo the mistake we made seventeen hundred years ago which started this war, but we'll be able to save hundreds of thousands whom the demons have tricked into a life of darkness, whom they've turned with fear, intimidation and cunning. Not all who've fallen wished for that life—even you know that. Our true business is the saving of souls. And those who've been confused and tormented and tortured into darkness need salvation more than any other. But first we must determine if this miracle exists. And if so—if this proves to be the task God chooses for us—then we must not fail Him."

Henrick stared at Bishop Messini for a long, drawn out moment. It was the gaze of a man willing to live and die for a cause, the gaze of a man would choose to face a demon, even the King of the Demons, and not back down. That much Messini was certain of. Henrick was a solider forged from molten rock, turned into iron by the pain he'd experienced and sharpened by years of struggle. But even the greatest warrior was of no use if he could not follow orders.

"How am I supposed to find an angel that doesn't even know what it is?"

"Proceed to the Bernese Highlands. At our hospice in Interlaken you will find your brother in arms Aldo Gruvaleu."

"Aldo?" Henrick said with surprise. "Surely you must be kidding. His mind was taken by a demon in the mountains of Croatia. He's been dismissed. He can never re-join us again. That is the law."

"I know the law, Henrick. But you will do as I say. And if my instinct is true you will find him useful."

"How is that possible?"

"He claims he can hear the voices of the dammed," Bishop Messini said.

"Of course," Henrick scoffed, "It's happened before. But they're just echoes."

"If they were echoes of the demon who possessed him, they would have ended by now. Instead he has filled journals with the thoughts he hears."

"Journals?"

"Hundreds of them. Rantings of pain and anger, of greed and lust. Many speak of acts that have occurred in the time *after* you and Simon dispatched the demon that possessed him. They cannot be echoes."

"Madness then."

"Perhaps," Messini said.

Henrick's gaze sharpened. "How is this possible?"

"When the demon possessed his mind, part of Aldo was dragged into the void. The demon died without releasing him. A final act of bitterness. But if it's true, then it's possible that part of Aldo's mind was caught there. Stranded on the other side.

"And if it's just a derangement?"

"Then Aldo is to be mourned even though he lives."

Henrick nodded, he seemed to understand. And finally he seemed to be in agreement. "But if he can hear them…"

"Then he can find those whom the angel is calling," Messini said. "And you can find the angel, if it exists at all."

Henrick sighed and nodded. "I don't agree with this approach," he said. "But I will obey your authority. However, if Aldo is mad or this seems fruitless after a time, I will renew my request to go after our enemies. And if necessary, I will go above you, to the Quorum of Five for permission. For even you serve your office at the pleasure of others."

Chapter 11

New York City

Red and blue light painted Kate's face as she sat in the corner of her darkened motel room. The wallpaper was dingy, the carpet old and tired. It reminded her of a crime scene. Fortunately the light wasn't coming from police cruisers parked outside. It was a flashing neon sign just beyond her window.

She stared at it for a while. Red, then blue, then red and then blue again. An endless beacon, forever shining in the night at a dingy refuge for the unwanted of Manhattan. It called to the pimps and hookers and the addicts and the lost. At forty dollars an hour the rooms were always full. Kate paid a hundred for the night, no questions asked. And since the flimsy door provided little safety, she'd un-holstered her weapon and placed it on the table beside her. Since then, she'd stared out the window, waiting for someone to come for her, and hoping it wouldn't be the police or FBI.

"Where are you?" she whispered to the night, thinking of the blond man. She'd sensed he was in New York but now that she was here it seemed nothing more than insanity.

A knock at the door startled her. She put a hand on her Glock. "Who is it?"

"Who the hell do you think it is?" a voice called back. "Open the damn door."

Kate unlocked the door and let a skinny man, wearing wire rimmed glasses into the room. Barton Hall, an informant of hers. He wore an old suit from J.C. Penny. His hair was thin and greasy. He looked like he hadn't showered in days.

Kate had busted him years ago when he was a small-time hood trying to go big time by purchasing guns in the US and shipping them to countries where the right to bear arms was limited to the police and military.

Since then, the FBI had used him to stop a half-dozen similar operations before giving him immunity. Instead of witness protection, they'd faked his death and snuck him out of LA. He'd chosen to come to New York and apparently—almost inconceivably—had picked up right where he'd left off. Although he now ran a smaller, more discreet operation. Maybe that's why he was still alive.

"What's with the no lights?" he asked. "You staking someone out?"

"Don't ask questions, Barton. Just show me what you've got."

He flicked a switch and the crummy room revealed all its defects. To Kate's surprise the light didn't bother her eyes.

"You alright, agent?"

"What the hell is that supposed to mean?"

"You don't look well," Barton said. "Unless you're going for some new Goth image or something. I mean don't get me wrong; I find it kind of hot myself. And if you wanted to frisk me or strip search me, or something, I might not be unhappy about it you know, but—"

"Barton," she said, interrupting. "I haven't killed anyone today. But I'm not above starting right now. Do you understand me?"

"Sure," he said. "Sure."

He turned to the duffel bag he carried. "Look, I couldn't find everything you asked for on such short notice. So I brought the best I had."

As Kate watched, he unzipped the bag and removed the contents.

"First, I brought you a modified Taser. This thing will stop a charging bull or a meth addict whose mind has been blown to the moon. Next, I have the biggest machine gun I own, an M-16 with grenade launcher."

"And what the hell am I supposed to do with that? I can't just walk around New York carrying an assault rifle with a 40 mm launcher on the bottom rail. This isn't Baghdad, you dumb-ass."

Stunned, Barton looked into the bag.

"You said heavy weapons. I figured you were looking to set up a fake buy, not arm yourself. Besides, this is all I had on two hour's notice. Look, if you don't want it, I can come back tomorrow, maybe by late afternoon. And next time be more specific. You can't get what you want if you don't ask for it. In fact, sometimes even if you do, even then problems crop up, issues, supply constraints…"

"I told you to bring me a nine millimeter Mac-10. Two of them, if you had them. How much more specific do I have to be?"

Kate tuned Barton out as he went on and on about the hardships of illegal gun running. An image of the blond man had flashed into her head. She froze. The image was powerful and she could see the surrounding area. Tribeca. He was walking the streets in the old meatpacking district.

The image faded as Barton's babbling voice returned.

"…and that's just here in America. You can't imagine what it's like overseas." He stopped. "Are you even listening to me? What Kind of Fed ignores an informant when he's spilling his guts out."

"Time to go," she said. "I'll take both of them. You have any ammo for this monstrosity?"

"I do, but hold up," Barton said. "I need some cabbage before I hand this stuff over. And to be honest, I'd like to know what you're going to do with this? I don't want to be part of anything weird here. You know, FBI agent goes postal or something."

"Is that what you think this is?" she asked, wondering if he'd heard about her fugitive status.

So far the FBI had refrained from blasting it all over the national news, probably because they were embarrassed or confused and would rather capture her themselves than tell the whole world one of their own had gone rogue.

"I think… you're undercover," he managed.

"And what happens if my cover is blown?"

He thought for a minute. "My cover gets blown."

"That's right," she said. "Word of my location gets out, I'm not going to bother having you arrested. I'm just going to let the wrong people know you're alive and where you can be found."

"Not a problem," he said. "I was never here. And neither were you."

"Just leave the stuff and get out," she said. "Your money's in the drawer over there."

As he went to the dresser Kate picked up the rifle, testing the weight. She held it firmly, with the butt pressed into her shoulder. "This will do nicely, actually. Good work, Barton."

He looked up from counting the money and seemed to look right through her for a second. His face was a little white. "There's more here than we agreed on."

"Lucky for you," she said. "Now leave."

He held up a hand and backed out the door, shutting it behind him. Kate sat and loaded the weapon. *Tonight,* she thought, *tonight she would get her answers. Tonight she'd find out what the hell the blond man had done to her.*

Chapter 12

The fluorescent lights flickered above Christian as he rode the B train downtown and the subway cars rumbled from station to empty station. The flickering made Christian think of himself and all the other members of the Fallen, caught between heaven, hell and the earthly domain. He lived in no-man's land. He flashed in and out, just like the lights. And his life was one empty station after another for seventeen hundred years.

As the train pulled into another station and stopped, Christian noticed some graffiti written on the wall across the tracks. It was the title of a book, a biography about Jim Morrison. *No One Here Gets Out Alive.*

That statement was true as well, even for an immortal. Even he and Drake would have to meet their maker one day.

Christian turned his eyes from the window in an attempt to shut his brain off from the endless questions it kept asking. He controlled his breathing and cleared his mind trying to meditate, but the quieter his thoughts got the more one image kept coming back to him. It was the image of a woman filled with anger. The sensation reminded him of the brief glimpse he'd had into Anya's soul.

Finally the train arrived at his stop, and here Christian felt the presence more acutely. He stepped from the subway car and glanced around. The platform was empty. The walkover that crossed the tracks to the other line was vacant. Not a soul could be seen at three in the morning, but Christian knew he wasn't alone.

The doors shut behind him, and the train pulled away heading down the tube, on about its business, but the sensation did not leave. He wondered if Anya was stalking him, if her presence in Boston had been part of the trap. Certainly her warnings had made him feel strangely overconfident. If she wasn't to be trusted, perhaps she was back here to finish the job.

He tried to stretch his mind. To feel the shape of the image the way one reaches around in a darkened room to find the walls. The truth came slowly. It wasn't Anya. *It was Kate.*

He climbed the stairs quickly and stepped out into the night and turned to see her waiting for him. He could feel her anger, confusion, and loss.

"I can help you," he said.

She stepped from the shadows carrying a military rifle with a grenade launcher attached. The rifle was locked and loaded. A laser sight illuminated his chest. "I'm not going to miss you this time."

"You didn't miss me last time," he said. "In fact, you ruined one of my best shirts."

"You think that's funny?" she said stepping forward.

"No," he replied. "But it was expensive."

They stared at each other for a moment like alley cats meeting on a midsummer's night, taking inventory of each other. Gauging each other's condition.

"You're troubled," Christian said. "Let me help you."

"And you're wounded," she replied. "Maybe I should finish you off."

Obviously Kate had begun to discover some of her telekinetic powers.

"I am wounded," he said. "Don't be foolish enough to think it will stop me from taking you."

"What did you do to me?" she yelled, her voice echoing down the alleyway.

"I'll explain, but this is not the time or place."

She pressed the rifle to her shoulder. "I say it is. Now tell me what you've done."

He sighed with frustration. He would try to explain. But he knew it would only lead to more questions. "I did what you asked," he replied. "I healed you. I can see that was a mistake. I should have let you die."

"Is this some trick?" she asked. "What's happening to me? Is it radiation? Poison?"

"No trick," he said. "I told you there were darker things in this world than what you were after. To keep you from dying, I had to turn you into one of them."

"One of what?"

He let a raft of images drift from his mind. Things he'd seen, places he'd been. She picked up his stream of consciousness.

"This isn't possible," she said, starting to shake with rage and confusion. "This isn't real. This can't be real."

"I'm sorry, but it is."

Her eyes narrowed. Her voice firmed. Her grip on the rifle constricted. "I don't believe you."

"Then pull the trigger," he said.

A part of her wanted to shoot; he could feel that. But she was conflicted. As she struggled with the anger he saw the truth. She was on the run and not interested in drawing attention to herself. For another, she was a soldier of law and order, not given to shooting people without absolute cause. But above all else, she was afraid. Afraid she'd kill him, but more afraid that she wouldn't.

So he pressed her.

Aim for my heart.

The laser dot dropped to his exact center of mass.

Pull the trigger.

She shook her head.

Pull it!

Almost instantly she responded. The rifle cracked twice. The strange feeling of matter passing through his body took Christian's breath away. Instantly, two clouds of dust exploded out of the brick wall behind him, but he stood, unmoved by the attack.

"Soon you'll be like this," he said. "You'll appear to be alive, but it'll be a deception. Your body is slowly dying. Your humanity is slipping away. Before long you'll feel nothing except pain, then your transformation will be complete. You will be one of us. The undead. The Nosferatu. A demon of the night."

"Turn me back!"

"I can't."

"Turn me back, I said!"

She was coming unglued as the truth hit. Her thoughts were jumping all over the place. Her son. Her mother. Her dead partner. The gate closed in her mind; the switch went off and she attacked.

He dove to the side as she opened up on full auto, blasting away at him, and trying to track him with the weapon. She was accurate, but he was way too fast. She couldn't keep up. Across the street, vacant storefronts took the brunt of the assault as shop windows were blasted out and mannequins riddled with bullets.

She turned further and launched a grenade. Christian dove to avoid the projectile as it whizzed past him, hitting a parked car and blasting it to pieces in a fireball.

As she tried to pump another grenade into the launcher, Christian charged, hitting her in a flash. He knocked the weapon from her grip with one hand and grabbed her by the collar with the other.

Alarms were howling up and down the street. New York's finest would be on their way in seconds, armed to the teeth for a battle with terrorists. They needed to leave. And fast.

"Come with me."

Her mind was overloaded and spinning. In that state, it gave itself to this command, welcoming the clarity that following orders brought. But before they could get far, police cars swooped into the area.

Gun-toting officers popped out and took positions behind their doors. "Freeze! On the ground! Now!"

Christian surveyed the situation. He was impervious to their bullets, but Kate was still mired in the Half-Life. She would die as easily as any human. He didn't want to hurt any of the police officers, but they could never understand. Nor could they be allowed to stop him from continuing on.

Christian looked down at his feet where the rifle had fallen. He flipped it up with his foot like a soccer player flicking a ball and caught it in midair and began firing before the police even knew what had happened. Bullets were streaking everywhere. Kate lay on the ground covering up. The police were diving for cover as the headlights, spotlights and blue and red light bars on the roofs of their cars were blasted out in quick succession.

Streetlights went next. Up and down the road, one after another. In a moment it was dark.

When the echoes of the gunfire faded, one of the brave officers risked a glance around the armored door of his cruiser. Aside from the burning car they'd been called to investigate, the street was empty. The suspect was gone.

Chapter 13

The sound of explosions rocked Ida Washington from her sleep.

She struggled to get into her wheel chair, heaving herself from the bed into the seat and pushing forward. She raced towards the window to see what was going on, only to remember that in Christian's lair the windows were covered by blackened steel plates.

The security cameras!

She wheeled over to the computer console, rolling across everything in her way like a monster truck. She flicked the monitor on, but the sounds of destruction had already died. She switched from one camera to another, there were police in the alleyway several blocks over, fire trucks on the main street. She saw a car burning and a crew preparing to douse it but nothing to indicate what had happened.

The sound of locks turning in the stainless steel door came next. She turned to see Christian carrying a woman over his shoulder. As he laid her on the couch, Ida shut the door.

"I should have known it was you!" Ida said. "Who else wakes an old woman up with explosions in the middle of the night?"

"Not my doing," he said, and then pointed to Kate's unconscious form. "All her fault."

Ida's brow went up. "Agent Pfeiffer."

"Yeah. The woman I sent you to find."

"About that," Ida muttered. "I had a little problem getting her attention. And then it turned out the FBI was looking for her, so I stopped asking questions and came home."

Christian nodded, looking around at the mess, books and notes and empty cups were scattered all over the room. "Is that why this place looks like a tornado came thru here? It was neat and tidy when I left."

"I don't have time to clean up," Ida said. "While you were out gallivanting around, I've been working. Very hard, I might add."

"Gallivanting?" he said. "I've been stabbed, shot at, half drowned and almost blown up – most recently by her. You call that gallivanting?"

She dismissed him with a wave of her hand. "That's common place in your line of work. Now, like I was saying. While you've been off playing, I've actually been getting some solid work done and I have much to tell you. Now be a good boy, and make me some tea since you woke me up at this ridiculous hour of the night."

It dawned on Christian that Ida had been lonely. And that this little display was her way of telling him she was glad he'd come home.

He went to the kitchen, wondering what Drake might think if he saw his mortal enemy being bossed around by a frail, seventy-year-old woman in wheelchair. Maybe, he thought, the King of the Nosferatu would die laughing.

Before Christian could answer, Kate began to stir and Ida wheeled herself over to the bar.

"Where are you going?" Christian asked.

"Poor thing is going to need a drink once you tell her all your *secrets of the night* stuff."

"I already told her."

"Then I'll make it a double."

"Well, that's not a bad idea," Christian said. "She seems to have lost her mind."

As Ida mixed a drink for their new guest, Christian went to check the camera feeds himself. He had a four block radius around his home under constant surveillance. He found the cops were still on the street that Kate had littered with shell casings. They seemed baffled and showed no sign of picking up the trail. The fire department had arrived and were dousing the burning car with foam. "There goes the neighborhood," he muttered.

"Where am I?" Kate said, coming out of her delirium.

Christian turned. "You're safe. This is my home. And you're in luck. The police don't seem to be coming our way. Although, I could call them if you'd rather go explain things to them than stay here?"

Kate looked at him nervously.

"I'm not going to hurt you," he said. "If that was my goal, I'd have done it while you were unconscious or before the cops came. Or I'd have let you die in the swamps, or in the 9th ward before that."

He sensed her searching him and calming down. "I'm sorry about the shooting… I wasn't thinking."

As Kate spoke, Ida rolled up and offered her a tumbler of Jack Daniel's on the rocks. "You drink this sweetie," she said. "I even put some honey in it, because you sound like you have a sore throat."

Kate's eyes grew wide. "You!"

"Yes me," Ida said. "A lot of chaos could have been avoided if you'd have just slowed down and talked to me. You young people are always in such a hurry."

Kate took a quick drink. Her mind grew more focused. "What about the cameras in the squad cars?" She seemed more worried about getting arrested than anything at this point.

"The video will be blurry at best," he said. "And I took us the long way around before doubling back. If they pick up our trail at all, they'll be going the wrong way."

Kate sat back. She was shaking, but her mind had finally stopped spinning. She almost felt as if something beyond her had stopped it, like a foot dragging in the dirt off the edge of the merry-go-round.

"Who are you people?" she asked.

Ida spoke first. "My name's Ida," she said. "He has a lot of names, but he prefers to be called Sonny."

"And she lies a lot," Christian said, before giving his name and explaining the situation in the best way he could.

Kate took it all with surprising calm. After an hour of back and forth, she ran out of deeper questions and sat there numb and still.

With Kate seeming to understand what she found herself in, he explained who Drake was, what had really happened in the swamps, and why he needed to hunt for Drake now more than ever.

"I can't wrap my head around all this," Kate said. "But I guess I'm not going to wake up and find out I'm dreaming."

"It's not a dream," Christian said. "For any of us."

"So what do I do?"

"The only way back is forward," he said. "You have two choices. If you this think this messenger of forgiveness is out there somewhere, you're welcome to go look for it. But I can't tell you how to search or where to start, and I can't come with you, even though you'll be a danger to yourself and everyone around you before too long. I have to find this weapon before Drake does. If I don't, it won't matter whether this angel is real or not, because Drake will turn *everything* to darkness."

"And where do you start that quest?" she asked.

"I know someone, like our friend Ida here, who's spent all his life studying the past, collecting books and records and knowledge." He glanced at Ida. "You should meet him actually, you two would hit it off I think. He lives in Germany. He's the caretaker of a vast, secret library. If anyone has a clue that can lead us to this weapon, it'll be him."

Kate sat back. Christian didn't pry into her thoughts but she was broadcasting them unconsciously. She was thinking of going back to Washington and turning herself in just to see her son once more. She was also considering going to New Orleans since that was where everyone had expected to find this healer. But now that she'd seen Drake through Christian's eyes, she could not shake the image of him conquering and destroying, turning all to slaves whether they were human or members of the Fallen.

"I suppose I could go down south," she said. "But if it's all the same, I'd rather go with you."

"To Germany?"

She nodded. "To Germany. Together."

Chapter 14

Port au Prince, Haiti

The sun beat down on the roof deck of a small hotel in the city of Port au Prince. The hotel was a ramshackle place with rusted iron railings, cracks in the plaster and a faded yellow coat of paint that looked worse from all the touch up jobs that had been attempted on it.

It was late afternoon. The heat of the day was slowly passing, and the air was thick with the promise of thunder.

Sitting in the shade of an orange umbrella, Terrance sipped his ice tea, fanning himself with a straw hat. "And I thought New Orleans was nasty in the summer."

Across the table, Leroy wiped the sweat from his face with a towel but didn't reply.

Terrance could feel the tension in Leroy. He could feel the conflict and the dread. He heard Leroy stand and take a few steps.

"Why are we here?" Leroy asked.

"Because there's work to be done," Terrance replied.

"But why this place?" Leroy asked. "It's depressing. Makes Compton look like Beverly Hills."

Terrance had seen Port au Prince years ago, before he went blind. Funny, he thought, it smelled the same, sounded the same, even hummed with the same vibe, but he knew it looked completely different. Even years after the earthquake, crumbled buildings lay where they'd fallen. Weeds grew everywhere because of the weather, but there wasn't a single tree in sight—not in the city, not up on the hills. They'd all been cut down for wood to make fires and charcoal. Every time it rained the hillsides washed away, and the water became putrid and bacteria ridden once again. All of which meant more wood was needed to boil it and make it drinkable.

"Did God forget this place?" Leroy said. "It's like He washed his hands of these people."

Terrance understood that thought. Between the earthquakes, the mud and diseases, not to mention the dictators, and the *Tonton Macoute*—a para-military group that committed so much evil their leader was once called the Vampire of the Caribbean—it certainly seemed as if this place had been abandoned by the Almighty.

But if that was the case, it didn't explain the presence of hundreds of missionary groups and charity organizations that struggled here every day, most of which were affiliated with one church or another.

"Not God's fault," Terrance said. "Human choice ruined this half of the island. The other side is the Dominican Republic. Clean beaches, plenty of trees, nice houses and paved roads. Poor in some places, but not destitute, not given to endless violence and anger like in this place."

Leroy turned. "Maybe we could go there."

"Some other time," Terrance said chuckling. "When your work is done."

The Half Life

Terrance had brought Leroy here for several reasons. To begin with, he knew that this was the city foretold in the prophecy. The church had guessed wrong, as had Drake and everyone else. The angel's work was to begin in the new world, in a city by the sea, whose heart was French, whose people had suffered from a natural disaster. Everyone who'd read the prophecy thought that was to be New Orleans still recovering from Hurricane Katrina, but Terrance knew differently; he knew it was Port au Prince. He'd known it for most of his life. And with that in mind, who was he to take a detour?

More importantly, the city became the darkest of places after nightfall. Because of its people's voodoo and pagan backgrounds, Port Au Prince had been a haven for the undead even before the earthquake. But afterwards... Afterwards a flood of vampires had entered the city, settling in its ruins and festering sores as they always did in lawless areas of the world. With so much death, chaos and destruction they could go unseen and uncountable. Here they could feed to their dead heart's content and so many did. People went missing in the city nightly and no one looked for them.

"This place is filled with evil," Leroy said. "With vampires. I can feel them gathered together in dark spaces, hiding like rats."

"Yes," Terrance said. "Being near the equator this city is not greatly suited for the undead, but the devastation makes up for that."

Leroy came back and sat next to Terrance in the shade. "How are we gonna find them?"

"Finding them won't be the problem," Terrance said. "The ones in the Half-Life will seek you out. They'll call to you. Most of them want to return to their human form. But those who are long passed have grown set in their ways."

"Like the two in the warehouse."

Terrance nodded. "It takes an extraordinary soul to want to return to the light once they've transformed totally. The longer they live in total darkness the more completely it consumes them."

"Why not leave them there," Leroy asked. "Go looking for more who want to change. Seems to me that would be a far better use of our time."

"Because the power of light still hides in most of them. In some deep place within their souls. Some of the demons can reach it. Some still remember their humanity."

Leroy listened intently but he still had questions. "And what about the ones who can't, or who don't want to find it?"

Terrance took another sip of his iced tea. "Well Leroy, I'm afraid they will probably try to kill you."

"What?" Leroy stood in shock.

"You're freeing their slaves," Terrance explained. "You think they're going to like that? Just take it lying down? You're the enemy. The light to their darkness. The music to their love of cold silence."

"But I…"

"But nothin'," Terrance lifted a hand testing the air. "The sun's setting. It's time to get moving. Are you ready?"

Leroy nodded, a nod which Terrance couldn't see and then said, "As ready as I'm gonna be, I guess."

The Half Life

Leroy's nerves were on edge, but Terrance wasn't worried. Tonight would be the easiest test of all; it was what happened after that worried him.

A short time later Terrance and Leroy walked from their hotel, taking the lane that ran beside the ocean. Leroy marveled at the sunset, the way the light caught the tops of the waves and sparkled and flicked like diamonds floating out at sea. Even though he lived in LA all those years he rarely ventured out to the beach. And when he did, the Pacific was always dark and cold.

They passed by the bars and dingy nightclubs, went past the brothels, drug dealers and the thieves who stood on every corner. No one bothered with them; no one gave them trouble. A fact which surprised Leroy. "In South Central, we'd have been mugged three times by now," he joked. "What's the deal?"

"They know me here," Terrance said.

"All of them?"

"Most," Terrance said, tapping his walking stick on the ground.

Leroy glanced at the stick and realized it was a different cane than the one Terrance had used in New Orleans. Carved into the staff was a snake and dagger intertwined. Around its center was a chain of small bones. "Oh... They're afraid of the voodoo."

"Not afraid," Terrance told him. "Respectful."

Knowing that, Leroy began to walk taller, looking over his shoulder a little less. He suddenly felt a burst of confidence, they were important people after all.

The spring in his step lasted all of five minutes, at which point they came to an unlit intersection.

"Which way?" Terrance asked.

"How should I know?" Leroy replied.

"What do you feel?"

Leroy looked around. The street turned to rubble a short ways down and a track had been worn in the weeds, where cars and trucks avoided the broken pavement. To the left, a road snaked up hill and between buildings that were nothing more than caved-in shells. More casualties from the earthquake.

"Do you feel it?" Terrance asked.

Leroy could feel a heart beating somewhere in the ruins.

"The young ones."

Terrance took a step backward and Leroy stepped forward. He closed his eyes. He felt their fear.

"Three of them," Leroy said. "They're afraid. The boy is thinking about killing himself. He doesn't understand what he's become."

"Then it's time." Terrance said.

Leroy took a deep breath and took Terrance by the arm and stepped forward.

As they got close to the burned out, broken building, a human yelled from the street. The words were French, in a Haitian accent.

"What'd she say?" Leroy asked.

"She said, you're entering the house of the dead. All those that go in never come out.'"

Leroy gulped at a lump in his throat but continued on into the crumbling building. The old wood boards creaked under their feet. Stairs led up into darkness and a hall beckoned in front of them. The smell was unbearable. Flies could be heard buzzing around something in the corner.

"Don't look." Terrance told him. "You don't want to know the evil that these thing spread in the world. If you see too much, you may not want to help them."

Leroy looked anyway. Rotting carcasses lay one on top of each other in the corner. Flies everywhere, rats stealing pieces of meat from the dead humans. Some bodies were decayed, others looked as if they'd been last night's meal.

"The new ones did this?"

"No, these were brought in by the clan leaders. To help the process along."

Leroy thought he'd be sick, but he held it together.

"We must be cautious," Terrance said. "This means the clan leaders are near. They're probably watching us, unsure what to make of us since no one dares to come in here."

Leroy was beginning to think he should have gone elsewhere. This was too much. But he went forward and stepped into the next room.

There he found some light. A candle in the center of the room with two teenage girls huddled together beside a male who appeared to be praying.

Leroy's arrival startled them, and they backed into a corner.

Terrance pulled free of Leroy's arm and whispered, "Ask the question."

"What question?

"THE question."

Leroy stepped forward and opened up his arms. "Do you want to be saved?"

They stared at him. Maybe that wasn't it.

"Do you want…" Leroy needed a word that could reach them, "…life?"

And then he saw it. Images in their minds. Moments they were clinging to. Pictures slowly fading. The two girls were sisters. Their mother had sewn them new dresses for their twelfth birthday. He focused on this thought, this happy moment, and tried in whatever way he could to make it brighter.

One of the girls broke free and crawled towards him. "Who are you?"

"I'm…" he hesitated and almost lost her. *What was he supposed to say? I'm an angel named Leroy?* "I can help you," he said. "Let me show you."

She was crying. She still had the ability to cry. Half human, half vampire was a terrible place to be, he thought.

"I can take you home," he said. "But you have to choose. Do you want to rejoin the light?"

The girl looked up, her face thin.

The Half Life

A hushed, "Yes," came forth through the sobbing. Like a slight wind on a midsummer's day, it could just barely be heard. She waved to her sister and the boy. Both came over.

Leroy put his hands on them. A light began to emanate from beneath his fingers. Brilliant and colorful, like a churning, glowing palate. Soon it filled the room, spilling out and chasing the darkness from every crevice, every broken hole and boarded up window, pouring through every crack in the wall, spilling out into the street.

Even though the light was warm and wonderful and living, Leroy shut his eyes. But the black eyes of the Nosferatu remained open. And the blinding palette of color danced on them, soaking into them and bringing back the soft brown color of the young trio's irises.

Outside, at the far end of the street as close as people were willing to come to this evil place, a crowd had gathered as soon as Leroy and Terrance went inside. Everyone knew that some great evil went on in there, but this was different. The light was mesmerizing. It seemed to change and move as if it were alive. They gazed in amazement and many crossed themselves while others chanted voodoo incantations.

"What is dis'?" one woman kept asking. "What is it?"

And then, the crumbling shack went dark. Instantly, something fled from the house. Something dark and evil. They saw it run up into the hills, fleeing in panic like a frightened animal.

They watched as Terrance and Leroy came out with the three children in front of them.

"He da priest," a woman said, in a singsong Caribbean accent.

"Ee' not 'posed to be here," another bystander said. "Dis not his place."

"Whatchu care for?" the woman replied. "Dey chase out the darkness, chase out de' evil. Why not he allowed to be here?"

"Cause dis just gonna make it worse," someone else added.

The first woman waved them off, saying something about scared fools and where they could go. But then another member of the crowd whispered a name which they all feared. "Papa Legba ain't gonna like dis. Trus' me. He ain't gonna like dis one bit."

They looked at each other. A few nodded. All kept silent until the last speaker muttered something under her breath. "Papa Legba," she said. And then she crossed herself, gripped her crucifix and whispered another prayer.

Chapter 15

Paris, France

Drake stood motionless under a bridge on the west bank of the river Seine. He watched the water play with the lights of Paris as it streamed past him in an endless effort to reach the sea. *The circle of existence*, he thought. *Ocean waters to vapor, clouds to rain, rain to river and all of it ended up back in the sea.* Somehow he and his kind had eluded the hard and fast laws of the universe, the cycle of life to death and perhaps back to life again somewhere.

In his case, he felt he'd eluded it by the skin of his teeth. He was not completely healed—the fact that he was pondering such things told him that—but he would be soon.

Having sent Zwana, Tereza and Akash in search of this great weapon, he'd come to a place he'd avoided for centuries. Paris had once been Drake's home. But a betrayal had made him feel unwelcome within its borders. He'd abandoned this city in favor of the new world. He'd certainly believed new opportunities awaited him in the Americas, but the lack of the Church's power there was also inviting.

Only his great need brought him back. And he hoped it would not mean a new front in the war.

A thirty-foot speedboat pulled up alongside. Three figures stood on the front deck. They wore modern clothing, jeans, boots, and hoody sweatshirts. They could blend in with the nightlife of Paris perfectly, but they were anything but modern humans.

Drake stepped aboard. The boat accelerated and turned around, heading down river. It would soon arrive at the entrance to the catacombs: the great stronghold of the undead in Paris.

The city had many catacombs. Most were known, but deeper than the caves which tourists flocked to were another set of tunnels and warrens. These were used by the undead. They were concealed, protected. One of the three hooded vampires tuned to Drake.

"Artimous is expecting you."

"Good," Drake said.

Drake had turned Artimous in 1514. Artimous in many ways had proven to be Christian's opposite. Where Christian was boring, dark and morose, but loyal until the falling out, Artimous, was a clever man, witty, arrogant and one who always wanted more than his fair share.

Drake had always known his intelligence and desire would be helpful, and the fact that Artimous loved to fight was a great asset at times. But his greed made him a problem, and his distrust of Christian became an issue. The two could not be in the same room.

So when Drake left Paris for good, he gave Artimous the city but warned him never to expand beyond it. Artimous had kept his word and Drake had let him live. A rare moment of mercy he was now thankful for.

The Half Life

The wind picked up as the watercraft pulled to a stop underneath a bridge near Villeneuve-Saint-Georges. Drake stepped ashore beneath the five-hundred-year-old bridge as the sound of stone on stone began to emanate from the shadows. A gap in the wall appeared and one of the entrances to the Catacombs of the Undead opened up before him.

Drake walked in and was greeted by more hooded vampires. Their looks and stations in society were as different as their ages, but all wore hoods when in the underground to shade the eyes and keep their telekinetic powers at bay. It seemed that Artimous ran a tight ship.

A torch was lit and Drake was led deeper into the catacombs to the grand chamber of the undead, a room that Drake had built five hundred years ago. He continued past ranks of vampires. It dawned on him that the entire clan was assembled, a show of great respect. He passed through them all the way to the Chair of the King. Sitting in that golden chair was a huge bearded figure with a scepter in his hand.

Artimous.

As Drake reached the first of the five marble steps that led to the chair, Artimous began to clap slowly and in an arrogant manner which was his way. "Yes, all Hail the King, the mighty Drakos who returns alone."

Perhaps the show of respect was facetious. "You've been busy," Drake said.

"I've built a civilization down here."

"And what good is it?"

"I have learned that not all of our souls are as dark and barren as yours… or mine," Artimous said. "There are some who play music.

Others who sculpt and dance. I have learned that gold, pure gold feels warm even to a vampire and that wine, if mixed with the smallest amount of blood, can bring taste without destruction."

Drake almost laughed. "So you get weak with pleasures. And you horde the yellow metal like humans. To what end, Artimous? To live in a hole in the ground?"

"The church is still strong here."

"I told you I'd break the church one day," Drake said.

"And I told you Christian would turn traitor," Artimous said.

Drake nodded. "It seems we were both right."

Artimous shook his huge, shaggy face. "No," he said. "I was right. The church still hunts, but I don't see Christian at your side."

"The church is in disarray," Drake said. "And I will soon have the power to defeat them."

"I would say it's *their* power that grows."

"What do you mean by that?"

"We've heard rumors," Artimous said.

"About?"

"The coming of angels."

"Yes," Drake said. "The prophecy of Jocasta. It's true."

At this, Artimous leaned forward. "You've seen the angel?"

"No," Drake replied. "But it *has* come into existence. We have little time. Unless you prefer to fight with me, or be returned to your wretched human life, you will do as I command."

"I will do as you command?" Artimous said, a look of surprise on his face. "Did you not come here to beg my help?"

"I do not beg," Drake said. "You will either fall into line, or I will destroy you and take your clan as my own."

Artimous sat taller and then stood upon his podium. "You're surrounded and defenseless," Artimous said.

"And if I choose, I will take the minds of your army and conform them to my own. And then *you* will be surrounded and defenseless."

"You would find them ill-suited for war."

"They can learn," Drake said. "Now answer me! Do we fight each other, or do we fight together?"

For a moment the two of them locked metal horns, but Artimous was only testing him. He had heard Drake was weakened but found it not to be the case. Not enough that he would challenge him. He moved from the chair with its high back and golden arms and bowed before his king: Drake.

Perhaps, these years had changed Artimous, for he had not just given him a King's welcome, but conceded the throne. Drake searched Artimous's mind. He was filled with fear. Fear that Drake had come there to kill him. Fear that the angel would undo all he'd done. Fear that even if there was forgiveness for the foot-soldiers, there was no mercy for those who'd turned them.

As it turned out, he was tired of worrying, tired of leading. In fact, he was glad to relinquish the throne.

"Rise Artimous," Drake said.

"What do you ask of me?"

"I seek a learned man whose mind I once saw into," Drake said. "He knows much about the past. You will accompany me, and we will extract from his memory all that we need to know."

"Who is this man?" Artimous said.

"His name is Faust."

Chapter 16

Cologne, Germany

The aroma of the hazelnut drifted on the air, surrounding the patrons of the coffee house and mixing with a hint of pumpkin spice. Dr. Morgan Faust didn't have a need for such frothy drinks. A strong cappuccino and the New York Times were his companions. Like the new-fangled beverages with names he couldn't pronounce, the modern newspapers and magazines were all fluff and no substance in his estimation.

He took a sip, read a snippet and looked out the window, a routine he had kept up for nearly two hours.

The rain was pouring down outside, adding the kind of darkness to the night that made lights all but useless. Though the weather was expected to clear in the morning, it had been pouring for days.

"Not fit for man nor beast," one patron remarked as he rushed into the safety and warmth of the coffee shop. Dr. Faust wished that statement were true, but as he stared out the window the thought of a beast haunted him as it had since the moment one of the undead had come into his church in Cologne.

No, he corrected himself, *not a mere church, The Cathedral, The Kohler Dom.* The largest, most important church in all of Germany. Since the demons had set foot there, Faust had been gripped with a kind of hidden fear. If they could walk there, they could walk anywhere.

Unlike most, he knew of the battle between the Church and the Fallen. He'd studied tales of both victories and defeat. In some ways he was like an armchair general looking over the follies and triumphs of a war long past. He'd even likened himself to the great Josephus, a Jewish scholar who wrote about Roman power in the second century and whose name was better known than most of the generals.

He'd rather enjoyed his life, but then one of the demons entered the cathedral and another had dug its claws into his mind. And suddenly the war was not some far off thing to be pondered and studied, but a close thing to be feared. And yet, he still lived.

Could a demon commit an act of mercy?

Had the church not investigated his claims and verified them by reviewing the blurred videotapes from the Cathedral's security cameras, he would have thought it madness or a fevered dream, since he actually remembered very little. But the truth was there. With Drakos trying to control his mind and drag him out into the night, the blond demon had literally thrown him not out into darkness but towards the altar of the church where even Drake's will could not touch him.

A war, he wrote on the paper almost unconsciously. *A war between the demons. But what could they be fighting for?*

He took another sip and looked out into the wet gloom of High Street wondering what was out there.

The Half Life

Are you listening in? Do you hear my madness?

He half hoped one of them would speak to him, and feared it like the devil at the same time.

In a fit of paranoia—or an act of extreme prudence—he'd set up cameras outside his flat, put motion detectors in. He'd even bought himself a dog and covered the place with holy relics *borrowed* from the church—in hopes they would keep the demons at bay. But even though the alarm never sounded and the dog never barked, Faust was positive that something was out there, something that refused to show itself.

On the worst nights he couldn't stay home. His first stop was the Café Bruner where the patrons numbered in the dozens even late into the night. What good that would do him he didn't know, but he had a feeling that even demons preferred to avoid public spectacles.

And when the fear got to him or when the crowd failed to last until dawn, Faust had a second place of hiding. But he tried not to use it for fear that if it did not work, he would have no place left to feel safe.

He peered out the window again, nothing but cars and people and rain.

He looked around the coffee shop. Not an unkind face among the bunch. But still the feeling persisted. *Something was watching him.*

Quickly he folded the paper and put it down. He stood, put on his raincoat and stepped toward the exit. Out the door and down the street, he moved as fast as his old legs could carry him. His heart pumped deep and heavy. He was sure if the vampires didn't get him that he would have a heart attack, but maybe that would be better.

He dashed across a street without looking, almost getting hit by a car that skidded to a halt on the wet pavement.

A window went down and German curses came flying out by the bushel, nasty words but nothing to take his soul. Very good, he thought. *Yes, yes I'm a fool and a schwein. Have to go now, must keep moving.*

He tipped his hat to the driver, ran another block and ducked beneath an overhang.

The rain continued to stream from the sky. The streetlights fought uselessly against the night and nothing on the road looked out of place. The church was only two blocks away. He could make it.

As soon as he was breathing halfway normally, he moved from the doorway back out into the rain. With that first step a cold wind blew through him. He stopped dead in his tracks and looked across the street to a blonde woman standing in the rain. The water streaked her face and left her flaxen hair matted. She had no umbrella or hat. She didn't seem to care.

She stared at him.

"The eyes of the Nosferatu," he whispered to himself.

She was pretty, but evil. He could feel her eyes boring a path deep into his mind.

"Leave me alone!" he said.

Words formed in his mind. *Don't run. It's of no use.*

He took off running anyway, cutting down an alley and glancing back. Nothing. He continued on. Made a turn and risked another glance. Still nothing. He came to the end of the alley and the blonde woman stepped out in front of him.

He crashed into her at full speed and fell to the ground, but she didn't even flinch. She picked him up and shoved him back into the narrow cut between the two buildings.

In the darkness of the alleyway, she would have her way. "You have much that I need," she said. "And you *will* help me."

"I won't," he said. With that, Faust went for his crucifix but she grabbed his arm and stopped his hand from reaching the cross. "You really should wear these on the outside of your clothes, Dr. Faust. But at any rate they don't affect me."

"How is that?"

"Wouldn't you like to know," she said. "Perhaps you can chronicle it in your treatise on *The War of the Demons.*"

"I… I wasn't really going to write it," he said. "It's just a silly notion."

"I think you should write it," she said smiling at him. Her lips were pale like blue ice. Her teeth so white they almost blinded him.

"Whose side…whose side are you on?" he asked, unable to stem his curiosity.

"I think you know that, already," she said. The image of Drakos came into his mind and he began to tremble with fear.

"I need you to think about something Mr. Faust," she said, sliding her hands on either side of his head to keep him from turning away. "The Dark-Star. What do you know of it?"

He was startled. Her hands were like frost on his skin. And yet, he was mesmerized as much by her beauty as her powers.

"Hey!" A voice shouted. "What do you think you're doing to that old man?!"

She glanced back just long enough to break the trance and Faust slipped free. He took off running again. Never looking back. He heard a scuffle and the sound of shattering glass and the loud metallic bang of a body being hurled against a dumpster.

By then he was around the corner and running the final block. Up ahead was salvation. The church of Saint Martin. She could not enter there, and if she did, she would be weak and blind like the blond one in Cologne.

He stumbled and crashed through the door knocking down a couple of tourists who'd made a midnight pilgrimage to the venerable building. He fell forward, crawling deeper into the refuge.

"Dr. Faust?" one of the monks asked. Saint Martin's was run by monks who named their order The Monastic Fraternity of Jerusalem. They knew Faust well.

"Please," he gasped. "Bar the door. I'm being pursued."

As one of the monks helped him to a sitting position, another went to the door. "There's no one out there, Dr. Faust."

But Faust could see her in his mind, obscured by the heavy rain. And then he heard her as well. *I will find you wherever you go, Dr. Faust, and soon, for I require what you know.*

Chapter 17

Interlaken, Switzerland

"I will see Aldo Gruvaleu, now."

Henrick spoke these words the way a commander spoke to a subordinate. The man and woman on the receiving end were not used to being treated this way.

"I'm afraid he's not in any condition to be seen," the man said. "Doctor's orders."

Henrick had come to the Lake District of Switzerland, to a Monastery for Spiritual Health and Well Being, owned and operated by the Catholic Church. It was a fancy description for an insane asylum. It bothered him. It reminded him of… the past.

"I don't care," Henrick said. "Take me to him. Those are *my* orders."

As he spoke he laid his hands on the desk. The ring of the hunter sparkled on his index finger. The man stared at it. The woman ignored it. He knew of the order. She didn't.

"Follow me," he said.

As the grey haired man led him down a high ceilinged corridor, it echoed with their footsteps. Henrick had mixed feelings for the Swiss. The Swiss Guards were the only other force attached to the Vatican. That, and the Swiss penchant for hard work, order and the creation of wealth appealed to his meticulous side.

On the other hand they had a nasty habit of sitting out the world's wars while safeguarding money deposited in their banks by both sides, traits he saw as cowardice and avarice. But worst of all, Simon Lathatch had been Swiss, and his stubborn unflinching manner had grated on Henrick for years.

"I warn you…" the man said, stopping at a door with triple locks, "…you may be surprised by what you see."

"Open it," Henrick demanded.

The man used the keys on his ring to unlatch all three locks, one at a time. *Click, click, clunk.*

The door opened to darkness. Henrick reached for the light switch and flicked it but nothing happened.

"He smashes the bulbs," the man said. "We've stopped replacing them for his own good."

"Hmmm…" Henrick said. "Is there a window?"

"Of course not," the man said. "Here." He handed over a flashlight and switched on one of his own. Henrick took both. "Leave me."

"It may not be safe to be alone with him."

"I said, *leave!*"

The man stood back and then stepped out. Once the door had closed, the locks could be heard turning again. *Click, click, clunk.*

The Half Life

Henrick walked into the dark unafraid of Aldo or anything else that might be there. He passed stack upon stack of notebooks piled up like towers in the dark. He opened one, able to read it by the modicum of light that came in through a narrow slit up high in the room.

The notebook read strangely.

Take them to the dark, take them to hell.

Yes bring them with us. Why should we go alone?

This is hell. We're in it.

This is hell!

The next page held some fanciful drawing of an eyeless corpse and symbols that Henrick recognized as the markings of a clan of vampires. Page after page were marked with similar rantings.

"Madness," he whispered, putting the book down. "Aldo?"

No response.

He walked in further. In the dark, huddled beneath a desk he saw a small figure rocking back and forth and writing vigorously. His lips trembled as he scribbled. Speaking words, alternating voices.

"To the death they hunt us, *to the death.*"

The next words were in Spanish and then what Henrick thought was Mandarin.

"Aldo!"

The young man looked out at him.

"What the hell is all this?" Henrick asked.

Aldo shouted something in a language that Henrick had never heard. In response, Henrick stepped forward, grabbed Aldo's arm and dragged him out from under the desk.

Aldo tried to squirm away, but Henrick held him tight. From a pocket he pulled out the flashlight and aimed it at Aldo's eyes. Aldo's pupils constricted and he turned away.

"I can't get them out," Aldo whined. "I can't."

"Is that what this is all about?" Henrick said, waving at the notebooks scattered around. "A way to get them out of your head?"

"I see things," Aldo insisted. "I see what they do. Horrible things... the evil they sow... murder, murder, murder, every night. I have to see it. I *have* to watch. I get no choice!"

Henrick wasn't sure what to make of this. For the most part, he'd believed this was a fool's errand, and came just to satisfy Messini, planning to get it over with as quickly as possible. After all, Aldo's condition had been seen before in many who'd been on the front lines. Once taken over by a demon who was subsequently destroyed, the demon's mind seemed to have the power to transfer its memories to the human it had taken control of. As if it was some last ditch effort to keep from being erased from existence. Most recovered in a week or two. Some remained depressed for long years, but Henrick had never heard of someone being incapacitated like this. Driven to utter madness.

Instead of pulling Aldo up, Henrick sat beside him. "What do you see right now, Aldo?"

Aldo stared into the light and his pupils dilated once again.

"He's going to kill the one who offered to help. The one who acted with pity. He's going steal his blood."

"Who is?"

"I don't know. He's stalking him. He's cutting a symbol into the wall."

"Draw it."

"I can't see."

"Draw it!"

Aldo grabbed his pencil and began to scribble. Half a symbol came out. But then Aldo seized up.

"Fire," he said. "She's on fire." He began to shout in Spanish. "The hunters in Panama. She's dying. Burning. She's burning!"

The door burst open as Aldo screamed and two doctors rushed in with the grey haired man from the front desk.

"What are you doing to him?" one doctor shouted.

"I've done nothing," Henrick said.

The doctors were on Aldo like a shot. One calmed him and whispered something. The other administered a drug.

Henrick ignored them and began walking around. He noticed some strange markings on the wall, where a dresser had been pushed away. He aimed his light and switched it on. There was something scribbled there. At first he couldn't quite make out what it was, a smudge or a…

An odd thought came to him and he flipped the switch on his flashlight changing the bulb from regular to black. More writing appeared, like that from Aldo's notebooks, but it was written with something other than ink. Henrick followed the lines which ran between various names and drawings. He recognized some symbols, a few names, and then he froze in horror.

"Out!" he shouted, switching off the light. "Everyone out!"

He moved toward them, pushing the doctors away from Aldo and grabbing the grey haired man by the shoulder.

"Get your hands off me!" the man shouted.

"This is ridiculous! We're trying to treat the patient!" one the doctors said.

"You can't—"

Henrick pushed them toward the door. "I'm the leader of the Righteous Fire, the Primus of the Holy Order of the Ignis Purgata, and by God I've told you to get out! Now leave!"

"Righteous Fire?" one of the doctors asked.

"Explain it to him," Henrick ordered, looking at the grey haired man. With that, he shoved them into the hall and slammed the door.

Alone now, he stormed back to Aldo who was half-sedated and dragged Aldo to the hidden drawing on the wall.

"What is this?" he shouted. "What does this mean?"

Aldo's eyes wavered in his head. He only stood because Henrick's iron grip held him up. Henrick pointed to a symbol. "What is it?"

"Staff of Constantine," Aldo said. "Given to the demon who calls himself Christian."

"Yes," Henrick said. "Exactly. And this?" he demanded, pointing to another note.

"The demon grieved for Simon."

"What demon?"

"The one in the church."

"You lie!"

"I saw it," Aldo mumbled. The drug was now taking full effect, he was slurring his words. "Simon was murdered…"

"What did you say?"

"He was murdered. I saw it."

"By the Nosferatu!" Henrick insisted.

"No," Aldo said, sounding as if he were begging. "By… one… of the Hunters."

Henrick knew this. For he'd killed Simon himself. Killed him for his treachery. But how could Aldo know? He'd been here in the asylum for several weeks before that and had never left.

"The demon put this in your head," Henrick insisted.

"No," Aldo said. "I saw it… through his eyes."

Henrick was gripped with fear. He considered slaying Aldo right then and there. He could claim Aldo was possessed by a demon and had attacked him. The proof lay all about them. No one could doubt that. But then Aldo spoke.

"The demon was half blind," Aldo said. "From the light and the pain. He didn't see the hunter's faces."

Henrick's hand had gone to his dagger. It was halfway out of the sheath. Cautiously, he slid it back in. It locked with a click.

"The light of the church," Aldo said.

Of course, Henrick thought. In the church, the demons were all but powerless. He wouldn't have guessed them to be blind, but it made sense—creatures of the night never see well in the bright light of day.

"It was too bright," Aldo added. "He could barely see. He could barely hear."

As the fear of discovery left him, a moment of clarity dawned on Henrick. He began to marvel at what he'd found. *Here in front of him sat a miracle. A gift from God sent directly to him. Sent to help him exterminate the demons for all time.*

"Can you find this demon?" Henrick asked. "This one who mocks us by using the name of our faith?"

"I..." Aldo said. "I can... try..."

But even as he spoke, Aldo's legs buckled.

"Aldo... Aldo?"

Aldo went limp, his eyes rolled up in his head and he crumbled to the floor.

Henrick let him go and then grabbed a cup of water from the table and heaved it at the wall. The contents splattered over the surface in an explosion-like pattern. Without delay, he grabbed a towel and began wiping the wall in great, swirling circles, doing all he could to erase what Aldo had marked upon it.

When he was satisfied, Henrick dropped the towel and heaved Aldo's unconscious form up over his shoulder. Carrying him like a fireman, Henrick stormed through the door and out into the hall.

The doctors sprang to their feet.

"What are you doing?" one of them asked. "Put him down."

Henrick ignored them, striding past.

"Mr. Vanderwall, this is *not* allowed," the grey haired man said.

"Where are you taking him?" the second doctor demanded to know.

Fools, Henrick thought. Even now they had the questions wrong. It wasn't where he would take Aldo, but where Aldo would be taking him.

Chapter 18

Cologne, Germany

The city of Cologne was different from the last time Christian had been there. The trees were now full with green leaves, not brown. The flowers popped with brilliant colors beneath the streetlights.

As he walked with Kate he stared at the roses in the park. The dark, rich red color of one rose reminded him of wine. The yellow roses were so bright, he imagined that as the color of the sun at high noon. *One day*, he dreamed, *he would see it again without being subjected to excruciating pain.*

"Kate," he asked. "Can you still smell? Have you lost that sense yet?"

"No, not completely."

"Smell the roses for me."

"You literally want me to stop and smell the roses?" she said, eyebrows up.

"Trust me," he said. "If you don't now, you'll wish you had one day."

She was impatient, pushy and a lot like him, he thought. And he wished he'd spent more time in the light before it went out.

Kate reached for one of them and happened to get her finger stuck by a thorn.

She pulled back. The blood that came forth was an orange, rusted color. It clotted fast. Kate looked at Christian. "What is this?"

"Your future. A few more shades of orange and you'll be unable to go out in the light, unable to smell or taste anything."

"Great," she said.

"Hold on to your humanity as long as you can."

Kate nodded. Christian knew she understood. "You think I'll want to taste life again once it leaves me completely, once I'm dead?"

"We all do Kate. It's confusing."

"And you. Did you ever kill? Did you murder for a taste of life?"

"No."

"How did you resist?"

He hesitated. "I guess I'd seen enough blood and dying before I ever became like this. People of this age can't possibly imagine what it was like. A hundred thousand men on a field, hacking and stabbing and slashing at each other."

She said nothing.

"If you want to resist, you either focus on something you love or something you hate. I hated the carnage. The waste. But if you have something you love, I'd choose that instead."

She nodded. "My son," she said. "He's all I have left. My husband was murdered. That's how I ended up on this case."

Christian nodded. "Lock onto that thought and hide it; protect it deep down inside you where no one can find it. Don't show it to the world anymore, not even me. They'll use it against you if they can. They'll get your own mind to lie to you. I know. Drake poisoned mine for years."

Suddenly Christian felt something looking at them. He stopped.

"What is it?"

"I don't know. There was something there," he said. "Now it's gone. Come on. Let's get off this street. Faust's place is only a mile from here."

"Wait." Kate bent down and sniffed the rose a final time. "They smell rich and warm with a hint of sweetness."

A few minutes later they approached Faust's building. A spiral staircase made of wood awaited them. An old time elevator with a gate that pulled across was on the far side of lobby. "We'll take the stairs."

"Why?"

"Elevators are traps waiting to happen."

Up the stairs the two walked, keeping alert. At the top there was Faust's flat. Number five, zero, one. Christian reached for the door, but Kate stopped him. "Let me do it."

"Let you do what?" Christian said.

"Get us inside."

"Give it a quick pull, the lock will break." Christian said.

"And if we do it my way we don't have to break anything." She pulled out the tools of a locksmith, and the bolt clicked in seconds.

"Stick around," She said. "I'll teach you some more tricks later."

She opened the door, and immediately both of their moods went south.

"Someone got here before us."

The apartment had been ransacked. Books and photo albums littered the floors. Memories, personal effect were ripped from their place. Everything that was precious to Dr. Morgan Faust destroyed or discarded.

They moved through the room like sharks in the murkiest of waters. Slowly looking through every piece of rubble that was Faust's possessions.

"There's nothing here of value," Kate said. "Whoever did this took whatever they were looking for."

"I agree. The question is: do they have Faust or not?"

"They don't have him." Kate said.

"How do you know?"

"Because they wouldn't do this if they had him."

Christian felt that made sense. "So he's gone into hiding. That's going to make him very hard to find."

"Maybe I can help," she said. "I have a friend who owes me big time. A high up director at Interpol. He actually lives here in Germany."

"Why would he help us?"

"Because I saved his life."

"Is there any chance he knows you're on the run?"

Kate stared down at her hands and the dried orange blood from where the thorn had pricked her. "There's no chance he *doesn't* know," she replied. "But unless you have some magic way of finding this guy, it's all we have."

Christian shook his head. There was no magic, only a long shot and even greater risk.

Chapter 19

Libyan Desert, North Africa

Tereza stared at the bullet hole in the gray concrete wall in front of her. These walls had once been manned by the Afrika Korps of the Nazi war machine. Bunkers from World War II littered the deserts of North Africa. Some, like this one, which Rommel himself commanded from, ran deep into the earth: fortified, cold, and dark. Perfect hiding spots for the Fallen when the sun took command of this side of the planet.

It was high noon above ground and Tereza and Akash could do nothing but wait. Zwana was still in the midst of his change, but the light was too much for him already.

Trapped, she thought. Trapped if anyone came.

She didn't like this assignment, didn't like being teamed with a half transformed wizard and a psychotic vampire who was too damaged to be trusted. They were below her on every level. But very dangerous.

Akash had a mind that flitted from madness to a blank state and then back. How he'd managed to avoid the blood lust she didn't know. Zwana was much like him and it dawned on her that once Zwana was fully turned, these two would be natural allies.

Danger. Trapped with danger. The only way out was to find this weapon Drake had sent them after and maybe even kill these two with it.

Her lip curled with the thought and then a scream of agony rang out from another part of the abandoned bunker.

It was true they couldn't go outside, but that didn't mean others couldn't be brought in.

She wandered back though corridors half-filled with sand and found a man being tortured by Akash. All through the day screams, cries, and pleading had come from the depths of the bunker, pried from men and women who were believed to have knowledge of this Dark Star. But none had spoken. And now their broken bodies littered this concrete coffin.

The last was an old man who had no idea what was in store for him when he indicated he had heard of the legend of the power of the rock.

"Why must you make them scream?" she said to Akash.

"It's part of the process."

"It's annoying."

The torturer just glared at her. The wizard replied. "The legend tells of an order who guard the Dark Star's resting place. They trained their minds to be shut."

She doubted this. Zwana was not far enough along in his transformation to understand his powers and Akash was a sadistic thug, little more than a Drone. More than likely the reason for all this torture was that they enjoyed bringing harm to these humans.

She crouched down and studied the old man. "Tell me what you know."

His broken body was weak, but his mind remained strong.

"Tell me!"

She forced her will upon him. Prying into him, like nails into soft wood.

He began to squirm and twist and finally went still as if he'd become calm. The cement tomb went dead quiet once again.

Images came to light, but they were false fronts designed to hide his thoughts.

"I will let them begin again if you don't speak," she warned.

Finally a phrase came through that she could trust: *The People of the Stone. The Guardians*

"Are you part of the Church?"

No, much older, four thousand years older.

The man was hiding something. His eyes went to the blade in Akash's hand. He wanted to die rather than give it up. He didn't know where the stone was. Only one of them knew. One they called… *the Watcher.*

"Where is he?" she demanded.

The man shook his head.

She put her hands on his neck. "Tell me!"

The man squirmed and fought; he cursed and shouted in more agony than he'd been from Akash's physical punishment.

Finally the details started to come forth. *The Arabian Peninsula. An ocean of sand. A journey that began in the city of Muscat, in Oman. And ended...*

"Where?" she demanded.

He tried to look a way, shutting his eyes.

She opened them with her thumbs. "Tell me and I'll let you sleep!"

But he didn't know where the stone was. Only those who were called *Guardians* knew. She saw a flash. An image of a man in Muscat. One they called... *the Watcher*.

She released the old man and left him to Akash. She would report to Drake, and once it got dark they would make her way to the nearest airport and charter a flight to Oman.

She climbed the stairs and found a spot near the entrance of the bunker, hoping she could get a signal there. She held out the satellite phone and waited. Nothing. She took another step toward the entrance, her feet sinking into the soft sand. It was no good. The walls and the overhang were too thick. It would have to wait for nightfall, eight hours away.

Suddenly there was more shouting from the depths of the bunker, but it wasn't the old man. It was Zwana. "Tereza!" he called out.

She ran back into the darkness, flew down the steps and found Zwana chained to the prisoner, drenched in human blood and stabbed in the stomach with a small knife.

"What have you done?" she cried. Though it was clear what he'd done. Like so many in the Half-Life he'd given into the calling of the blood. "You coward," she sneered. "Just couldn't resist."

Zwana had fed off the man, that much was clear, but how had he been stabbed?

"It was Akash," Zwana said. "He tricked me. He told me it would be good. It would ease the pain."

"Where is he?"

The sound of heavy footsteps pounding the metal grates above them gave her the answer. Akash was racing from the deeper section of the bunker toward the exit.

Tereza left Zwana where he was and rushed up the stairs, chasing Akash toward the entrance. She sprinted down the tunnel after him. "Akash no!"

But he didn't slow, he didn't turn. He ran right out into the blazing daylight of high noon. She tried to stop at the last second and went to the ground, sliding though the sand. She stopped with half her body in the sun, feeling as if she'd caught fire. As quickly as she could, she scrambled back into the cavern and its deep, dark shade.

Akash kept running. He jumped into their 4x4 and started it.

Don't, she willed him. *Drake will torture you for this. He'll take you to the edge of death a thousand times over before he kills you.*

But Akash wasn't listening. In fact, he probably couldn't hear her anymore. He was half human again. It was obvious what he'd done. He'd drank the old man's blood, drained it down as quickly as he could. It turned him human, allowing him to brave the sunlight. It wouldn't last long but they were only fifty miles from Tripoli. He could make it if he drove like mad.

The four wheel drive truck roared off into the distance, leaving her and Zwana behind.

Why, she wondered, would do this? There could be only one reason. The timing proved it for her. Akash wanted the Dark Star for himself. He was going for it. Going to find the Watcher on his own.

Tereza ran back to check on Zwana, broke him loose and checked his wound. It wasn't too deep. He'd live. They'd both live, at least until Drake heard about their failure.

"Is he insane?" Zwana asked.

"He's always been insane," she replied. "But he wants power of his own. Power to defeat anyone, even Drake."

Zwana seemed to understand that. She was actually surprised it had been Akash who made the move and not Zwana himself. But Zwana was still mired in the Half-Life. He was feeling weaker not stronger. The lust for power came only when everything else had been stripped away.

"I saw it in his mind," Zwana said. "He wanted me to join him. When I refused he stabbed me. He tried to kill me."

"No," she said. "He used you to distract me. But if he gets the Dark Star he might kill us all. And if Drake thinks we've failed we might die long before that."

"What do we do?" Zwana asked.

"As soon as night falls we run."

"Tripoli is a long way," he said.

"With luck we'll encounter someone on the road," she said.

Zwana sat back, clutching his side in pain. He almost seemed to enjoy it. It wouldn't last. The pain and the brief spurt of humanity would soon wear off. But it would leave him wanting more.

She turned toward the distant opening, the blazing white light of the desert lay beyond. Nightfall was still eight hours away. Akash would be in Oman by then.

Chapter 20

Prague, Czech Republic

The streets of Prague were quiet on a night with no moon. Under cover of this darkness, three Range Rovers left a secure garage and began to move north toward the ancient center of the city. On its surface, Prague looked clean and well kept. But it held secrets, one of which, Henrick thought, had festered in this city for far too long.

"Double check your armor," he said, adjusting the Kevlar wrapped, titanium plate that covered his chest. "Make sure your rifles are powered."

This was the new militarized army Henrick had envisioned. The new weapons he'd designed and the new tactics he'd personally devised would be tested in battle tonight. The batteries on his rifle showed a full charge. Of course he still carried a huge knife and, though it had been forbidden to the *Ignis Purgata* for years, a sidearm. He chose a Russian made pistol that fired hardened steel bullets and could even shoot underwater.

"Put on your helmets," he said. "Switch to night vision."

The angled helmets were pulled over the hunter's heads shielding their eyes from direct contact with those of the demons. In tests with lesser members of the Fallen, this had given the hunters the ability to look into the faces of their enemy without being vulnerable to their mind games.

Henrick envisioned a whole army of these new soldiers, and he would lead them like the great generals of old.

One of the men pulled from his pocket a wooden crucifix on a thick black cord and went to sling it around his neck before grabbing his helmet.

"You won't need that tonight," Henrick said.

"But I always wear this."

"Keep it under your tunic then," Henrick said. "As a last resort perhaps."

The man hesitated and then did as told. Minutes later they were in the oldest part of town, headed for an abandoned aqueduct from the fifteenth century which led to a series of tunnels, and deep within these tunnels, a chamber. The *Chamber of Bones*, as the demons called it.

Henrick turned to Aldo, who under a cocktail of drugs seemed stable for the moment. "Do you hear them?"

"They're preparing to go out," Aldo said. "You must hurry. They're hungry. Agitated. And there are many of them."

In the past, some hunters had waited for demons to feed before slaying them. Or had approached only in daylight when the demons had nowhere to run. Cowardice, Henrick thought. He and his men would attack in places no hunters would have dared venture before. They were now taking the fight directly to the enemy strongholds.

If his weapons were proved effective, if the body armor held against their foes and the system of filters and video screens repelled the demons telepathic powers, he would prove unstoppable. But most of all—even amid all the technology—if Aldo's gift of hearing the damned could be trusted, then this was the beginning of the end for the Fallen.

The convoy pulled to a stop. "We can't go any further. The entrance to the tunnel is up ahead."

Henrick locked his helmet into place and took a second to get used to the view through the night vision scope. Having only one eye put him at a slight disadvantage, but no matter. He stepped out of the SUV and powered up his rifle. "Let the extermination begin!"

They moved into the forest. The crumbling aqueduct was barely visible for all the trees and weeds growing around it. "Fan out," Henrick said. "It's here. It's close."

"Here," Aldo said, heading toward what looked like a pile of deadwood.

While two of the hunters cleared the entrance, Henrick fought to contain his adrenaline. "Can you feel the rush?" he said to Aldo.

"I feel only what they feel now," he said. "Blood lust. They're coming."

Henrick singled out two of the hunters and pointed to Aldo, "Guard him with your lives."

They nodded and the rest of the force marched into the tunnel and the subterranean darkness. From time to time a voice cracked the radio silence. It would state position and direction. Aside from that, no one spoke. Only the trickle of water and sound of their boots hitting the ground could be heard.

Suddenly, Henrick held up his fist. His soldiers stopped dead in their tracks. In the distance, through the night vision goggles, he could see movement. A group of figures were running their way.

Strange grunting noises like those of rooting animals preceded them, distorted by the acoustics of the tunnel.

"Steady," Henrick said, crouching.

The figures rushing towards them were almost naked.

"I see two…four of them," a voice whispered over the intercom. "Maybe five."

Aldo had insisted he could hear at least fifty different voices from here. Henrick hadn't given his crew that number, lest they question his sanity. "Steady."

The wilding pack was closing in on them. Henrick counted seven and then eight of them. "Now!"

The Nova rifles came on instantly. The tunnel lit up with ten million watts of UV light, the charging demons covered their faces and screamed in hideous tones. The leading group stumbled down and fell to their knees and faces. They tried to crawl away. The second group fared little better, crying out and dropping down to the ground.

"Forward," Henrick said.

His army moved in unison. Their lights blinding and burning the demons, who seemed to be aging before Henrick's eyes. When three lights focused on the closest vampire it shriveled up like a wilting flower and caught fire. The others soon followed, but these fires were not like the Ignatorum. Instead of a blue white flame that burned hotter than a gas fire, these demons burned away slowly like charred paper. Turning to piles of ash and red embers.

Henrick hadn't expected that, but it was merely interesting, not concerning. *Dead was still dead.*

They moved on and came to a curved wall that resembled the turret of a castle. Candles burned in recesses along its face, a row of skulls sat at the foot and everything was covered with centuries of wax. In a huge pit beneath the wall lay piles of human bones like nothing Henrick had ever seen on the outside. The bones of hundreds lay there.

"Aldo says they wait inside for the hunting party to return with victims," Henrick explained. "If he's right there are almost fifty of them in there, with only one way in or out."

"Fifty?" one of his men replied in shock.

"Almost fifty," Henrick corrected. "But their leader is the danger. He's a crafty, powerful demon named Tyrian."

All of the hunters knew who Tyrian was. He'd killed members of the Righteous Fire before. In fact, he'd nearly killed Henrick. Simon saved him by pulling him from the demon's grasp and stabbing Tyrian with a bayonet.

The incident had cost Henrick time in recovery, but unlike Aldo his mind hadn't been taken and so he was allowed to continue on in the order. And yet, the incident affected his stature in other ways. As Simon had saved him, Henrick always needed to show gratitude to the older man. It made Henrick appear the weaker of the two when, in fact, he was bolder and stronger. The thoughts burned like acid in his mind.

The Half Life

To hate a man for saving you, even Henrick understood how twisted that was.

"You have us come for Tyrian on our first mission?" a hunter named Doros asked.

"I hear fear in your voice, Doros. Are you afraid?"

"I've killed these things all over the world," Doros said. "But we fight one or two of them at a time, not fifty. Nor would I be stupid enough to lock myself in a small room with them while relying on weapons we've never tested before."

"We just tested them," Henrick insisted.

"On naked weaklings."

"Sometimes a leap of faith is required," Henrick said. "Today is one of those days."

"We've found the entrance," one of the men said. "It's sealed from the inside."

"Use the explosives." Henrick ordered.

Explosives were placed and weapons checked one last time. Henrick gave the signal to blow the doorway.

The explosion blew the iron door off its frame and sent it flying into the chamber.

Henrick rushed in, his men right behind him. The gathering of hungry demons turned in shock, and then they charged.

These demons were cloaked in heavy leather armor, their bodies thicker and more powerful. But their eyes and faces were still vulnerable, and as the Nova rifles came on their assault was turned back.

"Use the spikes," Henrick ordered. He tapped a switch on the side of his rifle and a barbed spike shot out, impaling the closest demon. His men did the same. Ten of the undead were quickly dispatched and burning. Some of the others raced for the door, but two of Henrick's men stood their ground, Nova rifles turning night into day.

One of the larger nosferatu tackled Henrick, its clawed fingers trying to dig into his throat. An armored collar protected Henrick and it went for his heart next, but the sharpened nails of its hand raked uselessly across Henrick's chest, unable to penetrate the breastplate.

Henrick managed to throw the demon off and then kicked it with his booted foot. The blow was strong, but not enough to injure such a creature.

A second switch on the rifle deployed a bayonet and Henrick jabbed with it, slicing the demon's wrist. The protective arm came away from its face and the creature's face took the full brunt of the Nova rifle's power at point blank range. Its eyes turned red, like glowing lava, and then burst into flame. The vampire peeled back, smoke pouring from its eye sockets. It collapsed and began to burn.

"Get their faces!" Henrick yelled.

The melee continued and one by one the vampires fell and began to burn. Two of the hunters were injured. One was dead with a broken neck. But fifty dead vampires was a fair trade for that.

The temperature in the chamber began to rise. The searing white fire of the Ignatorum spreading panic among the Fallen. It was madness and it was beautiful. Demons burning in a chamber of their own creation. A pit of fire. A reasonable facsimile to Hell.

"Yes!" Henrick shouted, his suit and the gas filter of his mask allowing him to breathe and not overheat. "Yes, this is it! The anteroom to Hell where you will spend eternity for your crimes against man and God!" He lunged and stabbed a dying vampire.

"For you too, Henrick," a deep voice growled.

Henrick turned to see Tyrian, his hand up under one of the hunter's helmets, blood pouring down the demon's muscled forearm as it burrowed its claws into the dead hunter's brain.

"This is you're end Tyrian," Henrick said. "Not mine."

Tyrian was huge, clothed in thick, medieval leather. He was staring at Henrick, trying to get into his mind.

Henrick laughed from behind the filtered shield. "Sorry," he said, tapping the side of his helmet. "Must be a bad connection."

By now the other hunters had brought their lights to bear on Tyrian, and in the crossfire the huge vampire fell to its knees.

Henrick walked slowly towards this demon, the one who had set him back. The one who had made him feel inferior all those years. A million times he killed Tyrian in his dreams and now, finally, his dreams and reality were colliding.

With a sudden move, Tyrian ripped the helmet from the dead hunter and lunged for the man's open neck.

"No!" Henrick shouted. He grabbed Tyrian by his long hair and yanked his face back. "You will not die as a human. Not after all you've done." He turned quickly to Doros. "Give me Simon's hunting knife."

Doros pulled the twelve-inch weapon from its sheath and handed it over.

"Let's see how you like feeling helpless!" He stabbed the creature in both legs and then pulled the demon's arm taut and sliced the flesh down to the bone. "Enjoying it?"

Tyrian didn't say a thing. In a rage, Henrick proceeded to hack off Tyrian's ears, first one and then the other.

Watching him, Doros shouted: "Just finish it! Give him the poison so we can see if it works and then we can get out of this hellhole."

Henrick didn't want Tyrian to die from poison. He wanted him to beg and suffer and show his fear. But there was none of this from the creature. Nothing but utter defiance and hatred.

A sudden emptiness consumed Henrick. This wasn't working. He wasn't getting the satisfaction he'd waited for. For years, he'd thought about this moment. He thought he'd be filled with pride and gratification, but there was none of that. He stared at the vampire. Was it a demon's trick? Was he somehow stealing from Henrick yet again, even here at the last?

Emptiness was replaced by fury and Henrick plunged the knife into Tyrian's chest. Over and over he raised and thrust the blade down with every ounce of strength he had. Flesh was torn, ribs cracked, rusted blood flying. He continued on even as the fires of hell began to flare around him.

"Henrick!" Doros yelled, grabbing at him.

"Get off me!" Henrick shouted.

Doros yelled to another hunter for help. Together they pulled Henrick off the burning vampire.

"You're on fire," Doros said, patting down the flames with his hands.

Henrick's body armor was smoldering and melting. His hair and skin were singed where gaps in the helmet and collar left them exposed. More scars he would carry with him proudly.

"I'm fine," Henrick grunted.

"Let's go," Doros yelled to the group.

They moved quickly, carrying the wounded and the dead, leaving the horror chamber behind as the fires within it purged the world of a great evil.

Though he was the leader, Henrick was dragged along like a sullen child, marching up the tunnel in a trance-like state.

"What was that all about?" Doros asked. "What were you thinking?"

Henrick didn't engage. He was trying to fathom the emptiness that came with his act. The complete lack of satisfaction—as if he couldn't kill Tyrian enough. As if a thousand times wouldn't be enough.

Why, he thought. *Why?*

An answer came to him slowly. It was the only answer that made any sense. Tyrian was not his real enemy. He was an old foe, of course. He was evil and depraved, yes, but in the greater scheme of things he was worthless. He was nothing. It was the *blasphemer* that Henrick must destroy. The invader of churches. The one who'd taken half his sight. Christian was the real enemy and only when Henrick made him beg for death and then delivered it would he feel any satisfaction.

Chapter 21

Central Haiti

The red Jeep Wrangler cruised along the country road with its top down heading towards the mountains of Haiti. The sun was high and the sky blue, though a band of clouds could be seen clinging to the ridge high above. As they climbed higher into the mountains the air-cooled enough to make it pleasant.

Another beautiful day on a troubled island. *All a disguise*, Leroy thought. Nothing in this place was pleasant. He downshifted the Jeep and turned onto an even more primitive road, as he and Terrance continued a long ascent.

"I don't understand why we're going this way," Leroy said.

"Which way are we going?" Terrance asked. "I can't see, remember."

"You think that's funny?"

"It's not too bad."

"Why do we have to go up here if these demons don't want to be saved?"

"You don't know that until you ask," Terrance said. "Maybe they do. Maybe they want to be saved and they don't even know it."

"And I'm supposed to convince them? Like some traveling preacher?"

"No," Terrance said. "You're supposed to show them the light. They'll decide for themselves."

Leroy wasn't sure he liked any of this. After weeks on the island and thirty conversions or rebirths of the souls of the dammed, they were venturing into the heart of darkness in an attempt to reach those who'd become demons long ago. These vampires would be hostile. Dark. Evil. And they served one so depraved, so vile that even the voodoo priests were afraid of him.

"What about Papa Legba?"

"He uses the name," Terrance said. "But Papa Legba he is not."

Terrance had explained before that Papa Legba was a voodoo Loa, a god of sorts, who commanded the keys to eternity. Modern culture had corrupted the image, making him into a mad demon, which he wasn't; and this vampire, the one who ruled the underworld on Haiti had stolen the name and used it for himself.

"Okay, but what about him?"

"Even he must be given a choice."

"And what happens if he becomes human?" Leroy asked. "Is he forgiven of all his crimes?"

"I don't know," Terrance admitted. "But if there is still punishment for one so evil, then at least he faces the sentence as a human."

Near the top of the foothills they came to an abandoned sugar cane plantation.

"And what about Drakos?" Leroy asked. "I've had dreams of him. He wanted to kill me; Elsa took my place."

Terrance nodded slowly at the mention of Elsa's name. "She sacrificed herself for us. She tried to destroy Drake even though she knew it couldn't be done. She did it to buy you some time."

"Does Drake know about me?" Leroy asked nervously.

"He knows of you," Terrance said. "But he doesn't know who you are. And he's wounded now. He won't come for you until he's strong again. And when he does you'll have to be ready. You can't fear him. He'll destroy you if you're afraid."

"So that's why we're coming here," Leroy said. "You're testing me."

Terrance grinned. "No test, just a lesson," he said. "Unfortunately in this world we tend to only find our most lasting faith in the darkest moments of our life. That's where the lesson lies. Only when we let go of old beliefs can new ideas and new power flow in."

"You think I'm carrying around old beliefs?" Leroy asked confused. "I barely even believe all this stuff I seen with my own eyes."

Terrance just hummed.

Leroy shook his head. "Who ever heard of having a blind man for a guide," he muttered under his breath.

"Who ever heard of an angel from the streets of Compton," Terrance replied. "You forget I can't see but I can hear really well."

The dirt road topped out on a plateau, and far in the distance the old sugarcane plantation loomed. Leroy pulled through a crumbling archway with one rusted gate still barely hanging on. Someone had scrawled graffiti on the wall beside the arch. It read; *Abandon all hope.*

Just inside the gate, perhaps a hundred yards from the house, he brought the Jeep to a stop.

"At least it's daylight," Leroy muttered.

"There won't be any light once you step inside."

"What do you mean once *I* step inside?"

Terrance put his hand on Leroy's. "My path has come to an end. It's time for you to go alone and for me to go back home and enjoy what little time I have left with my family in New Orleans."

Leroy stared at Terrance.

"You knew as well as I did that this day would come. Now, don't be afraid. You've been handpicked from billions of souls, and that's a promising thought. If I know anything, I know you were chosen because you *will* succeed, not because you might."

Leroy continued to stare at him. He didn't want to get out of the Jeep, didn't want to move a muscle until a sudden flash of a memory popped into his mind: the dream of his son months before asking why he was still in the old apartment in Compton. *What was he waiting for?*

Time to move, he thought. "Okay," he said taking a deep breath. "Here I go."

He stepped from the Jeep and walked toward the old plantation house. The rocks and dirt beneath his feet made a distinct crunching sound.

He turned back to Terrance, who was sitting in the Jeep. "I guess after tonight I'll take you home."

Terrance nodded. "And when you're done saving the world you come back and see your old friend."

As he walked the long gravel path toward the house Leroy felt the air growing cold. The shadow beneath his feet began to fade as the clouds above moved in.

As he approached the house, dead leaves began to swirl around his ankles, tumbling with the wind. A storm was definitely coming.

He thought about turning around, but as he looked back, he saw Terrance shaking his head and pointing with his cane. *They'd come here for a reason and there was no turning back now.*

Leroy stepped up on the great wrap-around porch of the old plantation house. Grand old columns of the fifty-room master's house still held up the dilapidated roof, inhabited now by only the birds. The paint was worn and totally ravaged. The plants and grasses had long encroached on the once proud manor and now covered it like camouflage. Vines snaked everywhere and the wood was cracked and splintered in places - brittle to the touch.

Leroy looked down, careful where to place each footstep. He saw footprints and scuff marks everywhere. Many different kinds and sizes.

There's a lot of Nosferatu here, he thought.

Leroy shut his eyes and listened. At first, the wind was all he heard as it whistled though the overgrown fields outside and through cracks and broken windows in the house. Then, as if it were carried on the wind, he heard voices and the minds of those inside the manor house. They were awake. Many were scared, living in fear. They sensed him. They knew something was out there. Something of great power. Certainly he was the first human to approach the plantation in fifty years, as all in Port Au Prince knew it was cursed.

Leroy took a deep breath and opened his eyes. He was about to go push the door open when the raindrops began to fall. His thoughts turned to Terrance in the open Jeep. He wondered if Terrance could actually pull the top up and secure it by himself. He turned back and saw Terrance moving around agitated.

Back in the Jeep, Terrance felt the wind blow cold just as the first raindrops hit his face. He looked to the sky. "No," he said. "No."

He grabbed the roll bar of the Jeep and stood, yelling to Leroy. "Is there a storm coming?"

Leroy couldn't hear him as the wind whipped through the fields.

Terrance repeated his question. "Is there a storm?"

"Yes! Why?"

"Damn!" Terrance yelled. "We got to get out of here, Leroy. The vampires have the high ground! The clouds turn day into night! You should have told me!"

"What are you talking about?"

"Run Leroy!" Terrance shouted. "Run!"

But even as the words left Terrance's mouth, the front double doors of the grand old house flew open and Leroy was trampled by a stampede of charging figures. He tried to get up but one of them swung a bat that connected with the side of his head. He fell to the ground and blacked out.

The Half Life

Terrance couldn't see what happened, but he could hear it, he could feel it. The rain came down with a rush. It sounded like slop on the dirt road, like a thousand rash whispers in the overgrown fields. Hail began peppering the old manor house.

He heard the door come flying open, shouts and cackling screams and running feet.

"Leroy!" He shouted uselessly.

There was no answer but the sound of thunder as it rocked the mountainside and echoed down the passes.

"Leroy?! Are you okay?"

A voice replied, but it was dark and malignant.

"He cannot 'elp you little man. Nothing can 'elp you now!"

Terrance had never feared being blind. It was a fair trade off for what he'd seen in his world. But the sound of that voice struck him to his core.

He stood and pulled the sheath from the outside of his cane exposing a rapier-like weapon.

"Hahahaha," the deep voice growled. "Blind man gonna fight us. Come on blind man, come an' get me!"

Terrance knew who was speaking. The demon of Haiti. The one who called himself after the voodoo god, Papa Legba. *Eight feet tall*, they said. *Teeth made of ivory*, they said. *Hands that could crush a pig's skull*. Whatever the truth, this was the image Terrance saw in his mind.

The sound of footsteps rushed around the Jeep. Terrance turned and swung the blade this way and that, like a man trying to swat invisible flies. He hit something; it could have been a man or a vampire or the padded roll bar of the Jeep.

A hand grabbed his leg and Terrance slashed downward. This drew a high-pierced shriek from some creature of the night. Another hand grabbed at his collar and the sound of the windshield smashing startled him.

Then all activity stopped and the harsh voice returned much closer this time. Terrance could smell death and decay on the breath. "I was told you would come, voodoo priest. I heard you've been leading my children back into the light."

Terrance slashed with the saber and considered jumping out of the Jeep. He knew the sugar cane fields were east of him, the manor house was in front of him and the way they drove in behind him. He couldn't feel the sun at all now as the cloud and rain ruled the mountaintop.

He wanted to run, but he couldn't. He had to stand and fight. He had to give Leroy time to work, if he was still alive.

He took a great gulp of nothing, as he had no spit. "I know who and what you are – a false imitation of the Loa. You hold only the keys to darkness. If you were really Papa Legba, you would be able to give the keys to the light as well. Which is what I bring to you. I come with absolution. Freedom from evil. The chance to become human again. This offer is to all of you who want it."

A hush ran through all the vampires followed by a slight chatter that moved around the circle, but no voice spoke except that of their master.

"Stop wasting your breath, little man."

The Half Life

Terrance was stalling, hoping that Leroy wasn't dead. He was trying to keep their focus on him and away from Leroy. "You fear the return to your human form," he said. "But it's not something to be feared. Only your master fears it because then he won't rule over you."

He received no answer.

"They serve me," Papa Legba said sharply. "Whether they want to or not!"

A huge paw of a hand grabbed Terrance and flung him to the ground. As he landed, the rapier was knocked from his hand.

"I'm going to dismember you piece by piece and then feed on you slowly."

Fear gripped Terrance. He scrambled for the Jeep and tried to get back in, but it was no use. In a second the vampire had him again, grabbing him and tossing him further this time.

Terrance landed and rolled in the mud. Before he could move, a heavy boot stepped on him. Terrance felt his ribs crack as if they were matchsticks.

He was gasping for air as the others surrounded him. He could hear a frenzy among them, like a pack hungry jackals.

"You don't have to do this," Terrance managed.

If any of them heard him, Terrance would have been shocked. The wind and the rain were too loud. Their own cackling too hideous and constant for the soft pleas of a broken man to overcome.

Papa Legba slammed a fist into Terrance's face. Another blow landed and then another and then another. Battered and bloody,

Terrance felt Papa Legba leaning in close, sniffing him and putting his ear to Terrance's lips. "What was that?"

Terrance had no strength left to talk and Papa Legba pulled back laughing. "The voodoo priest says we're all forgiven!"

A wave of sick laughter rose up.

"Tonight we can go home, and tomorrow we can bask in the sun. Or maybe we roast you on a barbeque spit, voodoo man."

More laughter. And then, to Terrance's utter surprise, a human voice, "You can be forgiven, but you need to take what's been offered!"

Terrance could barely believe his ears. It was Leroy. *Thank God he was alive!*

"I came to bring you back to the light," Leroy shouted. "I come to end this curse. And from this day forward, I don't need your permission!"

The depth of Leroy's voice, the deep baritone thunder of his words were like nothing Terrance had ever heard from the soft-spoken, unassuming man. He felt the demons pulling away. Not in hope, but in fear. *What was this? What power was in this man who stood before them?*

"Kill him!" Papa Legba shouted.

They didn't move.

"Then I kill you myself!" Legba dropped Terrance and charged for Leroy.

"No!"

The Half Life

Papa Legba lunged forward, his hands outstretched for Leroy's throat, but the instant they touched Leroy's skin he was thrown back by a shockwave of power and light that flashed from Leroy's body. The sound of thunder crashed right over them and a pressure wave blasted forth like a nuclear explosion. Terrance felt a spray of gravel, rain and leaves rake him. He covered his own face as the light burned in his mind's eye.

The vampires were blown off their feet like bits of straw in a hurricane. A concussive wave louder than the thunder echoed across the plantation grounds and boomed its way up into the hills. It blocked out all other sound as it rolled forth and then came back, echoing longer and deeper than any thunderclap Terrance had ever heard.

It seemed a minute or two before it finally faded. But when it was gone, the sound of the rain returned. Steady. Strong. Peaceful.

"Leroy," Terrance whispered. "Leroy, what happened?"

A pair of hands found Terrance, kind hands that helped him to sit up.

"I was knocked out." Leroy said. "I'm sorry."

"Don't be," Terrance said. "Just tell me what happened. Are they gone?"

"No," Leroy said. "They're all around us."

Terrance froze. "What?"

Terrance tried to envision it. Lost souls, standing in the rain, encircling two small humans on the muddy ground. "Their eyes?" he asked. "Can you see their eyes?"

"Human again." Leroy said. "Crying."

The blast of light had transformed the vampires instantaneously back into human beings. They stood in shock, staring at Leroy. Weeping in the rain.

"What about Legba?" Terrance asked.

"He's gone. Gone from this place."

"He ran?"

"No," Leroy said. "He vanished."

Terrance nodded slowly. He could only guess that Legba rejected the chance at mercy and was destroyed.

As Terrance thought about this he felt Leroy's hands touching his wounds. "What are you doing?"

"I have to save you," Leroy said. "I couldn't save my son, but I can save you."

Terrance held up his hand. "You already did. Besides, this is my destiny. I was born in Haiti and I always knew this was where I'd die."

"But I have the power. I can..."

"Your power is meant for the dead," Terrance said. "Not the living. You were sent here to help those in the darkness. That's the mission. You must stay true to your gift."

"But I can't do it alone."

"You've been doing it alone already," Terrance said. "I've just held your hand... a little."

Before Leroy could speak Terrance began to cough. His clothes were soaked with blood and rain and the tawny, clay-like mud of Haiti. "Me and the mud," Terrance muttered. "One and the same."

"Please," Leroy said. "Please don't go."

"I'm proud of you," Terrance whispered. "Proud of a good son…"

Terrance said nothing more. There he died, lying in the mud on that high plateau, surrounded by twenty healed souls and the Angel of Redemption as the rain fell down on them from above.

Chapter 22

Cologne, Germany

Christian and Kate waited in a fashionable district surrounded by upscale shops, outdoor cafes, and nightclubs that bustled with foot traffic. The corner café they sat at had a clear view of everything that was going on up and down the boulevard, and from it they surveyed the crowds filtering in and out of the various restaurants and clubs.

Kate watched with amused wonderment. There, in the faces of those that passed by, life existed: life and love, laughter and anger. She had undervalued all that was human, reduced it to a trivial race for tomorrow. All the emotions that made it worth living were slipping ever so slightly into the distance and soon would exist only in her memory. The invisible wall that separated her from all those around her was growing with every second, she'd be just like Christian soon, surrounded by thousands of people yet totally alone.

"Where's this friend of yours?" Christian asked.

Her contact was nearly two hours late. Both of them understood the implication. He must be comprised, or he'd set a trap for them and was about to spring it.

She shook her head.

"We need to get moving Kate. He's not going to show, and we're in a bad spot sitting out here in the open."

Kate agreed. The two companions, their destinies now intertwined, headed up the boulevard passing couples and party goers in the night. As they were about to leave the area, a young boy, totally out of place, ran up to Kate. Kate's eyes were drawn to him as he reminded her of Calvin.

She kneeled down and looked at the boy. "Are you lost?"

"No." The young boy said. "A man named Nicodemus told me to give this to you."

He held out his tiny arm and handed Kate a note. She stood quickly, casting her gaze over the crowds that mingled about the area, but Nicodemus was not to be seen.

Nicodemus was the code name of her former Interpol assignment. As the boy ran off, she opened the note.

Your FBI friends are here, Kathrine. I didn't burn you. I was informed that they were here earlier today. Meet me at the "Cathedral" at midnight. I have the whereabouts of your subject, and new documents for you to travel under.

"A cathedral is not the best place for us to meet," Christian informed her. "Our powers will be diminished there."

"This *Cathedral* is a Goth club down town. It was the focal point of the case we were working on when I was last here. A human trafficking case."

"Oh," he said. "Goths are not exactly my favorite either."

"Why not? They seem kind of vampire-like to me."

"My last battle for the Roman empire was against the Goths. Trust me, they were not fun people to deal with."

She almost laughed. Perhaps there was a little humanity left in her after all.

Twenty minutes later they were approaching the Cathedral. It was now an upscale nightclub catering to the new elite of Cologne with a line-up around the block.

"We're a little underdressed," she said.

"I'll get us in."

Christian dragged her to the front of the line, where a pair of security guards bristled at the intrusion; then suddenly, one guard pulled the rope aside and ushered them through.

"Changed their minds did you?"

"Don't worry I wasn't mean. I made them think we're huge A–list celebrities and that we're going to get them into our next movie."

"Gonna have to teach me that trick sometime," she said.

They moved through the club. It had been redesigned since the raid five years ago. It was disorientating to her. What had been a warren of purple velvet drapes and small candlelit alcoves was now a multilevel, wide open amphitheater with everything facing toward the center dance floor.

How the hell am I going to find Nick in here? As she stared into the darkness a hand landed on her shoulder. Kate turned ready to fight, but instantly recognized her friend.

"Good to see you, Kathrine," he said in an Italian accent.

The Half Life

Kate thought back to when she first meet Nicolas Kempt. Nick was as cool as they come. He never let his emotions surface. She never could tell if he was excited, angry or saddened. And yet at sixty, and ready to retire, time did not seem to have been kind to him. He had a lot more grey hair and had put on thirty pounds.

"I was sorry to hear about your husband," he said, "but that's for another day. We don't have much time. Your coworkers are here in Cologne."

"Did they contact you?"

"Of course. They expect you to reach out to me. They may even be here now. So let us be quick."

He led them to a dark corner. "The back office is a safe spot for us. I know the new owners, and from there you can get out via the fire escape and leave unseen."

As they made their way to the back of the club one level up, Kate couldn't help but feel the tension from Nick. She couldn't read his mind like Christian might have been able to do, but she could sense that he was frightened. She could sense a conflict in him, too. He felt he owed her some loyalty for saving his life from the Russian mob, but he was also helping a known fugitive escape capture.

He glared at Christian.

"I'll wait outside," Christian said.

He left and Kate entered the back office with Nick, who asked the manager to give them a minute.

"Nick, let me tell you what's going on," she began.

He cut her off. "No, don't tell me anything. I don't want to know. I hope you're innocent of what they've accused you of, but it doesn't matter to me. I owe you, but the tab is cleared after this."

She nodded. *How much more could she expect?*

He handed her a small shopping bag. "I brought you a new passport and identity card along with some spending money. It's not much, a thousand euros. It's all I could get my hands on."

"What about Faust?"

"He's not in Germany anymore. He's hiding in Amsterdam."

"We'll have to get there fast."

"I suggest you drive," he said. "They're watching the airports."

She nodded, "Thanks."

He held up his hands. "That's all I have for you. Now I must go. Your exit is through that window, down the fire escape."

The two stared at each other for a second and then Nick moved toward the office door. Kate grabbed his arm for a second. He turned. "What are they saying I've done?"

Nick stopped in his tracks, his hand on the door. "You don't know?"

"I punched agent Blackburn in the face," she said, "but that's not worth an all-out manhunt."

A long silence hung in the air. "They're saying you've teamed up with a suspect and killed your partner. Why, they've never explained. I can read a trumped up charge when I see one. But you're here, looking for God knows what, and you're not alone. He's the one isn't he?"

She didn't answer. She couldn't. She felt as if she'd just been slapped across the face.

Nick pushed through the door. "God speed Kathrine. I hope you survive whatever it is you're mixed up in."

He said nothing more and left the room. Kate lingered. She'd never felt more alone than at that precise moment. Accused of Billy Ray's murder. *Damn them. How the hell could they possibly think that?*

A wave of uncontrollable rage bubbled up. The first thought in her mind was to find these agents. Confront them. If they wanted to see killing, she'd show it to them. Make them bleed. And if Christian was right, maybe she'd have a little taste of what being human felt like afterwards.

She heard the thoughts in her mind, felt the pull of adrenaline they gave her.

"Stop it," she said aloud. "Just stop."

It took a few minutes for her to settle down, but she managed to calm herself. And then she made a mistake; instead of taking the fire escape, she opened the door. To her surprise, Ashley Blackburn and a trio of Cologne's finest were standing there.

"Going somewhere?" Ashley said, the dark bruise still visible on her face from where Kate had clubbed her.

They pushed in through the door, grabbing her before she could form a plan. Two of the officers sat her in a chair. The third stood beside Ashley.

"Kate Pfeiffer, you are arrested and to be placed in custody," the lead German said.

"We followed you from the square," Ashley informed her. "Where's your partner?"

"I don't know what you're talking about," Kate said. "You saw how little I like having partners."

"Very funny."

Ashley whispered to the one of the Germans, who turned to his men. "Get the others and search the club. We'll take care of her."

Two of the men left while the third held out his cuffs. "Please turn around."

Don't do it, Kate thought with her mind focused on the German. *Don't cuff me. No need. I'm not dangerous.*

"Hands behind your back," he said.

Damn.

"Did you really think we were just going to let this all go?" Ashley said.

Shut up! Kate thought, focusing on Ashley now. If it wouldn't work on the German maybe it would work on Ashley. At least she'd have silence.

Once the German had cuffed her and spun her around, Ashley stepped forward and sucker punched Kate in the stomach sending her to the ground. "That's for the bathroom, bitch."

Kate crumbled to the ground, but in truth she barely felt it.

Ashley seemed satisfied though; she turned from Kate and picked up the package, dumping the contents out on the desk. "Let's see what we got here."

The Half Life

As Ashley looked through the materials in the manila envelope, Kate tested her strength. Straining with all her might, she felt the chain between the cuffs bending and then it snapped with a quiet click. She kept her hands behind her back as Ashley walked over with her new passport.

"Where were you going to run to this time?"

"I'm not running," Kate said. "I'm searching for answers."

"Not anymore you're not."

As the words left Ashley's mouth, Kate gave her a sweeping kick, chopping her legs out from under her and dropping Ashley to her knees. She followed that with a kick to the chest that sent Ashley flying backwards into the desk. The German was so stunned it took him a moment to react.

He went for his gun, but Kate sprung from the floor and knocked the pistol out of his hand. She followed up with a forearm to the face that sent him into the wall and knocked him unconscious.

Turning back, Kate spotted Ashley lying on the floor, clutching her ribs.

Kate knelt down next to her, and whispered in her ear, "I didn't kill Billy Ray. If I had, I'd kill you right now. But if I told you the truth, you'd never believe me. I barely believe it myself. Tell the Director and that snake, Serrano, that I'm hunting for the person responsible and once I've found him, I'll be back."

Kate stood, gathered up the documents and money that Nick had provided for her and turned to the window. She smashed it open with a chair and climbed through. Just as she was about to jump, the hammering of a pistol rang out, five or six shots in rapid succession.

Kate leapt through the air, dropping the manila package with all the documents. She'd been hit, and she could feel it. It burned like acid inside her. One bullet hit her shoulder, the other her lower back. She dropped twenty-feet to the road below and hit her head.

The last thing she remembered were the headlights of a car racing towards her.

Chapter 23

Muscat, Oman

Akash hid in the shadows of an overcrowded shanty town on the outskirts of Muscat watching the comings and goings of the people, waiting for one particular soul.

Fires burned here and there and incandescent lights flickered. The light reflected off his eyes as he peered through the night.

It had been three days since he'd fled from Teresa and Zwana. Three days since he'd decided to go for the Dark Star on his own. Thinking back now, he should have killed them. But the old wizard scared him and Tereza was not easy to fool or to defeat. And, having drunk the human's blood he was no match for either of them.

No, he decided, there was no more he could have done. But three days was a day too long. He was now in danger. He tried to stretch his senses into the night, searching for Tereza or the witch doctor. He felt nothing, but that didn't mean they weren't out there.

He considered hiding, running away. But in his human life that had never worked. Nothing worked to free you from slavery, nothing but killing the master and becoming the master yourself.

He settled down and focused on the task at hand. Waiting, until finally, his prey came into view.

The man he had been waiting for, *the Watcher*. The Watcher had a single job among the people of the stone, to keep view over the others, to make sure they remained loyal. As such he was like the patriarch of a family, a family whose roots stretched back into time, millennia before Drake had even been born.

Akash stared as the Watcher entered one of the low white buildings made of adobe.

Finally.

He stole across the alleyway and pushed into the small home, surprising everyone inside.

A shout rang out in Arabic and three men rose up. Akash grabbed a baby from the lap of a woman near the entrance and ran. The men chased him, the Watcher among them.

Akash darted through the back alleys, jumped a small ditch filled with a muddy trickle of water and kept running. He made sure not to outpace his pursuers by too much.

Shouts in the distance suggested more men and women had joined the chase. That was fine, he'd give them what they wanted, but he would take something in exchange.

He turned down a darkened alley, placed the infant down and hid. As the men turned the corner they saw the child sitting in the middle of the street, they rushed forward and Akash jumped from the side of a building and landed behind them. In seconds he'd killed the first two and dragged the Watcher back into the darkness.

Willing him into silence, Akash drove the Watcher before him, like one might drive a tired horse. They ran several blocks and eventually came back to a different part of the muddy ditch.

Here Akash began to dig into the man's mind. He saw that there were others of the family in Muscat. Generation upon generation remaining anonymous as they protected the hiding place of the Dark Star.

Tell me! Tell me!

The town of Ibis flashed into the man's mind. More family members were there. Akash saw a rental place where heavy trucks and four wheel drive vehicles could be rented. He saw a course on the compass on the dashboard of one, saw an oasis which the Watcher had driven to.

"Akash!"

The voice echoed down the length of the ditch. Akash looked up to see Tereza standing there with her sword in hand.

"Time to pay for your treachery," she yelled.

Akash threw the Watcher aside and pulled out his machete. He and Tereza clashed in the ditch and despite his fury, Tereza quickly got the upper hand. She knocked his weapon from his hand and threw him through the walls of one of the nearby homes like it was paper.

As she rushed in, Akash got her with a forearm to the face and then kicked her through a window. She landed hard and her sword was knocked free. He charged forward, determined to finish her. But she spun his way with long knife in her hand.

Shadows II

It almost decapitated him, but he ducked at the last second and the blade missed the mark. Instead of killing him, it carved the flesh from the left side of his face.

He screamed in agony and sprinted off into the night, clutching his face and blind with the pain.

Chapter 24

Overleek Village,
North of Amsterdam

The light from the setting sun filtered through the broken slats of the old barn. Specks of dust caught in the light glowed as if powered from within.

Naturally, Christian avoided every last photon, but its beauty did not escape him.

From the shelter of the upper level he watched a small figure hike up a dirt path and across a cow pasture to his fortress of solitude, an old church. As he had earlier, Faust entered the church and barred the door. At that point Christian got bored with the show.

Christian needed Faust to leave at night, but he wasn't about to do that for the same reason he was hiding in a church in the first place. Faust knew there were Nosferatu after him. And he wasn't interested in seeing them face-to-face.

Little progress, Christian thought, but the surveillance was worthwhile based on something Christian overheard.

He put the binoculars down and descended a wooden ladder to the level below. The car he'd stolen was there along with his passenger.

She'd been recovering for three days. At times Christian thought she wouldn't last the next five minutes, but she was a survivor and she never gave in.

He opened the door to check on her. She was awake for the first time in days.

"What happened?"

"Your ex-partner, Ashley, shot you."

Kate held her head in her hands as she tried to focus and make sense of where she was. "I was hoping this nightmare was going to be over when I woke up."

"Be glad you woke up at all," he said. "Ashley hit you once in the center of your back and once in the right shoulder blade. I took the bullets out and sewed you up, but the damage was done."

"I don't understand?" Kate said. "I thought we were bulletproof. Or invisible or something."

"I am," he said. "But you're still part human, so the bullets didn't pass through you. Truthfully, I wasn't sure what was going to happen. I've never seen a Half-Lifer shot before."

The two stared at each other.

"What aren't you telling me?" Kate asked.

"I just..."

"You just what?"

"I don't know what to expect when we finally get you to the angel. Your body took a pounding; it's pretty bad. We never repair once we've changed. You know that. I have burns and scars, like my neck wound. I just don't know what will happen if the angel turns you back."

"You mean the wounds might kill me?" she said.

"They might kill us all."

"What does it matter?" she said. "I'll never see my family again, even if I do live. With what just happened to Ashley and her team, the FBI isn't just going to forget that and let me play soccer mom for the rest of my life. You saved me. But I'm just as dead as you. Even if this insanity ends, the only way I'll see my son is when he visits me in prison."

Christian recognized the despondence, the blackness enshrouding Kate's mind. This was an extremely dangerous place for a Half-Lifer to go. He'd felt it many times himself. Most of what she was saying was true, but he couldn't let her fall into despair.

"Yeah, you're right," he said. "You're doomed."

She cocked her head at him.

"I'm just being honest," he said. "There's no hope for you. No chance. No way at all that it can work out."

She looked at him harshly. "Clearly you're not a grief counselor."

"Not my strong suit."

"In that case, shut your pie hole," she said.

He grinned. "That's more like it. Now listen. One thing long life brings is money. I have it. Lots and lots of it. You'd be shocked what compounding interest can do for you over fifteen hundred years."

"You have bank accounts?"

"Hundreds of them. For centuries."

"Where?"

"All over the world. At one time I banked with the Medici and the Rothschilds."

She laughed for a second and then winced as it sent waves of pain through her. "That's absurd."

"If we live," he continued, "you can have a bunch of it. Go to a country with no extradition. Bribe the hell out of someone. I'm sure you've chased enough criminals that bought their way out of prison in your time. Why shouldn't you be able to do the same?"

She smiled. "I just want my son back. I want to see him smile. He means everything to me."

He nodded. "Hang onto that thought. It'll save you."

"And what saves you?"

He hesitated.

"Come on," she said. "Fess up."

He looked away. "I want to feel the sun again. When I was young I worked in the fields planting crops. I used to work till the late afternoon and then jump in the river to clean off and then climb out and dry in the sun. I want to feel that again."

She stared at him and then reached up and kissed him. Pressing her lips to his and pulling him close. He kissed her back once, but only because he knew what she wanted.

"Do you feel that?" she asked.

He could feel it. Somehow, perhaps because she was still in the Half-Life or because he turned her, he could feel the passion flowing through her to him. But he hesitated.

"I'm sorry," she said. "I shouldn't have…"

"No," he said. "Don't be."

"I've lived without passion for long enough," she said. "I just thought we could share some, before the feeling dies."

"I want to feel passion again, too," he said. "But there's…"

She sat up taller. "What?"

"It's just…"

"Oh my God," she said. "You're holding a candle for someone. Who is she? Is she alive? Is she a vampire?"

He held up a hand. "Stop."

She shook her head. "Sorry, persistent questioning is my business. Now who is it? Who are you saving yourself for Christian Hannover?"

"Her name is Elsa," he said. "She's waiting for me on the other side. At least I'd like to believe that."

Kate smiled. "That's so romantic I could punch you in the face."

"Don't," he said. "You'll pull your stiches out."

"You really think you'll see her again?"

"Maybe," he said. "If we can finish this and I can die as a human. Then maybe. I hope so anyway."

"Pretend I'm her," Kate said. "And kiss me one more time."

He leaned forward and held her face and kissed her softly and for a long moment it almost seemed like he was human again. And then they parted.

"Yeah, I'd wait for that," she said, grinning.

He smiled. "Back to work," he said. "Faust is about to make a move; he's heading into Amsterdam and we need to follow him."

Kate's eyes lit up. "We found him? You mean we're not just hiding out?"

"No," he said. "We're multi-tasking. We're camped outside his sanctuary. He's found himself an old church. But he's tired of being cooped up. He's been hiding here for weeks. Later today, he's going to see a friend at the new Van Gogh exhibit at the art museum in Amsterdam."

She glanced out through the gap into the pasture beyond, studying the distance. "You can read all that in his mind from this far away?"

Christian laughed. "No," he said, pulling a hi-tech scanner from his pocket. "But I can listen to his phone calls on this."

"You'd have made a good FBI agent," she said. "Bullet proof, mind reader, with no need for sleep. I'm thinking if this angel thing doesn't work out, maybe you can change the whole bureau into vampires. We could put a stop to crime in all fifty states."

"Except for the ones we'd cause ourselves."

"There's always a catch," she said, then added. "You know, back when I was still an agent I met your friend, Drake, once. We thought Vivian Dasher was our number one suspect in the Boston murders and went to find her. He ran interference for her. I felt something was off that day with that man; in fact, I knew something was wrong."

"Well if you ever see Drake again, you run."

"Why? You don't think I can handle myself."

"He's the King of the Undead. His abilities are extremely powerful, and he is highly intelligent with a psychopathic personality. He likes to inflict pain and, more so, he loves to deceive and distort others' thoughts and reality. No need for you to ever interact with him. Our goal is to find the angel and get you back to your son. Period. So if you meet Drake again, you run and keep running."

A strange look came over her face as if she didn't quite believe him, but she nodded. "I got it. Run."

Chapter 25

Central Amsterdam,
Museum of Art

Dr. Faust and his longtime friend, Hans Daimler, slowly toured the museum with glasses of red wine in hand. Faust could not describe the relief he felt at being out of the small church, though he knew he'd be back there by nightfall.

With this sense of fleeting freedom on his mind, Faust strolled through the Van Gogh exhibit, it was comprised mostly of his early works. Daimler spoke about each piece, but it wasn't the artwork that Faust was interested in as much as the knowledge that his friend was reiterating about the life and death of the master painter. Besides, the more his friend spoke, the more Faust could drink and the longer the tour went. Soon he'd forgotten all about the demons and the danger and the time of day.

"…and unfortunately Van Gogh was misunderstood," Daimler continued. "Trouble followed him wherever he went. After some years, the citizens of Arles signed a petition saying that Van Gogh was a dangerous man and he was forced to leave."

"He had some kind of mental illness," Faust said. "Didn't he?"

Daimler nodded. "No one's quite certain of the diagnosis, but even Van Gogh seemed to know something was wrong. He moved to an asylum in Provence. In May of that year he began painting in the hospital garden. The next year he was invited to exhibit his art in Brussels. He sent six paintings including 'Irises' and 'Starry Night' to the exhibit. Can you imagine seeing all those paintings in one showing?"

"I can hardly think of it," Faust admitted. "They probably rode together in the back of some carriage, handled by the most regular of people, placed and delivered for a pittance."

"Little did they know," Daimler said, "that angels were rubbing shoulders with the common folk."

Faust paused, taken aback by the statement. "Yes. Of course."

"Shortly thereafter, Van Gogh traveled to Auvers. He did less well there, I'm afraid, and soon became distraught. It seems he thought his brother, Theo—who had been his most stalwart guardian—had grown tired of helping him sell his paintings."

Faust took another sip of wine. "He shot himself, didn't he?"

Daimler nodded. "On July 27, 1890, Van Gogh went off to paint, but he took a loaded pistol with him. He shot himself in the chest, but the bullet did not kill him. Theo arrived and tried to nurse him back to health and for two days they talked, brother to brother. Man to man."

"What did they talk about?"

"Van Gogh, wanted Theo to take him home," Daimler said. "He didn't want money or an apology or anything at all; he just wanted to go home. Two days later he died in his brother's arms. He was only 37."

"So young."

The sound of clapping arose from somewhere behind them. It was slow and almost mocking in its tone. "An excellent story," a voice announced.

Both Faust and Daimler turned. A group of men stood on the far side of the exhibit room. They were well dressed and wearing long black overcoats. Funny, Dr. Faust thought, since it was summer. Even in Amsterdam, no one needed a long coat at this time of year.

The tallest of them stepped forward, his boots clomping on the floor like wooden blocks.

At the sight of him, Faust dropped the glass of wine from his hand. It fell as if in slow motion and shattered against the marble floor, the red wine spilling out in all directions like blood from a terrible wound.

Faust went weak in the knees and had to put a hand to the wall to keep himself up.

"Morgan?" Daimler cried out, grasping at his friend.

"Let him fall," the tall man suggested. "He knows what's about to occur. It's not fair to ask him to stand against it."

"Who are you?" Daimler said. "What are you talking about? And how the hell did you get in here? The museum is closed except for private guests."

"How the *hell* indeed," the man said.

"Don't…" Faust managed, shaking and pawing at his friend, "…don't antagonize him."

Daimler looked confused but acted quickly, lunging for the emergency alarm button.

The tall figure shot forward, grabbed Daimler by the collar and flung him back, slamming him to the ground in what appeared like the blink of an eye. "That won't be necessary, Herr Daimler," the tall man said. "Dr. Faust and I are old friends."

Faust wanted to run, but couldn't move. His legs were jelly. His heart pounding uncontrollably, he wanted to tell Daimler to run, to tell him the truth, but who would believe it?

"Now…" the tall man said, lifting Daimler back up and shoving him against the wall with Faust. "I'd like to thank you for that wonderful history lesson. However, like most of the history told and retold on this planet, the truth has been lost with time, replaced by fiction, and then myth. The ending of your glorified tale about Mr. Van Gogh is incorrect. On that fateful day in July, I remember it was hot and the breeze was from the southwest. Mr. Van Gogh was painting in the fields that morning, but he didn't shoot himself.

"The truth is that some children in the town knew him and how different he was. They knew of his mental illness, his strangeness, and his proclivity for talking to himself. They teased him relentlessly, but for some reason, Van Gogh not only put up with them, he seemed to take a liking to them. Perhaps they were his only friends—how pathetic. At any rate, on that fateful day, the boldest of these young men took Van Gogh's pistol and while showing off to his girlfriend— waving it around in the air like a fool—he shot Van Gogh in the chest."

Drake paused before finishing. "Van Gogh's death was no suicide. He was murdered by those who couldn't accept what is different. The great irony of story is that he didn't tell anyone because he didn't want the children to have their lives ruined. A very selfless final act, wouldn't you say, Dr. Faust?"

"Angels," Faust said, repeating what Daimler had said. "Rubbing shoulders with the common man."

"Fools," the tall man replied. "Dead ones at that."

By now Daimler seemed to be getting his wits together. "Morgan, what is this man taking about? What does he mean, *he remembers that day?*

"I'm sorry," Faust said. "I shouldn't have come. I thought that in the day I would be safe. But I stayed too long. I'm so sorry."

"Safe from what?"

Faust trembled with fear. "From the King of the Nosferatu," he said, nodding towards the tall man. "Or as he's called by the Church, Drakos."

"What on Earth are you talking about?" Daimler said. Confused or not, Daimler had had enough. "That's it. I'm getting security."

Daimler went for the alarm button again. This time Drake cocked his head and instantly reached into Daimler's mind. The torment was fast and painful, and before he'd taken another step, Daimler crumbled to the ground and began screaming.

Dr. Faust tried to aid his friend, stepping in front of Drake and holding up his crucifix.

Drake reacted as if he'd been blinded. He covered his eyes and buckled back in pain. But one of the Drones ran forward and snatched the crucifix from Faust, crushing the small medallion in his hands, and tossing it to the floor. As the Drone stepped back, smoke poured from his palm.

Drake straightened up, regaining his strength. He looked at the Drone. "You shall be made a Prince in my new world for your actions."

Drake looked back at Dr. Faust still standing foolishly in front of Daimler as if he could do anything to stop Drake or the Drones at this point.

"Please," Faust said. "I beg of you. Don't harm Hans. He has nothing to do with this. I will help. I will go with you willingly."

"Of course you will," Drake said. But he didn't stop. And within seconds Daimler was screaming in torment again and then foaming at the mouth, his body in full convulsions.

When Drake was satisfied, he released the man and turned to Faust. "You understand, that if you do not help me I will force you to. And furthermore that I'll harm you and then hunt down all that is precious to you in this world if you try to deceive me."

"I know what you're capable of," Faust managed. "I know you can force me, so why would I fight? I also know that once you have what you're looking for, you'll kill me. Just don't turn me into what you are. That's all I ask."

Drake almost seemed magnanimous. "And that I shall grant you, but first you must tell me all that you know about a weapon the Church calls the Dark Star of Power."

Dr. Faust looked confused. "The Dark Star?" he shook his head. "It's just an old myth, or perhaps a metaphor, but it's certainly not real."

"I beg to differ, Dr. Faust, and you're going to help me find it."

"How? I don't know anything about it."

"You'll do what you're trained to do," Drake said. "Access records. Specifically, Vatican records and documents. You'll search for me until you find its origin. Then you will bring the information to me."

Faust listened and his mind began to whirl.

"I already see your thoughts turning to escape. To hiding in the Vatican or some other church. That will not avail you, unless you have no care for others."

"What are you talking about?" Faust asked. "I wasn't-"

Drake didn't let him finish. "I'll be taking your friend here as my captive. Perhaps I'll even regale him with stories of his favorite artists, truths from the past the world has long since forgotten. But I won't wait long. You will work quickly, ruthlessly and without deception or he will begin to suffer."

Faust looked at Drake, he couldn't imagine what would happen to Daimler if he didn't comply, though he doubted it would be a pleasant end for either of them anyway. "I'll do as you ask," he said, nodding in agreement.

"Help him up," Drake ordered. "We begin at once."

As Faust bent down to assist Daimler, the main lights went dark and the secondary security lights come on. The room was now bathed in a dim glow.

Faust stood quickly, not sure what to make of it. In the dim lighting, he saw Drake pull his sword and whirl around. Apparently this wasn't Drake's doing. In fact, Drake seemed to be in a state of surprise, of shock, even fear. *Yes*, Faust thought, *the King of the Undead is afraid.*

Drake's servants turned in lockstep with him. And the four of them stood gazing down the long, dark corridor. Something was out there. Something was coming for them.

Chapter 26

Drake waited in the soft glow of the emergency lighting, his eyes darting from left to right. Searching. Watching. Under normal conditions the dark would have only enhanced his vision, but he was still healing and it seemed as if a haze lay between him and anything beyond the room.

"Hunters?" One of the Drones asked. "Police?"

Drake shook his head. "No," he said. "Something worse."

The sound of boots hitting the marble floor could be heard coming down the hall. From the far end, a shadowy figure passed through one of the floor lights then back into the darkness, and then back into the light of another beam. Drake began to see, began to focus. It was a man in a long coat, running toward them all as if in slow motion passing through the dark and back into the light again.

"Christian," he muttered.

In a blink of an eye, the battle was on. Christian rushed into the room swinging his sword, and the Drones charged at him as commanded by their master. Christian parried them away with ease, flinging one into the wall and another down the hall. The third attacker managed to stay in combat with him for a few seconds longer but was battered to the ground and then thrown into a priceless statue that stood near the center of the room.

It crashed to the ground, shattering on impact. The alarms sounded and the security doors began to drop. Drake moved first and quickest, diving under the hardened steel shutter. Christian was left with the Drones, Faust and Daimler.

Without their master to give them strength, the Drones drew back. Christian ignored them and raced to the door. He tried to force it, but it wouldn't budge. He pounded his fist on the door like a hammer, but even with his supernatural strength there was no way to break it down.

"How do we open this?" he yelled at Faust.

"We don't," Faust said. "They can't be opened from here. Only someone in the control room can release the locks."

"The control room?" Kate was in the control room, as safe a place as Christian could think to put her. He cleared his mind.

Kate. I need your help. Find the controls. Open the doors.

Chapter 27

Kate was sitting in the dark, her eyes on the three guards Christian had subdued and tied up. None of them moved. Though one continued to stare at her.

She looked into his eyes, trying like Christian did to read the man's thoughts. What she got was a wave of confusion and emotion. It was disorienting, disturbing. "Stop looking at me!" she ordered.

The guard looked away and Kate stood, feeling pensive. Moments later the alarms rang out. Christian had been afraid this might happen. He'd prearranged a meeting place in case they got split up. She stood, went to the door and moved out into the hall. It looked clear but something felt wrong.

She took a few steps when she thought she heard a voice.

Kate. I need help.

She looked back to the control room. They weren't the guard's thoughts. They were Christian's.

Open the doors. I'm trapped. I need you to open the doors.

She rushed back inside the room and went to the control panel. Multiple lights were flashing. The schematic showed a group of doors closed on the third floor.

She grabbed one of the guards, heaved him up into the air and onto the seat, surprised at how easily he flew.

"Punch in the code," she demanded. "Release the doors."

He muttered something she couldn't hear through the gag. She ripped it off.

"I can't," he said.

This time she knew he was lying, and despite the sick feeling it gave her, she pried into his mind once again. *Tell me. Tell me the code!*

"D…L…W…4971," he blurted out.

She pushed him back to the floor and despite the fact that he was much larger than her, the guard scampered away, afraid.

She punched in the code. The alarms stopped instantly. The lights stopped flashing.

On the panel she found an intercom switch. "The doors should be open," she shouted.

Christian replied over the small speaker this time. "Drake's here," he shouted. "Run, Kate. Run!"

Kate stood up and bolted out the door only to find Drake himself standing in the hall.

"Agent Pfeiffer, isn't it?"

"Not anymore," she replied. "I've been forced into retirement."

He stepped toward her, but she moved with great speed herself, lunging for the wall, grabbing a fire hose form its hanger and spinning the valve.

Drake charged but was a fraction too late. The jet of water blasted into his chest and knocked him to the ground, with the hose on full blast she sent Drake sliding twenty yards down the hall, dropped the fire hose and sprinted for the door.

As she passed Drake, he grasped for her legs, but she hopped over his out stretched hands and continued to run.

She banged through the exit doors and raced down two flights of stairs. She came out into the basement, one level below where she wanted to be.

"Damn!"

She turned to go back up, but the door above flew open and Drake came rushing in.

She turned and ran the length of the basement looking for another stairway, elevator shaft or a window. She broke through a locked door and came to a room where a vast treasure of art was stored on mobile racks.

She searched through it for a way out. The area was cavernous, and to her horror, it was a dead end.

She had to go back. She turned around, but it was too late; Drake had entered the room. With her heart pounding she stopped in her tracks and crouched down.

"I know you're in here, Kate."

She didn't respond. She could see his feet and the tip of the sword in his hands.

"I can feel you," he added, searching for her. "Not as well as you can feel me. But then I burn brighter than you, don't I?"

Still, she held silent. If he would just go far enough toward the other side of the room she would make a break for the exit.

He continued to speak as he walked slowly, picking through the racks. "I know what you are. I know you're a changeling, caught up in the Half-Life. I hate to tell you, but the worst is yet to come. Why don't you let me help you?"

You can't help me, she thought.

"Oh, but I can," he said, suddenly turning her way.

Damn.

"And I would help you, because I also know how special you are."

She decided it was time to engage. She thought about a section in the far corner of the room. She saw Drake's feet turn. Next she thought about Christian. She sensed an uptick in the rate of Drake's dead heart.

Drake was afraid. He didn't want to be caught down here anymore than she did. *It's a dead end.*

Christian is coming. I released the doors.

"Christian is taking Faust to safety," Drake corrected. "An inconvenience for me. A death sentence for you."

He continued moving, sliding the racks this way and that, pushing through and coming closer.

"You're the first changeling Christian has created in a while," he said. "You should know that. But he didn't tell you that. Nor did he say why he created you, did he? And now he's left you here to die."

Kate closed her eyes and tried to let the tension leave her. She didn't move or breathe. She tried to make her mind a blank slate. It didn't matter. Drake kept talking and moving closer.

"He's using you."

Kate tried to keep her mind quiet, but it was no use. She thought back to her first meeting with Christian, to the moment in the swamp when he saved her, to their exchange in the freight car on the train. Even in New York when she'd attacked him, he'd never done anything to harm her.

No, she thought. *You're lying.* But even that thought betrayed her.

Drake plunged his sword through the racks, and it burst through the back of a painting and gashed her arm. Her response was instant and surprising even to her. She hit the racks in front of her with all her might, knocking them off their tracks. They collapsed fast, falling like dominoes, burying Drake and giving her the chance she needed.

She darted past him and this time ran up the stairs and onto the ground floor. Seconds later, she broke out into the evening air at the back of the museum by the loading docks.

She was instantly hit with multiple Taser weapons. Her body stiffened like a statue, and she crashed onto the cement as thousands of volts rushed through her body.

Lying there she heard a voice, "Drug her this time."

It can't be, Kate thought, as the needle punctured her arm and some kind of anesthetic began coursing through her body. *Ashley!*

The world blurred around her, but it didn't go black. She heard a van pull up, the doors slide open.

"Get her inside," Ashley shouted. "The jet is ready. We're taking her back to the States."

A hand grabbed the back of Kate's hair and lifted her head. "Nick told us about Faust. And we followed you right to him. I thought you'd be smarter than that. Turns out I was wrong."

Ashley dropped Kate's limp head, and three male agents picked her up and tossed her into the back of the van. Within seconds they were speeding off into Friday night Amsterdam traffic.

With her hands bound and her body weak, it was all Kate could do to stay awake. As the van moved along she tried to listen in but only caught fragments of conversation up front. They were speeding now, weaving through traffic beneath the orange halogen street lamps. The light came down through the windows and hit Kate's eyes in a hypnotic kaleidoscope of color.

And then, Kate sensed something approaching. *Coming on fast.*

At an intersection, the van was struck with tremendous force from the side. It rolled twice. One door flew off and side was torn open like a tin can, leaving jagged, twisted metal protruding everywhere.

When the van came to a stop the only sounds were grunts and groans from the injured agents and a strange hissing from the radiator.

Kate peered around the van, her eyes foggy, her vision unclear. Ashley lay unmoving in what was left of the passenger seat. The driver was trying to release his seat belt but was in so much pain he couldn't reach it.

Kate tried to break free of her restraints, but in her drugged state she lacked the strength. Suddenly, the back doors of the van were ripped open. A distorted image appeared: a man reaching in for her. He broke the restraints with ease and lifted Kate from the wreckage.

"Christian?" she said, as the image blurred in and out of focus.

The man carried her to another car, placed her down in the passenger seat and then got into the driver's side. As she looked over, the image cleared.

"We haven't been properly introduced," the bearded man said. "My name is Artimous."

"You work for Drake," she muttered, sensing his evil.

"I do," he said putting the car into gear. "And soon, you will too."

Chapter 28

A few blocks from the Amsterdam Central Train Station,
Christian Hannover walked through a sea of bicycles all chained up
together. He moved slowly as rain emptied from the dark clouds above.
It had been coming down for a day and a half. Pedestrians everywhere
ran for cover, ducking quickly in and out of doorways and jumping into
cabs. The city was very environmentally green with a lot of foot and
bicycle traffic, but on days like this, few were out and about and the
bike racks were packed with thousands of unused machines.

At the moment, Christian felt as forlorn as those machines. Empty
and unwanted. He'd spent the last forty-eight hours searching every
corner of the city for Kate. But she was gone. He'd told her to run.
He'd felt her fleeing, but then what?

With everything that happened, he'd hoped she would escape. But
she'd never showed at the rendezvous, and if she was still in the city,
he would have felt her. He would have been able to hone in on her.

In a rack beside the unused bikes, he saw a newspaper. Its
headline read: *American FBI Agents Critically Injured in Crash.*

He plucked the paper from the box and read all he needed to. It
wasn't Kate – it was Ashley Blackburn and her partners, operating this

time without any permission from the host country or Interpol. A big scandal was erupting, but the darker news to him was the eyewitness report of a bystander. It read that a bearded man had crashed his car into the van deliberately and had then pulled a woman from the back. A woman who matched Kate's description exactly.

There could be no doubt now, Kate was in Drake's hands. Where would he take her? There was really no way to know. Drake was incredibly wealthy, he had financial and personal resources that ran deep in both the human world and the world of the Fallen. By now she could be anywhere.

If she was still alive he would crack her mind and learn all she could about Christian. She was tough, but it wouldn't matter for long. Soon enough Drake would know what she knew. And that would endanger everything.

He glanced at his watch. It was quarter to five. Time to go.

He entered the train station to the sound of the public address system announcing in a metallic and reverberating sound that the five o'clock express train was leaving momentarily.

"We don't want to miss the train," Faust said, as Christian walked up to him.

"No," Christian said. "But I have a call to make first."

He dialed a number on his satellite phone. It was almost midnight across the pond. Ida answered on the first ring.

Her voice was warm as usual. "It's about time you called in, Sonny. You send a text that says, 'Hide in the church and don't come out,' and then you don't explain. I've been waiting on the apocalypse for two days."

"Kate's gone," Christian said explaining his text. "Until this moment I wasn't sure, but I'm certain now that Drake has her. That means he knows everything. Including where I live and who you are. He probably also knows you have the journal and that it might contain information about this Dark Star, so you stay put in that church."

"Damn," Ida said. "I'm sorry to hear that. She seemed like a decent woman."

"I doubt she's dead," he replied. "Drake's not that stupid. But she's not going to be able to hold out against him for long."

"Are you going to go after her?"

"If I had the slightest clue where he's taken her I would. But I have no idea. And I have a bad feeling she's going to become a bargaining chip sooner rather than later. So I'm going to need something to trade for her."

"I guess I'll stay put then," Ida replied sadly. "Although the preacher's going to think I'm crazy requesting sanctuary at this point."

"Maybe you should go on a vacation," he suggested. "I'm not sure the West Harlem Baptist church is going to keep you secure."

"No place safer," she insisted. "First of all, I'm never alone. And second of all, it's real easy to spot any of your sun deprived kind up here. You guys stand out like a sore thumb, if you know what I mean."

"Not all vampires are white, Ida. And none of us sparkle, no matter what you've heard."

"Black, white, red, yellow, it doesn't matter. You all have that same pasty, pale, I-need-a-mega-dose-of-vitamins look to you. Trust me."

"I'll take that as an insult," he said. "But good to know. Are you sure they're going to let you stay?"

"They think I'm crazy," she said. "But I made a donation from one of your slush funds and that seemed to smooth over the whole idea. The pastor even makes me coffee every morning."

"Glad to hear you helped yourself to one of my checkbooks," he said.

"It was the least I could do," she said. "Now what if Drake goes to your apartment? Do you want me to go back and shred everything?"

"Do you have the journal?"

"I do."

"Nothing else matters."

"Are you sure?"

"Positive," he said. "Don't, under any circumstances, go back there. I'm going to arm the system, and if Drake or his minions show up, you'll hear about it because the whole place will blow sky high."

"What do you mean, *sky high?*"

"The whole building is rigged with explosives. Don't worry, I had a demolitions expert put them in. The building will pancake on itself. Nothing but a pile of rubble."

"What about the other people who live there?" Ida asked.

"No one else lives there," he said. "I own the whole building."

"Of course you do," she said. "You might have told me the place was booby trapped. I've been poking into your stuff for days."

"Don't worry," he said. "It wasn't armed. But you might want to stop being nosy. Now, what have you got? Your text sounded a lot better than mine. Any idea where I can find this Dark Star? Or if it's even real?"

"Afraid not," she said, "But I've found something even more interesting."

Faust was standing a few feet away, nervously shifting his weight from one side to the other. The announcer was calling their train. Christian turned his attention back to the phone. "I'm not interested in story time right now, Ida."

She replied in her best school teacher tone. "Just listen for a minute, will you? Remember the inscription at the end of the journal? The one Simon wrote directly to you?"

"Of course I do." *You are not alone, my midnight son.*

"I think I know what it means," she replied. "I think his note is a reference to a Nosferatu named Jocasta of Crete. Have you ever heard of him?"

"Jocasta was a Greek trader," Christian said. "Drake turned him about fifteen hundred years ago. He was part of the early version of Drake's Brethren. At some point they had a falling out and Drake killed him. What does that have to do with me?"

According to the notes from the year 1054, Jocasta was the vampire who gave the prophecy of the angel to the church in the first place. It says, he was given the prophecy because he swore off the blood lust. A messenger was sent to him, an angel delivering to him the word of God, that he shall be released and that all who were willing to wait for it would be shown mercy and be forgiven for their sins."

"Jocasta," Christian said. "You're kidding me? I guess that explains why Drake killed him."

"Except he survived," Ida said. "At least at first. According to the journal, Jocasta survived Drake's fury and escaped, though he was badly wounded. He managed to make contact with one of the head masters of the *Ignis Purgata*—I believe you know who they are. The leader heard Jocasta's story and supposedly helped him find a place where he and others like him could go and wait for the coming of the angel. Jocasta went there and was never heard from again, not even unto this day. The church believes that Drake later found and killed him, and the idea of helping any demons find a sanctuary was labeled as heresy and the matter closed–except that the prophecy itself was left on the table."

"So if the church believes this prophecy why are they killing us?"

"They're still debating it," she said. "They seem to be mostly against it, from what I've read, but haven't strictly ruled it out yet. And here's one reason why. Over time, even after Jocasta disappeared, there are repeated instances of known vampires disappearing from the map without the hunters acting. Rumors of a gatherer, who comes and finds them. Some of the *Ignis Purgata* felt it was Jocasta continuing to act."

Christian had heard a similar tale from a dying bottom feeder who insisted he was going to be saved. It never happened. "Sounds like a Santa Claus story to me," Christian said. "Trust me, vampires go missing for many reasons."

"And yet a note from Simon, three weeks before he dies, references a dream about Jocasta the Gatherer, who leads the Fallen to the Land of Blinding Light."

"What exactly does that mean?"

"I don't know," she said, "But wherever this Land of Blinding Light is, Jocasta was tasked to gather the souls of all who would be willing to wait with him. All the souls who were cursed, but did not turn evil, did not turn to the blood lust or somehow found the strength to turn away from it. There they would pass the time and wait for the coming of the Angel of Forgiveness."

"Utopia," he muttered, "for demons. It sounds absurd."

"I think Simon was trying to tell you it exists," she said. "But he did it like this to keep the truth from Henrick, in case Henrick got the Journal instead of you. *You are not alone, my midnight son.—* Remember?"

"Then why not just tell me outright, in person?"

"At the time, you were going to face Drake in the swamps. What if you lost to Drake?"

"He would learn everything from me before he killed me," Christian said, half guessing but fairly certain. "And any who were hiding would be in danger."

"Exactly," she said. "Hence the secrecy."

Could it be? Christian wondered. "Does it say where this place is?"

"Not in anything I could find," she said. "But it seems likely that the head of the order would know about it."

For a minute Christian considered the information, but then he put it out of his mind. It was useless to him at the moment.

"If it's true," Ida said, "there might be hundreds, maybe thousands just like you out there somewhere. Lost souls waiting for deliverance. If you find them you don't have to live this nomadic life anymore."

"Good work," he said. "And thanks for telling me, but it doesn't matter at this point."

"You're wrong," she said. "It does matter. Three seconds ago you were alone in the world now you have a tribe, now you have a pathway. It gives you a point in the future to go after; it gives you meaning to a meaningless existence."

"I have meaning," he said. "The destruction of Drake is my meaning. Preventing him from finding this weapon is my purpose."

"You need more," she said. "I know you do."

Overhead, the PA system had begun to insist that the train would be leaving imminently. Christian nodded to Faust. "Stay put Ida. I have to go."

"I will," she said.

He hung up and slipped the phone in his pocket.

"Guess we won't need this," Faust said. He held the third ticket out for Christian who shook his head.

Faust ripped it in half, tossed it in the garbage, and the two of them hustled for the platform.

* * *

The Half Life

The compartment on the TGV line normally held eight passengers, but Christian had sprung for the entire cabin and he and Faust were alone as the train traced south at 175 miles per hour.

"Sure you want to go through with this?" Christian asked.

Faust cleared his throat. "You mean sneak into the Vatican on the suggestion of a demon, steal information only a few people in this world even know exists and risk being hunted down by Drake or the church for it?"

"Yeah, all that," Christian said. "You can bail at any moment."

"Really?"

"Did you think I was taking you hostage?"

"No," Faust admitted. "I thought you needed me."

"I do," Christian said. "You don't seem to be afraid."

"Not true," Faust insisted. "I'm afraid of everything. But for some reason, I feel safer with you than anywhere."

Faust pulled out a pipe and lit it.

"I didn't know you smoked?" Christian said. "How very professorish of you."

"I've just recently taken it up," Faust said. "After our first meeting."

"Can't say I blame you," Christian said, staring out the window.

It didn't take long for the heavy aroma of pipe tobacco to fill the cabin.

"What do you know about the Dark Star?" Christian asked.

"Only that it's a myth," Faust said.

"Myths all come from somewhere, Doctor. Somewhere far enough back, there is truth."

"Yes, six thousand years ago, well before your kind even existed."

"So you do know something," Christian said.

"The Dark Star is supposed to be, as legend has it, the stone that Jacob had when he wrestled with God or with the angel of God. Do you know the scripture?"

"*And Jacob was left alone*," Christian said, quoting Genesis. "*And a man wrestled with him until the break of the day. When the man saw that he couldn't prevail against Jacob, he touched Jacob's hip, and Jacob's hip was dislocated. Then the man said, 'Let me go, for the day is near'.* I have to tell you – that last verse is one I've always felt a certain understanding for."

Faust laughed. "Well, you would. Wouldn't you?"

Christian nodded and then Faust finished. "Jacob said, '*I won't release you unless you bless me. And the man said unto him, 'Your name shall no longer be called Jacob, but Israel, for you have striven with God and with men, and have prevailed.'*'"

"Yes," Christian said, "But if you notice, the verses say *a man* fought with Jacob."

"True," Faust said, waving the pipe around, "but classical interpretation is that the man was at least a messenger from God, thus an angel."

"Perhaps," Christian said. "But nowhere is there mention of a stone or rock or weapon."

"No," Faust said. "But there are fragments of papyrus in the Vatican that tell the story differently."

"So you've seen them."

"Heard of them is more accurate."

Christian was skeptical. "Even if the fragments are genuine, that doesn't mean the stone exists."

"No," Faust said. "But if it did, it supposedly disappeared soon after Jacob's death. Those who'd seen its power, hid it or destroyed it. Or so the legend says."

"Do you think the Vatican knows where it is?"

"I think," Faust began cautiously, "that no living human has thought of it in hundreds of years."

Christian wondered.

"Truthfully," Faust said, "if such a thing does exist, the world is better off not knowing where it hides."

"We don't have the luxury of hoping it stays hidden," Christian replied. "You have to find out what the archives say. And if it's real, we have to get to that stone before Drake does."

Chapter 29

Rome, Italy

The Rome Termini was bright, spacious, and modern. Its architecture was more like an airport than a train station from the old world. The straight lines, the metal and glass weaved to create beauty, it was something to behold. Shops and cafes littered the inside as passengers moved about.

Christian and Faust stepped off the train, and immediately both of them felt the tension in the air. Christian hadn't been to Rome in fifteen hundred years. Not since the power of the Church had nested in the Holy See and Vatican City. Nor was he alone. Very little vampirism, occurred in this city. There were too many churches, too many eyes, too many members of the *Ignis Purgata* about.

That Rome had once been Christian's home was part of the exile, he guessed. Ironically, it had also been Drake's ancestral home before he'd traveled with Pilate to Jerusalem. Drake wanted it back. Part of his master plan was to rule from high atop the Vatican, to return and crush his enemies like an emperor claiming his rightful kingdom. He wanted to destroy the Church, to make them pay for refusing him absolution;

after all, he was a son of Rome and they crush their enemies. They bow to no one.

As far as Christian knew, Drake had yet to cross the Rubicon as Caesar had. But if he put his hands on the weapon he sought, that day would not wait for long.

They walked through the terminal, stopping at a café. Faust had a cappuccino, which he lifted to his mouth with shaking hands.

"Something wrong Doc?"

"I'm worried. Am I making the right choice? Maybe we should tell the church about Drake. Tell them what he's after. The new head of the *Ignis Purgata* is a very zealous man. They say he's gone into strongholds of various clans and come out victorious. They say he's created new weapons. Perhaps these weapons would be useful against Drake. Perhaps they could reach this Dark Star faster and easier than we can. Maybe they already know where it is."

A smirk of disgust crossed Christian's face. "The new head of the *so called Righteous Fire* is the last person on earth you want to confide in. Trust me."

"He swears an oath," Faust replied. "When he became the leader he-"

"He only became the leader by murdering Simon Lathatch," Christian said sharply.

Faust went silent, then spoke. "A demon murdered Simon."

"That's right," Christian said, "And that demon's name was Henrick Vanderwall."

"I know that you're enemies but-"

"I could show you," Christian offered. "I could replay it from my own memory. You'll see everything."

Faust looked at his coffee. "No thanks. Not necessary."

Christian realized this new conversation had just made Faust more nervous, not less. "Maybe we should spike that coffee with a shot of whiskey."

Faust smiled. "I prefer cognac. The older the better."

"I'll see what I can do," he said. "And be careful. If they get onto you, pretend I hypnotized you. They'll believe that."

"You want me to lie in the Vatican?"

"No," Christian said. "I want you to avoid getting caught. If you have to lie, wait till they drag you out of the building."

He pulled out a map of Vatican City and pointed to an intersection. "I'll pick you up here. I don't want to get too close, so you'll have to walk a bit."

"Pick me up in what?" Faust asked. "We don't have a car."

"I'll find something to drive," he said. "Don't worry. You'll know it's me when you see it."

Faust took a sip of his cappuccino. "I'll need some time. It's not going to be a simple—how do you say it—smash-and-grab job. Just getting to the vault will take some time. To go through the vast amounts of documents and find the ones we're looking for will take hours, possibly days."

"If you're not out of there by dawn, I'll assume you're in their custody. But how long can they hold you?"

"Days. Weeks. Who knows? They call it being a guest, but you can't leave."

Christian tried to calculate their chances of success. Part of him didn't want Faust trying this. It felt like he was using the little man. Part of him wanted to cast off all allies. Certainly none of them seemed to fare well. But he had little choice at the moment.

He sat back, deciding a man with a dangerous task ahead was more likely to succeed if he had confidence. "I have faith in you Dr. Faust. And I'll be waiting with the best bottle of cognac you've ever laid eyes on."

Faust smiled, but his eyes suggested he was filled with doubt.

Chapter 30

Henrick Vanderwall moved through the Vatican, marveling at the power he felt. All the glory, splendor and beauty caught his eye. The spoils of war taken from other lands, things that told him conquest was indeed part of the Church's mission.

"Every time I enter this grand house of God I can't help but feel the authority flowing through it," he said. "And it's ours to command. That is our duty."

He and two of his lieutenants were making their way up a grand spiral staircase and into the administrative center of the Vatican where they would meet Bishop Messini and gain their just rewards. As he walked, Henrick wondered what Bishop Messini would bestow upon him when he announced the success of his new weapons and the revelation of Aldo—the oracle.

Not willing to wait, he walked past Messini's secretary and burst into the Bishop's office.

"I have glorious news, Bishop. For we have now built the army that will defeat the Fallen once and for all."

By chance Messini was on the phone, in mid-sentence. He shot Henrick a look of annoyance and then politely ended his phone call and returned the receiver to its proper resting place. At that same moment, his secretary came rushing in. She appeared visibly upset at the fact that Henrick had barged right past her.

Before she could speak, Messini raised a hand. "Not to worry, Maria. Finish up and head home. It appears I have some business with Mr. Vanderwall."

She gave Henrick a snide look, one that brought to Henrick's mind a yappy little dog upset that a bigger animal had just taken its bed. He almost laughed. *Who did she think she was?*

As she shut the door, Bishop Messini took a last look at the screen of his laptop and folded his hands. "So, Henrick, what is it that you wish to tell me?"

* * *

In a different part of the Vatican, Dr. Faust was entering through a small gate protected by minimal security. Only staff and those who had business with the Vatican could use this entrance. There was only one other person in line with him, a tall brunette in her twenties. She looked like she was the administrative type, all dressed up to the nines.

Upon entering the room his eyes darted from left to right; he was nervous and doing a poor job of not showing it. Three big security guards, a metal detector, and cameras everywhere - all these things stood in the way of accomplishing his goal. Sweat ran down his forehead as he waited for the security to clear the woman; he dabbed it away with his handkerchief.

Don't look at the cameras, he told himself, as he was doing just that.

Don't count the guards.

Don't act weird.

It was probably too late for that last part, he thought. Fortunately he was known as an eccentric. For once his reputation might help.

As he wiped the sweat from his forehead he thought to himself, *why are you getting yourself all worked up? What can they do to you, even if they catch you in here, nothing? You haven't done anything wrong yet!*

That thought made him a little calmer and once the woman had passed through, he stepped up to the security desk and handed his credentials to the guard. It seemed to take hours just to punch in Faust's clearance number.

"And what is your purpose for coming to the Vatican today, Dr. Faust?"

As Dr. Faust went to speak, he suddenly remembered that those thought to have been possessed by demons were confined in sanatoriums and banned from the Vatican even after their release. They were locked away and studied for years, like rats. Fear engulfed him, and all he could think to do was run.

"Dr. Faust?"

"Well, I'm not going to blow the place up if that's what you mean," he blurted out.

What's wrong with me?

"Excuse me?" the guard said, no doubt thinking the same thing.

"A little joke," Faust said. "I'm here for research, of course."

Faust wondered if they'd detain him. He thought they might not have to. He thought he might have a heart attack on the spot and save them the trouble.

The guard looked at the screen and then whispered something to the second guard. A snicker of laughter passed between the two.

Then the guard went back to the computer and typed a few words in rapid fashion. Dr. Faust tried to see what was on the monitor, but could only see a small section of the screen without being obvious. It read something about *contacting Bishop Messini if Dr. Faust…*

Faust looked away. This was it. He knew it. This was where these three giants in the room took him away, stashed him in some small cubbyhole and kept him there forever.

To his amazement, it didn't happen. The guard handed him back his credentials and buzzed him in. The door opened, "Please walk through the metal detector, Dr. Faust."

As Faust left the room he paused and took a deep breath. He couldn't believe it. The hard part was over, but then he overheard the security guards talking. The one that buzzed him through said something about, "*…Send Bishop Messini a message letting him know Dr. Faust is in the building. It says here the Bishop needs to speak with him.*"

Faust wasn't a fool. He knew it was just a matter of time before they came down to the vault and took him away. But he had to try, and he quickly scurried off through the great halls of the Vatican.

Chapter 31

Five stories below ground Faust sat in front of a giant panoramic window. On the other side of the window lay the vault, a vault that no human entered. This was more than a library; it was a storehouse of artifacts that told the saga of the humanity through the ages. He'd been here four times in his life on official church sanctioned business, and always it had awed him.

Putting aside the feelings of wonder, Faust got down to business and searched the computer database for anything that might lead them to the Dark Star. He scrolled through list after list of searches, entering different terms into the database, adjusting the search parameters, reviewing the results and moving on. He went as quickly as he could, taking few notes and trying to remember everything, like a concert pianist playing without sheet music.

He doubted he had much time and he knew for certain he'd never get another chance to access the vault, so he was going to take all the information he could out with him. When he began to find items relating to the stone of power, he reached into his pocket and pulled out a phone. He was surprised the guards hadn't asked for it at the security desk, then again he was one of the chief researchers of the Office of History. His clearance to this part of the building was very high. There was no cell signal but the camera worked. He began taking pictures of the computer screen, saving the data without having to read through it. The photos came out slightly distorted but readable. No printing required.

After an hour he came upon a new term, *the fallen stone.* At first he thought it referred to the Nosferatu, whom the church called the *Fallen,* but a quick study told him that was just a coincidence. The early church believed the Dark Star was not of this earth. It was a stone that had fallen from heaven, possibly during the battle between Lucifer and the other angels. That, they believed, was the reason for its power. The reason it gave Jacob the power to overcome God's messenger.

A later note indicated it had been found by a blacksmith, who'd seen it falling from heaven leaving a trail of smoke and fire against the sky. A meteorite, Faust thought. A meteorite from another realm that could upset the balance of power on Earth.

He sent a new request into the computer terminal, a short list of document and parchments appeared on the screen. He executed the command to get the first document, and beyond the giant glass window a robotic machine moved down the aisle towards the desired section and rack number. It stopped abruptly and rose upwards to a height of around ten feet. There, it extended a sterile metal claw and retrieved the Plexiglas slide in which the parchment was protected.

Glass slide in hand, the robot returned to the front of the vault and placed the document under a camera for Dr. Faust to view.

With his heart pounding, Faust glanced around. *I'd never make it as a criminal*, he thought to himself. *Too much stress.*

He looked back at the monitor, on screen was the parchment he'd wanted to see. He pulled out his phone and snapped a photo and then sent the robotic worker on another mission.

Chapter 32

Henrick Vanderwall stood boldly in Messini's office. "The end of the demon's scourge is near," he announced with great verve.

Bishop Messini looked surprised. He took off his reading glasses. "I thought you disagreed with that interpretation of the prophecy, Henrick."

"I'm not talking about the prophecy," Henrick said. "I'm talking about this office and our purpose being fulfilled."

Messini raised an eyebrow, "Go on."

Henrick had brought Doros and John Wellington with him. He waved for them to sit but he remained standing as he presented his case. "The Nova rifles worked to absolute perfection, Bishop. The new crossbows were also effective killing weapons. The armor plated suits, designed by John Wellington, held together as the demons clawed at them, and the new helmets kept the evil thoughts of their minds at bay. Even as the demons burned we were immune from the heat and flame."

He pointed to Wellington and the other lieutenant behind him. "With these suits, we were able to venture where no hunter has ever gone before, into the heart of the demon's lair. We destroyed a whole clan of extremely power Nosferatu. Something that has never before been accomplished in the history of the Order."

He placed a report on Messini's desk detailing the destruction of one of the more depraved clans in all of Europe.

"The entire clan?" Messini asked.

"More than fifty of them," Henrick said proudly. "And it was easy. Our communications were efficient, un-garbled and excellent, and the night vision enhancements evened the playing field for us. No longer do we fight bats by blindly swinging our fists in the air."

"I stand impressed," Messini said. "On the other hand, I never authorized you to go forth like this."

"It was a tactical decision," Henrick said. "Those remain in my purview."

"If the leader of my order gets killed, that is a strategic matter," Messini countered.

"I disagree," Henrick said.

"Yes," Messini replied. "I'm not surprised. I have a feeling we disagree on many things all of a sudden."

Henrick was taken aback and slightly confused.

The Bishop quickly clarified it for him, sliding a report of his own toward Henrick. It bore the imprint of the sanatorium in Interlaken. "Now tell me, what have you done with Aldo Gruvaleu?"

* * *

The Half Life

Into his second hour of research, Faust was sweating now, as much from adrenaline as anything else. He snapped more pictures, looked at more documents and tried to keep it all straight in his head.

He ran one more search, found nothing new and made a decision. *Time to go.* He put the camera away and fought to contain himself as a wave of joy, energy and exhilaration surged through his body. For a moment, he felt like James Bond. Now all he had to do was escape.

Logging out of the computer terminal, he took a deep breath and began the long march towards the outside world, five stories above. He reached the vault's anteroom, handed his credentials to the guard and waited.

"A good day for research?" the guard asked in Swiss accented English.

"Every day is a good day," Faust said.

That brought a nod, but instead of handing the identification cards back, the guard held onto them, tapping one of the computer keys repeatedly. A scowl came over his face. "I need you to stay here for a minute, Dr. Faust. We have an issue with the computer terminal. It will just take a second."

The guard disappeared into a back room and Faust felt his knees grow weak. He knew that his time was up. *He knew it.* He briefly thought of reaching around the desk for the switch that would let him through, but what was he going to do? Run? Fight?

Time to face the music, he thought. His James Bond moment was short lived. Now he felt powerless, impotent, a liability, and the only thought circling around in his mind was that he had let his new friend down.

Faust was white as any ghost by the time the security guard came out of the back room and handed his credentials back. "You're all clear, Doc. Have a great night."

"What was the problem?"

"A slight computer malfunction; it's all sorted out now. Everything checks out. Enjoy the rest of your time here in Vatican City."

Dr. Faust tipped his hat and thanked the guard but didn't hang around to chat. He got moving, astonished at the kind of luck he was having. He ran up the stairs as fast as he dared made it through one more check point and then, unbelievably, out into the night and freedom.

* * *

Henrick stared at Bishop Messini in shock. He'd thought the men at the sanatorium understood who he was and that Aldo belonged in his custody.

Messini did not wait long for an answer, nor give Henrick time to read the letter. "I ordered you to see if Aldo might be useful in finding this Angel of Forgiveness. Instead you abducted him and used him for your own purposes."

"It was necessary," Henrick said.

"Who are you to make such a judgment?"

"He was being abused," Henrick said. "Probed and drugged by quacks who know nothing of his mind or of our struggle. I would not allow a dog to be treated that way, let alone one of our bravest."

"So now you're protective of him?" Messini said. "It was not so when I sent you."

"I didn't know his condition at that time," Henrick said.

Messini narrowed his gaze as if, like a demon, he could see into Henrick's soul. "Where is Aldo now?"

"Safely in the custody of his brothers," Henrick said.

At this Messini snapped and stood up. "Aldo is not a hunter. His mind was taken by a demon. It is against the code to put him in their company! And when I ask you a question I expect a clear answer. Now tell me where he is!"

"I act on our behalf," Henrick insisted, still trying to be respectful, still trying to be reasonable with this foolish old man. "But you must understand what I see. God has seen fit to give us an oracle, created out of the fire of conflict. From the acts of evil he has given us something good. Aldo can hear these demons. His gift is true. He can find them anywhere, any one of them. Even Drakos!" Henrick's face was red by now. His fists were clenched. "None of them are safe from his sight. They have nowhere to hide. Is this not what we've been waiting for?"

The Bishop seemed stunned by the force in Henrick's voice. He wavered slightly and put a hand on the desk to steady himself. A sheen of sweat appeared on the old man's brow and a strange look in his eye. He began to speak but his voice was cowed, less strong than he had been only a moment ago. It almost seemed as if he was speaking to himself.

"I've failed you… I've failed you all… I …" He seemed to gather himself, meeting Henrick's gaze once more. "What did you have Aldo

do? What pressure did you put that poor boy under? You're reckless…
and I'm just realizing…"

As Messini continued to mutter this way, the phone began to ring,
but Messini let it be. Indeed he didn't seem to hear it.

"It was a mistake," he continued. "A mistake to promote you… I
must undo this before something else happens, something which
cannot be undone."

Messini was grasping the desk now, sweating profusely, but
through what seemed an act of shear will he managed to focus himself.
He looked squarely at Henrick once again. "There is an earnest untruth
in you," he said bitterly. "Simon warned me of this."

"This is absurd!" Henrick exploded. "I bring you news of a great
victory and you treat me with scorn. You question my methods? My
judgment? My honor? I am the one who takes the fight to the enemy.
Not you. You sit here in an office and ponder things you know little
about. Have ever you seen a demon up close? Have you ever felt the
unearthly cold of their claws around your neck? The tentacles of their
demonic minds trying to penetrate your brain with the poison of fear
and doubt?"

"It matters not," Messini croaked, his throat seemed dry from all
the yelling. "This mission is too…"

As Henrick watched, the Bishop wobbled once more. This time
his eyes squinted. He grabbed for the edge of the desk again but
missed, knocking a lamp off which smashed on the floor as he
collapsed into his chair.

Sitting, he raised a finger to point at Henrick but moved the hand to his chest instead. By now Doros and John Wellington had leapt from their chairs. They moved toward Messini with concern in their eyes.

"Bishop?" Doros asked.

Messini fell off his chair and landed on the floor, clutching at his chest.

Henrick crouched over him. Doros ran to the door shouting for help.

"You… are… removed," Messini grunted.

The words came as a raspy whisper. Only Henrick heard them. He looked into the Bishop's eyes and shook his head. "It appears, Bishop, that you're the one being removed."

John Wellington moved forward to administer CPR.

Henrick blocked him. "Let him go."

"But…"

The phone kept ringing.

"He's the leader of our order," Wellington said. "A Bishop of the Church. We have to help him."

Herrick found his mind spinning. He knew it was wrong, *but the Bishop had to die*. Otherwise his weakness would undermine the mission. And Henrick could not allow that to happen, not now, not ever.

The phone continued to ring, the Bishop began to gasp for air and the men at Henrick's side became frantic.

"Do you want him to take the suits away from us?" Henrick shouted. "Do you want him to send us into battle with nothing more than fifteenth century technology? Or disband us completely? All of you are associated with me. If I fall, you fall!"

"Are you insane?" Wellington said.

"Are you?" Henrick shot back.

The situation was getting out of hand; the phone continued to ring insistently as Henrick tried to keep the pressure up. "You must understand," he said, "...there's nothing to..." The ringing phone broke his concentration. "We are the only..." The ringing interrupted him again and Henrick stopped midsentence and turned to Doros who was just standing there. "Will you answer that goddamn phone?"

Doros did as ordered but Wellington used the moment to push past Henrick and begin CPR on Messini.

Henrick stood back. The bishop could not live, not now, not after all this. "Don't you see?" he whispered. "The Bishop was about to block us and God took him. God removed the obstacle from our path. Can't any of you see it?"

Wellington was pumping hard on the Bishop's chest, trying desperately to restart his heart. Henrick could see it was too late. He stepped back and turned to Doros. "Who was on the phone?"

"It was just security. I told them we were having an emergency."

"What did they want?" Henrick asked almost absentmindedly.

"They wanted to tell Bishop Messini that Dr. Faust was leaving the Vatican heading out to St. Peter's Square after being in the vault for the past couple of hours."

Henrick scratched his head. "Faust? Where do I know that name from?"

"He's the church caretaker from Cologne," Doros reminded him. "The one that led the demon into that vault there."

Henrick stared at Doros. "And he was here? Looking through Vatican archives? Why? For what purpose?" Henrick began to panic. Was something else going on here? Something deeper than his own war. One thought came to mind. Faust was in league with the blasphemer.

"Leave him," Henrick shouted. "He's dead. We have to find the caretaker. He'll lead us right to Christian."

Henrick grabbed Doros and the two stormed out. Wellington continued to work on Messini until the paramedics arrived a few moments later. He could see it was too late. He stood, sick to his stomach. And then he turned and ran, racing down the hall to catch up with the other warriors and the mysterious Dr. Faust.

Chapter 33

Faust stepped out into the night air, walking at a brisk pace. He could hardly believe it. This had been the most exciting few hours in his life. And he'd escaped to tell about it. Or so he thought. But as he moved through the square an alarm began to sound behind him.

He turned and looked back across the great square as a number of men came running out from one of the side entrances, moving in all directions. At almost the same moment an extra group of security guards appeared outside the front entrance to the Vatican. They moved past the empty barricades that kept people in line during the day and began to fan out.

They were obviously looking for someone. And Faust knew the truth immediately: that someone was him. He stopped looking back and tried to blend in with the people in the square.

He pulled his phone out and texted Christian.

Ready for pick up. Come fast, please!

***

Henrick ran out into St. Peter's Square and scanned the open space as quickly as possible. One of the security directors came up to him. "What's this all about?"

"We're looking for someone," Henrick replied.

"And who are you? By what authority are you sounding the alarm and giving orders?"

The double-edged sword of the Ignis Purgata, Henrick thought - so few were allowed to know of them it made things difficult at times.

"Listen to me," Henrick growled. "Bishop Messini has just died. A heart attack, possibly. But as he fell, he insisted that this Dr. Faust had given him something. Poison perhaps."

The security chief radioed his men. He'd heard the news. "Messini? That's a shame. Always a kind word from him."

"Then get off your ass and look for the man who might have killed him," Doros said. "He has to be here somewhere. He's old; he can't move that fast."

As the security director moved off to coordinate the search, Henrick gave Doros an approving nod. "That's more like it."

"In for a penny," Doros said.

Henrick was glad to hear that, but didn't respond. He was looking, looking, looking… "There!"

Most everyone else in the square was watching the commotion, but one figure was hustling towards the Via della Conciliazione, The Road of Conciliation, which led from St. Peter's Square to the Tiber River.

"That's him!"

***

Faust walked briskly across the Via Paolo, a curving road that followed the rounded boundary of St. Peter's Square. The Road of Conciliation was just up ahead. Two cars and a taxi whipped past him. A horn blared. Someone shouted a few choice words in Italian.

Faust marveled at how many languages had been used to swear at him lately. It had to be some kind of record. Safely to the other side, he risked a glance back. Two men were rushing across St. Peter's Square towards him.

This was terrible. This was a disaster. By the eye patch he recognized one of them—Henrick Vanderwall, leader of the *Ignis Purgata* and murderer of Simon Lathatch, if Christian was to be believed.

Faust stopped looking and kept moving. The same feeling he'd had when running from the female vampire weeks before came over him. Fear and panic and a sense that he could not compete.

Henrick and his friend were picking their way through the crowd. They waded into the street, boldly ordering moving vehicles to stop. Faust was struggling, lumbering along. He'd run more in the last month than in the past ten years, and he didn't like it.

He looked up ahead to the corner where Christian would meet him. But there was no car waiting, no savior, no chariot to carry him to safety. Christian was late, or not coming at all.

He turned down a side road in the vain hope that he'd somehow elude the hounds, but this was not the case. They were coming faster now, sprinting towards him.

Faust was hustling forward, looking back at his pursuers, when he ran smack into someone who grabbed him by the shoulders.

"Where do you think you're going, Dr. Faust?"

Vatican security had him. The pursuit was over. Henrick and his sidekick even slowed their pace going from a sprint to a walk.

"I was just heading for the bus stop," Faust stammered, out of breath.

"The bus stop is over there," the guard said.

Faust looked in the direction being indicated. He shrugged sheepishly. "Silly me. I get lost all the time. You wouldn't believe the trouble-"

The sound of a high-performance engine cut off his words as a red Ferrari came tearing through the traffic and screeched to a stop in front of them.

Release him!

The voice echoed in Faust's mind, but the attack was meant for the security guard. He let Faust go and stood like a statue as Faust rushed to the open door.

"No!" a voice shouted from across the street.

"Get down!" Christian yelled.

Faust ducked down as Christian pulled him into the car and stomped on the accelerator while simultaneously releasing the clutch and spinning the wheel to the right.

The engine's twelve cylinders howled and the tires spun. A cloud of blue smoke billowed into the night as Christian whipped the car around in a half-circle creating a smoke screen and then straightening the wheel.

At the same time, Henrick and his partner pulled their weapons and began firing. A half dozen bullet holes were punched in the pristine red sheet metal, but the Ferrari leapt forward with a suddenness the prancing horse on its hood would have been proud of. In seconds it had reached the nearest corner, carved a sharp turn and vanished out of sight.

Without the slightest hesitation they roared down the street and onto another boulevard. And just like that they were gone.

Faust looked back. He guessed that both he and Christian would have to deal with Henrick again someday, but for now, the nimble red car was racing into the night, picking up speed and weaving around other cars as if they were standing still.

Chapter 34

Christian got them out of Rome with surprising ease. It wasn't just the horsepower. He took an odd route that avoided most of the traffic. And when cars did get in front of him, they quickly pulled to the side and let the Ferrari pass. Even a police officer ignored them as they raced by at a hundred miles per hour.

Faust wasn't sure if the drivers gave way out of reverence for the roaring, half-million dollar champion of Italian motor vehicles or if Christian was willing the other motorists to get out of his lane. Either way it was helpful. In twenty minutes they were tearing south on Strada Statale 148, a newly reconstructed highway linking Rome to the southern part of Italy.

For his part, Christian was having flashbacks. As the concrete wound its way through the mountains, Christian remembered a march along a similar road when he was just sixteen and a new recruit for the Legions. So much had changed but the mountains were the same.

As for the road, he couldn't help but be impressed. *A perfect piece of engineering*, he thought to himself. The construction battalions of the Empire would be proud. It was also rather empty as the hour was late and most travelers took the larger A-1/E-45 superhighway.

As Christian drove, Faust spent time with his smart phone, paging through photo after photo, enlarging certain sections and then moving to the next page and back again.

"Anything?" Christian asked.

Faust ignored him and continued for almost an hour without speaking, except for the occasional grunt. All the while, Christian resisted the urge to listen to his thoughts, until finally he could wait no more.

"Doc!" he said abruptly.

Faust turned.

"Do we have anything or not?"

Faust sighed; he looked frustrated. His eyes were red from staring at the little screen. "Sorry," he said. "I get absorbed in my work. I forgot you were here."

"I'll try not to take that personally," Christian replied. "What do you have?"

"Muscat," he said.

"Muscat," Christian said. "As in the city?"

Faust nodded.

"The Dark-Star is in Muscat?" Christian asked.

"The ones who buried the Dark Star," Faust corrected. "They returned to Muscat. They call themselves the Guardians or the People of the Stone."

"I hope you got more than that, Doc."

"That's where the trail starts," he said.

"Where does it end," Christian said. "That's what matters."

"Well…"

"Do we at least have a map?"

"Sort of," Faust said, in a way that did not sound promising. He went back to the phone and pulled up another document. "This parchment is a map. It has a starting point, Muscat, but no end point. All that exists upon it are dots."

"Show me."

Faust held up the phone. He wasn't kidding, nothing but dots. Hundreds of them. "I don't suppose we could connect them and…"

"It's not a child's game," Faust said seriously.

Christian shrugged. "It was just a suggestion."

"I appreciate it, but leave this to me," Faust said. "I may not be sure what to make of it right now, but we'll get it to give up its secrets sooner or later."

"Well, that's a start," Christian said. "Good work, Agent Faust."

Faust looked over grinning.

Still driving but going the speed limit now, Christian reached into the foot well and pulled out a small wooden box. "Here," he said, handing it to Faust. "You've earned it."

Faust opened the box to discover a dust-covered bottle made of ancient, hand-blown glass. It was dark and wrapped in a handwritten label.

"You must be joking," Faust stammered.

"My kind aren't known for our sense of humor," Christian said. "This is yours. Gautier Cognac. Produced in 1840. There are less than a hundred bottles of this stuff left in the world."

"This had to cost…"

"As much as this car," Christian explained. "More, in fact, considering I borrowed the car and paid full price for the cognac."

"Borrowed it?" Faust said. "That sounds fishy to me. Won't someone be looking for it?"

"Not at all," Christian said. "The man who loaned it to me was only too happy to be rid of it for a while. He'd run out of parking spots in his villa and was taking delivery of a new Austin Martin. Once we reach Naples it will be returned with a full tank of gas, none the worse for wear."

"Except for the bullet holes," Faust said.

"Nothing a little patch job can't fix," Christian said.

"Hmm…" Faust said. He turned his attention back to the bottle, closed the box, and put the prize down by his feet.

"Aren't you even going to try it?" Christian asked.

"Heavens no," Faust said. "This is not something to be drunk. I can retire on that."

Christian shook his head. "That's it," he said. "Next time I'm getting you a *box of wine*."

Faust laughed and even Christian smiled, but the moment was short lived as the thunderous sound of a helicopter rushing over the top of the car shook them.

Christian's eyes snapped forward. The helicopter was no more than fifty feet off the deck. It passed them from behind and, once it was in front, it slewed to the side matching their speed. A powerful spotlight came on and night turned to blinding day as a stark white glare engulfed the car.

Chapter 35

Christian slammed on the brakes and the Ferrari screeched to a halt. The helicopter continued on, made a wide turn and came back towards the highway. It slowed to a hover no more than a hundred yards in front of them.

Christian stared into the floodlight, shielding his eyes with one hand, trying to see through it, but it was no use.

"Hang on," he said.

He put the Ferrari in reverse and looked over his shoulder, accelerating backwards only to see a second helicopter drop in behind them. He hit the brakes again and they stopped. They were caught, trapped between two hovering beasts, illuminated in their overlapping lights.

"Now what?" Faust asked. "Surrender?"

Christian wasn't sure. If it was the Italian Military or the Carabiniri, surrender might make sense. He could admit to kidnapping Faust and then trick the pilots into flying him away, much as Drake had done in the Gulf of Mexico. Before he could decide, a third light snapped on as bright as the other two but with a different hue, bright white, but tinted cobalt blue and purple. It came from the door of the helicopter ahead of them.

A second blue beam hit them from behind. With a flick of his hand, Christian knocked the rearview mirror from its perch. It clattered into Faust's lap.

"What's wrong?" Faust said.

"It burns."

The tint of the windows and the UV filtering effect of glass protected him from most of the pain, but not all.

"Nova rifle," Faust said.

Christian nodded. Surrender was off the table. "You might want to get out?"

Faust looked outside then back at Christian. He shook his head.

Christian revved the engine. "Last chance."

Faust clutched his phone, put his seat belt on and nodded. "Let's go!"

Christian dropped the car into first gear and stomped the gas pedal to the floor. The horsepower and torque of the Ferrari took over, the back wheels spun out and the car twisted sideways until the rubber gripped the road. From there the Ferrari shot forward as Christian straightened the red bullet out, roaring toward the helicopter ahead of them.

Inside the helicopter, Henrick shouted to the pilot. "Move, move, move!"

The pilot pulled back on the stick but the copter had moved only inches when the Ferrari shot beneath it and roared off down the road.

"Follow him!"

Within ten seconds Christian and Faust were moving at a hundred and twenty miles an hour. They caught up to and blew by the few other cars and drivers as if they were standing still.

The helicopters were in full pursuit now, one on their right, and one on their left. The colored beams of light came on once more, sweeping over the car time and again, sending shivers of pain through Christian each time they found the mark. He swerved like a mad man, tapped the brakes and slammed the throttle home to keep out of the swath of pain. As a result, the Nova rifles never held their target for more than a second or two.

"Those are the new weapons I was telling you about," Faust said. "UV rays. A million candle power."

"Thanks for the update," Christian said. "Remind me to pick up some sunblock when we stop for gas."

As he spoke, Christian whipped the car around a slower vehicle and ducked in beside a long haul truck. The big rig blocked the false sun from one side like a shade, but as the helicopters closed in, the trucker hit his brakes hard and Christian had no choice but to gun the engine again.

Around a sweeping right hand turn the Ferrari continued to pick up speed. And as the turn ran, the hills and trees on the right forced the helicopters to form up on the left side.

After one more pass with the Nova rifles, the strange beams of light went out.

"Now what?" Christian asked.

The answer came instantly as marksmen on the skids of the two helicopters opened fire with assault rifles. Flames from the barrels and tracers lit up the night, and Christian slammed on the brakes once again. He downshifted, slowing the car rapidly, switching lanes, and then flooring it again, getting back up to speed. The bullets missed, but their impact could be seen on the concrete barrier that divided the highway.

"That was close," Faust said. "How do we get out of this?"

"I don't know yet, but I'm working on it." Christian slammed his foot on the brakes again as another burst of gunfire came at them.

"We've got to get off the highway! We've got to hide!" Faust yelled.

That was true. But they needed an exit. For a second Christian wished he'd stolen a Humvee; that way he could have made his own exit.

The curve of the highway became a straightaway and Christian gunned it, hoping to put the helicopters behind him. Faust closed his eyes as the speedometer hit one hundred and sixty miles an hour.

The helicopters followed, slowly closing in. The gunfire erupted again, tracking him and trying to lead him. One of the shooters led them by too much and the armor piercing bullets hit a tanker carrying propane. A massive fireball rose up, engulfing the entire highway, the Ferrari and the helicopter itself.

The brunt of the explosion was channeled upward, back in the direction of the shells that had pierced the tanker. The Ferrari raced beneath the fire cloud and shot out the other side, singed and toasted but in one piece. The helicopter was a different story. Covered in burning fuel, it became a fireball of its own, careening forward and dropping until it hit the road and blew apart.

"My God," Faust whispered.

Up ahead Christian spotted their salvation, a long tunnel cut into a mountainside. They could get inside and commandeer another vehicle in the tunnel, escaping unnoticed, like a magic trick. Christian dropped the hammer on the Ferrari, flooring it in an effort to make the safety of the tunnel faster, leaving the destruction of the tanker and all its flames far behind.

The second helicopter was still chasing them. Flying at top speed only feet off the deck. Christian realized the pilot might not be aware of the landscape. He might not realize a tunnel was coming up and, if Christian could bait them a little bit, he might get them to crash into the mountainside.

He slowed for a second and then accelerated again.

The helicopter got close, drifted back and closed the gap again. *Just a few more seconds.*

The gunner on the skid opened fire again. This time he hit the mark and the armor piercing shells pounded the front wheel, driver's side door and the roof. Glass and metal fragments went flying everywhere. Flames shot from the engine and the Ferrari went sliding like an Indy Car with the tires blown out. It hit the middle of the concrete divider and then slid on into the tunnel. As the crippled machine dragged along the cement wall, its rims grinded into the highway, sparks flying in every direction until the car finally came to a stop.

When the violent ride ended, Christian turned back. There was no explosion at the entrance to the tunnel. The helicopter had pulled out.

He turned his eyes from the tunnel entrance to Faust. "Come on, Doc. We have to move."

Faust looked over at him, his hands were covered in blood. His white shirt was stained crimson red. Christian reached for him trying to stop the bleeding, but it was no use. Faust's life was pouring out of him by the liter.

"The bullets..." Faust said, "...they came through you."

Christian knew that. It only made it worse. Blood was everywhere. Christian's hands pressed hard on Faust's chest trying to stop the bleeding, but it was pointless.

"This can't be happening," Christian said. "Stay with me Doc." No response. "Doc, can you hear me? Faust?"

A whisper came forth, a whisper from a dying man. "Take... my... phone... the answer... is in there..."

Faust leaned back on the seat and spoke no more, and Christian's mind snapped. He turned from Faust's bullet riddled body to the tunnel entrance far behind. He could hear the helicopter hovering. The hunters were waiting.

He grabbed the blood soaked phone, put it in his pocket and then turned and kicked the door off the hinges.

He stepped out, grabbed a shaft of metal from the wreckage and marched toward the entrance to the tunnel. He walked in a blind rage, intending to find Henrick and beat him to death with the shaft, to break every bone in Henrick's damned body before plunging the shaft into his enemy's heart. Twice Henrick had stolen the life of a friend of his, and enough was enough.

Priests, angels and demons.

The thought came unasked for and unwanted.

At each turn he became more lost. Elsa was trying to show him the path, but it was not a path of revenge.

Every fiber in his body told him to go forward and punish Henrick for all he'd done. But somehow, he listened to the thought. Filled with hatred but unwilling to give all hope away, he stopped in his tracks, turned back the other way and ran off into the dark.

Chapter 36

Paris, France

Do you hear me Kate? Are you listening? I need you to remember.

Drake was in the depths of the Paris catacombs, images were streaming from Kate's mind to his. Childhood memories, her mother and father, her first boyfriend, then college, the academy, her wedding, the murder of her husband, finding him dead on the kitchen floor, case after worthless case, file names and numbers and images of the suspects.

Christian. I want you to think of Christian.

A trickle of images arrived. The bayou, Billy Ray, even Vivian Dasher, and finally her son. And then it was her son, her son, her son, until Drake was sick of it. "Focus! Or I will bring you pain like you've never imagined."

The connection broke and Kate fell to her knees, held up only by two of Drake's soldiers. He waved his hand. They let go of her and she hit the cold stone floor of the catacombs.

Drake looked at her. She was beaten. Physically, mentally, emotionally. He'd tortured her for the past three days in every way he could think of, and yet somehow, she'd held on. Something was giving her power, something was combating the onslaught and he was becoming increasingly frustrated.

Only one other ever gave him this much trouble and that was Anya.

"Maybe you should just kill her," Artimous said.

Drake turned. "You really don't see very far do you, Artimous?"

"This is dangerous," the bearded vampire replied. "She's not conforming. Perhaps she has special training from her days in the FBI. Perhaps she *can't* be made to be one of us. Meanwhile we're wasting time, while Christian escapes with Faust."

"Christian could go only one place with Faust: the Holy See. Do you want to go there?"

Artimous said nothing. *Of course he didn't.*

"If the Church knows of it, Christian will discover the location of the Dark Star," Drake continued. "But we'll have Kate to deceive him. And she will tell us. Mark my words: once I turn her, she'll become the key to defeating Christian."

"And if the church doesn't know?"

"Then Christian is wasting his time or getting himself killed by *Ignis Purgata*. And we will still have Tereza's path to follow."

Drake looked down at Kate. She was a shadow of herself now.

"She's falling into the abyss," Artimous said. "She wants to die. Without Christian here, she's given up hope."

Drake ignored him. He knelt down and whispered in Kate's ear. "You will help me; it's just a matter of time. Sooner or later, I'll find the key, and then you'll do my bidding…forever."

At that moment a door opened and one of the servants came in. "Tereza has arrived, as you requested."

Drake left Kate and returned to his throne as Tereza was shown in.

"Tell me good news," he demanded.

"We've found the location of the Dark Star," she said. "It lies in the Empty Quarter, hidden there by an order who still protect it. There's a single oasis from which can take our heading. From there it's no more than a day's journey, if we have the right vehicles."

Drake grinned. "You've done well, my princess, but what troubles you?"

"As I feared, Akash was pulled by the desire for the power."

"What do you mean?"

"He tried to kill Zwana and me. He's going for the Dark Star on his own."

"You fools!" Drake boomed.

"It's not our fault. He's broken. Beyond reason."

"How far behind are we?" Drake asked.

"Several days," she said. "But disfigured and must conceal himself. He no longer has a face. I tried to kill him, but he escaped. And he doesn't know the final heading. Whereas I do."

"Then how does he expect to find the prize?"

"There's little thinking in him," she said. "He's like an animal, but a cunning one. He'll try to find one of these guardians. In their foolish attempt to protect the stone, they might attack him, and you and I know what he'll do to them. They'll fail and he'll end up gaining the secret from them."

Drake turned, deep in thought; not only did he have Christian to deal with, but his own disciple. Drake searched the Court, looking over his army and his wealth, and all he had. Although he was the king, he was king alone. He couldn't really trust anyone. It was only fear that kept some sense of a semblance of order. The truth was that vultures and thieves stood all around. He had built an army of those that would usurp him if the chance presented itself. The worst type of minds inhabited his world. He could trust no one.

His mind drifted to a time he hadn't thought about in almost two thousand years: when he was a soldier of Rome there was honor, a code, duty. In this new empire there was none of that. It was survival. Every man for himself. Drake's mind flashed to Akash. He would make an example of this one, or someone. Order must be restored.

"We depart at once," he said to Artimous. "Bring thirty and leave the rest."

Tereza looked over at Kate. "And who is this mess on the floor? A new recruit?"

Drake looked at Tereza. "She could be, but I can't break her. She seems to be holding on to something that gives her great strength. I'll probably have to destroy her."

Tereza bent down. "She's pretty. Don't kill her yet. Let me take a run at her."

"You think you can do better than me?"

"I think you're not asking the right questions."

"What do you mean by that?"

"You're too much like all men, Drake," Tereza said. "You keep asking and demanding and you do everything but listen. But I can hear it already. She has questions of her own." Tereza looked down at Kate. "Don't you pretty one?"

Kate was too beaten to respond, but Drake sensed immediately what Tereza was suggesting.

"More than anything she wants to know who killed her husband," Tereza added. "Since we know, I believe we should tell her."

Chapter 37

Port of Qaboos, Muscat, Oman

Half an hour after sunset, the cargo ship *Fortune Hunter* bumped against the dock at Qaboos, the largest port in Oman. Christian stood on the deck as the lines were secured and the rusting old hulk was lashed to the concrete pier.

As he waited for the gangplank to be lowered, Christian stared at the phone Faust had given him and the strange document with the dots. The starting point was the city of Muscat, but the dots were still a mystery. They didn't line up with established settlements. A fact that didn't surprise him since the parchment was several thousand years old. But what could they be? Coordinates of some oasis? Resting places? Or some other creation of ancient men?

The ship's horn sounded letting all in port know they were docking. Christian shut off the phone and looked up into the sky. In the late twilight, the stars were beginning their magic act, appearing out of the darkness. Little dots all over the night's sky.

It couldn't be that simple.

But it was. As he stared, the map's meaning suddenly became clear. The map's directions had been charted in the sky like the navigators of the ancient world. He'd spent three days inside his cabin, looking down at the image, when he should have been looking up.

Of course, he thought. There were only two ways to navigate across the sea in the ancient times, by the sun and moon, or by the stars. And the desert was basically a sea made of sand. Follow the star pattern and one would find the stone that came to Earth from the heavens.

Christian knew the race was on, but he guessed that finally he'd put Drake behind him. Kate didn't know about the map and that meant she couldn't tell Drake about it, even if he broke her spirit. For once he was ahead of the game.

He stepped onto the dock alone, as it should have been from the start. Kate and Faust, Simon and Elsa, he was tired of seeing others suffer because of who and what he was. The only way to make their sacrifices worth anything was to find this weapon of the heavens before Drake did; otherwise, all of their deaths, all their agony, would be in vain.

He made his way from the docks to the streets of Muscat. As he walked, Christian noticed the pain in his arms and legs. His body had taken a pounding over the last few months. He was weaker than he could ever remember. Ever since Boston he'd been in one kind of confrontation or another. Burned, shot, stabbed, irradiated; even for a member of the Fallen, that took its toll. Maybe when it was all over he would rest. Maybe for eternity, the idea didn't sound too bad at all.

He entered the market looking for a rental shop that one of the sailors had referred him to. The owner apparently took many travelers into the Empty Quarter on expeditions.

He walked up to the shop, eyeing the Jeeps, Land Rovers, and a trio of squared off Mercedes Benz SUVs that sat in the yard beside it. They looked like they had a million miles on them but they also appeared to be formidable, with big knobby tires, extra fuel cans and shovels on the side, as well as battering rams, light bars and winches on the front. Exactly what he needed.

He stepped inside the shop, which was nothing more than a garage. In the far corner an old man sat staring into space, while a young boy was sweeping the floor. A clerk, whose age suggested he was one man's grandson and the other man's father, turned out to be the owner.

He looked over Christian with uncertainty. Christian didn't even have to read his mind: he knew he didn't fit in. He was an outlander, a foreigner here, an American traveler in a country that was not all that friendly to Westerners.

"I was referred to you by a sailor on the *Fortune Hunter*," Christian said. "A sailor named Aziz."

The clerk's face softened a bit. "Aziz, is a friend, yes."

"He told me you would rent me a Land Rover outfitted for the desert."

The clerk just shook his head. "No rent," he said. "Charter. A driver goes with you."

Christian leaned forward. *Not in this case.* He spread a large wad of cash on the desk. Enough to buy the Land Rover. After what happened to the Ferrari, he figured it was only fair.

The shopkeeper stared at the cash.

It will be okay.

The clerk took the cash, scribbled up some paperwork and then handed it over to Christian along with a set of keys. As he signed, Christian caught a sense of fear in the man's mind. It seemed Christian wasn't the first stranger to come here tonight. Another man had come in and forced them to give him a vehicle.

Christian saw the picture of the man. *A man without a face, wearing white gauze over everything but his eyes.* Christian released the shopkeeper. The man wobbled a bit. He was dizzy, light headed. He looked confused and sat down.

"When did this man leave?" Christian asked.

"An hour ago. He's heading for Ibis. Nothing but shifting sands and blistering heat after that, there is no gasoline or supplies. Ibis it the last stop before hell."

Christen had seen a glimpse or two of hell, and this desert was nothing like it. He took the keys and left. He'd landed in Oman thinking he was ahead. But as usual, he was one step behind.

Chapter 38

For years, Henrick Vanderwall had imagined the moment that was now upon him: validation, coronation, a moment of victory. In his vision of it, he wore the dress uniform of the *Ignis Purgata*; looking like a knight of the Crusades, he would be standing in front of the Quorum of Five—the group of bishops who'd foresworn any right to ascend to the Papacy in exchange for entry into the Righteous Fire.

As he imagined it, the moment came with long speeches in which they praised him and lauded his accomplishments, anointing him as their champion. There would be blessings and prayers and Holy Communion. At the conclusion of the ceremony, they would place in his hand the weapon he coveted above all else, the weapon he'd kept from the claws of the demon he now hunted – The Sword of God, made from the nails that pierced the hands and feet of Christ, two thousand years before.

But the moment came to him differently, he and the greatest of his hunters were in the noisy confines of a chartered cargo plane, descending towards the blazing sands of the Arabian Peninsula. Instead of dressing like a knight, Henrick wore tawny camouflage like a military man. Around him were armored Jeeps, stacks of supplies and the weapons of his trade. The honor itself was bestowed via the scratchy, intermittent signal relayed to them from the cockpit on a black, plastic phone.

"… the Quorum has met," a Bishop named Hershel told him.

"And?"

"Your request has been granted, Henrick. All of us realize this is a moment of danger. A moment to act."

Henrick allowed a slight sense of joy to course through his body; though in truth, he'd reached the point where approval mattered little, even the approval of the Quorum.

"Please understand," Bishop Hershel added, "this was not an easy decision. But these are desperate times. Simon's death, followed so closely by Messini's, has put us in a quandary. We are all but leaderless, and for that reason *and that reason only*, we're trusting in you. It could have gone otherwise; the incident on the highway has been difficult to accept."

Henrick thought the Bishop was overstating it a little. The incident along the SS 148 had been swept under the rug quite easily. All it took was a simple agreement between the Vatican and the Italian authorities. As the saying went, money changes everything and the Vatican was not short on cash while Italy was almost broke. The final report would read as nothing more than a tragic accident between a helicopter and fuel tanker, end of story.

Henrick chose not to point this out in his moment of victory. "I understand Bishop. I won't let you down. I firmly believe that Faust had something to do with Messini's death. And that he acted under the power of the demon who calls himself Christian. As you know, this was the same one who killed Simon. You, or whomever of the five assumes Messini's position, would do well to be cautious. You may all be targets of this demon. For reasons known only to him, he seems bent on destroying our leaders."

"Yes… well…no decision has been made yet. For now, the council will meet and allow you to lead as you will."

Henrick smiled. They were afraid. Old men who'd lived life behind the lines suddenly felt the battle coming to their doorstep. If he was right they would never appoint another, at least not until Henrick had rid the world of this vampire scourge. Then they'd need someone to take the credit.

"And the sword?" Henrick asked. "Will it be in Oman when I arrive?"

Henrick had asked for the sword, even as they spoke of dismissing him. It was a bold demand, but the revelation of what Faust was looking for in the archives combined with the thought of a demon wielding a thing such as the Dark Star—if it existed—had swung the vote opposite.

Henrick had them in a corner. In a moment of crisis he'd seized the reins. It was simple really. The men were already in disarray. The demons seemed to be on a rampage. There was no time to find another leader. And that leader needed a weapon like no other if he was to inspire them to victory.

"A Vatican aircraft left here an hour ago," Hershel said. "Bishop Milago is accompanying it. He should arrive in Oman a few hours after you. Be careful Henrick. You're entering a land we have little sway over."

"I'll be cautious."

John Wellington came up to him. "We touch down in thirty minutes."

Henrick covered the phone. "We'll have to divide up. The sword won't be arriving for several hours."

"I'm not sure we should delay," Wellington said. "If the demons find this Dark Star…"

Henrick nodded. "Take a scout team ahead," he said, then changed his mind. "Actually, take the main group. If you encounter them, you'll need numbers. I'll remain here with Doros and three others until the sword is delivered."

Wellington nodded and Henrick returned to the call. "I must go Bishop. I'll wait for the sword and then I'll find these demons before they discover the Dark Star."

"We can only hope," the Bishop said. "God be with you."

Chapter 39

The Empty Quarter, near the border with Saudi Arabia

The yellow, oxidized headlights on the fifteen-year-old Land Rover barely lit up the desert floor as Christian rumbled across it. The interior of the cabin was faded, the windshield cracked, even the seat was held together with duct tape, but the engine sounded like it was in good shape, well maintained as the clerk promised, and Christian was making good time.

The night's sky had given up its secrets hours earlier and Christian had found the stars he needed and plotted his course. Now all that mattered was catching up to Akash.

Christian had looked for him in the town of Ibis, but Akash had been there and gone and the town itself was in disarray after four bodies had been found. Akash had been busy, searching the town for anyone who knew of the legend. Christian guessed he'd found what he was looking for because the fourth murder was particularly brutal. Obviously the man had information he wouldn't part with, so Akash took it.

Christian guessed Akash was no more than an hour or two in front of him. By morning he'd be in sight, and Christian had the advantage; Akash didn't know he was coming.

The Land Rover climbed another huge dune, the big tires dug in and pushed it over the top. The next dune was smaller, and before long the sands began to flatten until Christian was driving across a dry lakebed. He stepped on the gas and picked up speed. It was like the Salt Flats in Utah. He couldn't see the other side, but based on the satellite view it was at least sixty, maybe seventy miles across.

After an hour on the flats he could see the beginning of a set of foothills worn down to the nub by time and wind. He slowed the vehicle and turned his attention back to the stars until he'd gotten his bearings, but when he pressed the pedal down again, the engine began to sputter.

Christian checked the instrument panel. He saw no problems, no warning lights.

After sputtering for a moment, the engine quit completely.

"You've got to be kidding me."

He cranked the ignition and the Land Rover started, but it stalled again seconds later. This time it would not refire.

He stepped out, popped the hood and looked over the engine. As far as he could see nothing was wrong with the vehicle.

He looked up. Dawn was not far off. With the morning sun coming, he was short on options. He turned and looked around the desert. It was salt flats as far as the eye could see, except for the small rocky outcroppings he'd been headed to. They looked like the best place to hide from the sun. He set out for them, thinking he'd find a cave and rest there and then head for the ruins the next night. His only hope was that Akash didn't know the correct bearing.

Grabbing what he needed from the back of the SUV, he hiked off towards the foothills and the shade they could offer. An hour into his hike, the sky began to lighten and the morning sun warned of its coming appearance.

The light refracting off the sky slowed him a bit, but he had bigger problem: the foothills were actually much further away than he thought. And they weren't foothills, they were mountains.

He quickly realized he should have stayed with the Land Rover, but now he was stuck in no man's land. Which way to turn? Which way to run?

He turned back and began to run, jogging at first and then sprinting, but the sun rose quickly near the equator and like an arc of fire, it crossed the horizon line before he was within a mile of the Land Rover.

It hit him as if it had him in its crosshairs. Christian pulled his long coat up over his head to hide from the light, but his pace slowed. He kept on, burning and feeling as if he was aging with every step.

The desert grew hot around him and he began to labor, pulling the coat down to check his progress. The light hitting his eyes was excruciating and the Rover was still a half mile away. He tried to run but his legs were losing coordination. This was unlike Boston where the waters had shielded him or the oil platform, where he hid in the shadows waiting for Drake. The power of the Sun was beating directly down on him and it was draining him.

He trudged along, fighting a great desire to lay down. He knew better. He knew that meant the end. A day of total pain where he would be charred to death in the blazing light.

He kept going, his exposed hands burning. He couldn't give up. He had to get to the Land Rover and shelter.

He fell to one knee, forced himself back up and pushed on. He wobbled like an old man. Five hundred yards to go but all he could think about was resting. He stumbled along towards salvation, fell again and found his legs would not answer the call to get back up.

He crawled for a few minutes before collapsing in the sand. It was hopeless. With all the energy he had left, he covered his face and arms with his long coat and burrowed his hands and feet into the sand, trying to force his way beneath it.

As the hours passed he became delirious and feverish, thinking he heard sounds in the distance. Before long he began to wonder. He heard the sound of an engine, and not just one, but many. And they were coming his way.

A small convoy pulled to a stop only a stone's throw from him. He could hear men milling around. He wanted to yell, but he couldn't talk, his throat was constricted.

"He's over there."

A minute later a boot was rolling him over. By some miracle, the man above him stood blocking the sunlight, his shadow protecting Christian. As the man's face came into focus, Christian saw who it was. "You?" he whispered, recognizing the shopkeeper.

"Yes, my friend, it is I."

"But how?"

The shopkeeper now looked like a Bedouin, a facial scarf unfurled and dangling down one side. "We were able to find you because the Rover had a tracking device in it. We knew to look for you, because we sabotaged it before you left."

"But why," Christian asked. "Who are you?"

"My name is Fahad," the man said. "But the real question is: who you are, Christian Hannover, and who is your friend?"

"My friend?" Christian was confused. "I have no friends with me."

"The man with no face," Fahad replied. "We found him out here, just like you, dying in the Ocean of Fire. We should let you both die and be absorbed by the sand, but we need something from you first."

"What could you possibly need from me?" Christian asked.

"Answers," Fahad said. "Answers to many questions."

Chapter 40

Christian was thrown into a cage that was secured in the bed of a pickup truck. A tarp was pulled over it covering it completely, perhaps to keep him from knowing where they were going. It also kept him alive. They began driving, but even when the tarp fluttered in the wind and he could see through it to the desert beyond, everything was blurred with the heat of the day.

Whatever their course, with every mile driven, he was getting further off track. The only comfort was that Akash was with them, but what of Drake? Akash belonged to him. Was he an advance scout of some kind? Was he alone?

Christian kicked himself for not taking the time to look deeper into Fahad's mind in the shop, but there was no reason to suspect anything. Fahad was just a clerk who rented vehicles.

The convoy pulled into a camp of some kind and stopped. As the tarp was pulled back, Christian could see a number of tents. Fahad's men got out and began to unload supplies. Five men walked over and dragged Akash's cage off the back of the truck. Akash was in the fetal position and crammed into the corner in a desperate attempt to hide from the light. He wore the mask of gauze Christian had seen in Fahad's thoughts.

Someone had taken a swipe at his head and just barely missed. But who?

Christian looked away from Akash and toward the main tent. Fahad and his men were sitting and talking, drinking water or maybe tea. He couldn't hear what they were saying. He tried to read their minds to no effect. He tried to read their lips, but they spoke a language he didn't know.

He guessed the topic of conversation was the people Akash had killed in Ibis, and how Christian knew him, and so on. It was clear they knew the half-faced man was a killer, but little did they know what really hid behind that mask.

He hoped they would come for him soon. If they brought him into the darkness of the main tent, a good portion of his strength would return, enough that he could regain control of the situation. Even beneath the tarp he felt better than he had in the desert.

In the tent, Fahad's men finished their tea and began to get ready. Electric cattle prods, knives and some type of plank with a chain wrapped around it were arranged. This was not going to be pleasant.

Fahad walked out of the tent, looked skyward and held up his palms as if he was saying a prayer. He then walked up to Christian's cage.

Good, Christian thought. *Take me first, so I can explain what's happening here.*

Fahad stood a few feet from the cage looking Christian over. He threw a bottle of water into Christian's cage. "Drink. Or you'll die out here."

"You're going to kill me anyway, aren't you?"

"That is yet to be decided," Fahad said. "First, your friend will pay for his crimes. We know he's the one who murdered our brothers in the town of Ibis. He's also responsible for several deaths in Muscat as well. There is no doubt about that. Since you just arrived, we can conclude that it happened before you got there. But if you're an accomplice, well then, you shall pay also."

Christian drank some of the water. "He's not my friend. He's my enemy. Kill him if you want. In fact, I suggest you do it right now. But do it out here. Out in the open. Out under the sun."

"I suppose you'd like us to kill him before he speaks, wouldn't you?"

"Listen to me," Christian begged. "He is a murderer, but others like him are almost certainly coming, others who are worse than him, far more dangerous."

"Coming here? To this desert?" Fahad spoke with disbelief in his voice.

"Yes. To this desert."

Fahad shook his head. "Listen to me friend, there is no hope of rescue. We've guarded this secret for thousands of years and never have two come at the same time, let alone others as you say. Intruders into our world are rare. We've had the occasional treasure hunter, sometimes an oil man, but they would always use us as guides and, of course, we never found anything."

"You don't understand what you're dealing with," Christian said. "We're not treasure hunters. We're not like anything you've ever known. Please, take me inside, get me out of the sun, I'll explain everything to you."

"Of course, of course. We would talk over tea, like civilized men, I suppose." He tapped on the cage. "Don't worry, my friend, we shall talk soon enough. And yes, *you will* tell me what you wanted with the Sphere of Power."

"I don't want the power, Fahad. I want to destroy it."

Fahad walked away, shaking his head at Christian's statement. He looked back as he spoke. "If it could be destroyed, we'd have done that four thousand years ago. The sphere is impervious. It is indestructible. It is not of this world."

Neither are we, Christian thought.

Fahad motioned to Akash. "Take him inside and chain him to the stone."

"No, Fahad!" Christian said, stumbling forward, falling into the sunny portion of his cage and crashing into the bars. "Don't take him out of the sunlight, you don't understand. Don't put him in the darkness."

Fahad ignored the warning, walking towards the tent even as Akash was being dragged from the cage.

"Listen to me Fahad!" Christian shouted with all the strength he had left. "Chain him outside. Keep him in the --.'

Christian's warning was cut short as one of Fahad's men jabbed him with a cattle prod. The electricity sent Christian flying back. He banged against the far side of the cage and crumbled to the floor.

He could barely move as he watched Fahad's men lead Akash into the tent by the chains around his neck. There Akash was shackled to a great block of stone. They bound his hands and feet and ripped the gauze from his hideously scarred face.

"Don't," Christian pleaded uselessly.

It was too late. Fahad entered the tent and closed the flap, cutting off the sunlight, and from that point on it was only a matter of time.

Christian fell back demoralized. He lay there, huddled in the only part of the cage that was out of the direct sunlight, listening to the interrogation.

Fahad's men were shouting at Akash, demanding answers. The sound of the cattle prods snapping came next and the stench of singed skin. He could hear them beating on him, pounding their fists and clubs on his dead body. They didn't know. They didn't understand. He felt none of it.

As Christian listened, he also counted the minutes that Akash had been in the darkness of the tent. It wouldn't be long now.

He looked around for a weapon, but there was nothing to be found. This situation was grave and getting worse by the second. And then suddenly, Christian heard the sound he'd been waiting for, the snapping of the chains followed by the shouts of the men. Shouts turned to screams and then to gunfire as chaos erupted in the darkness of the tent. Bullets ripped through the canvas walls, tearing the same useless holes they would punch in Akash's hide.

The screams continued and Fahad was thrown, bloody and beaten, through the tent flap. He crashed to the sand, half wrapped in the canvas. He tried to get up and then fell back to the ground.

Inside the tent, Akash was taking apart the last of Fahad's men. He ripped arms out of their sockets, broke necks and impaled one man on a cattle prod that had been used against him. The men outside rushed into the battle, but they were killed as easily as the first group.

When he'd choked the life out of the last one, Akash turned his attention to Christian, grabbed a weapon and took a step towards him. In his rage, Akash had forgotten the sun, he roared like a lion when the light hit him and was forced back into the tent.

A standoff ensued. Christian huddled in the corner of his cage, weak and defenseless, Akash inside the tent, pacing back and forth like a caged animal, never once losing eye contact with Christian.

Christian could see the future. Hours would pass, the sun would fall and Akash would burst from the tent, far stronger than Christian. He sat down in the only corner of shade and tried to rest and conserve all his energy. He could only hope it would be enough to defend against the onslaught that Akash would bring.

Chapter 41

The wind blew hot and dry as the sun made its long slow descent into the west. Aside from re-bandaging his face, Akash hadn't stopped moving the entire day. Back and forth, testing the shade, testing the sun.

Down range the blazing disk was being swallowed by the mountains.

"Night will be here soon," Akash growled.

"I can see that," Christian replied. "Looking forward to it, in fact." As he finished the statement of bravado, Christian began to cough. He coughed so furiously he was spitting by the end. It was a ruse. And Akash bought it fully.

"Are you sure of that," he mocked. "You sound like you might not make it to dusk."

"Maybe you should come for me now, before my strength is reborn in the dark," Christian warned. "You can't possibly hope to defeat me once the sun is gone."

Akash laughed. "I see you out there, hiding in the shade. You won't be ready for me. Don't worry, I'll finish you quick."

"Like you finished off whoever took half your face?"

At this Akash raged. "When I have the Dark Star, I will find her and torture her for all eternity. Drake too."

Drake too? This surprised Christian. He remembered Akash as a loyal zealot in Drake's hierarchy. But much had happened since the bayou. Anya's strange actions. Drake's incapacitation. Perhaps Drake's grip on these lost souls was failing. Even if that was the case, Christian wasn't sure it made things better. Instead of one enemy, he might face a hundred.

As he considered this, the first fingers of shade began to creep across the sand. Unfortunately they would envelop the tent, Christian's cage and the land in between almost simultaneously.

"So who was it?" Christian asked. "Anya? Teodora? Certainly not Lucinious of Albania? I mean come on Akash, she's a weakling."

"It was Tereza," Akash said.

"Ah," Christian replied. "Well, I must admit, I've had my own problems with her."

Akash stared at Christian.

"I'm just saying, at least we have that in common."

"Shut up. I won't let you trick me."

"Just trying to make conversation," Christian replied.

"I said shut up!" With that Akash launched one of the empty rifles at Christian, a lethal missile like projectile. It hit the bars of the cage and clanged off it. Christian fell back as if in shock and acted as if he could barely get up.

"You don't have to…" he said, as if short of breath. "…you don't have to kill me."

"True," Akash said. "But I want to."

Akash was crouching down now, watching the shade crawl across the sand towards him. When it stretched across the entire gap between him and Christian, Akash stood and walked calmly out of the tent with a spear of sorts in his hand.

Christian didn't make a move. He just stared like a cornered animal.

Akash reached the cage and lunged forward, extending the spear like a pike man of Sparta. Christian dodged it like a matador might dodge a bull's horns and waited for the next thrust. Akash pulled back and thrust the spear forward again. It nicked Christian's side leaving a diagonal slash from which Christian's rust colored blood oozed.

Christian had no time to contemplate the damage as Akash was trying to run him through yet again. He dropped to the bottom of the cage, ducking under the latest stab, rolling to the corner and springing up again.

"I will pin you like an insect," Akash raged.

Christian didn't reply. He was getting stronger. His time in the shade and the gathering dusk were regenerating his power.

He stood and wobbled against the back of the cage, trying to bait Akash into one more careless thrust. Seeing Christian vulnerable, Akash did just that. He jabbed forward recklessly. Christian dodged the spike yet again, and this time he grabbed onto the spear and yanked hard. Akash was pulled face first into the cage and Christian's free hand went to his enemy's neck.

Akashi released the spear and tried to pry Christian's hand from his throat. Christian grabbed him with both hands, trying to crush his enemy's windpipe.

The ruse had been played, but Christian was still caged.

Unable to break Christian's grasp, Akash punched at him furiously through the bars. His fists hit like steel hammers. Still Christian held. Next Akash pulled back with all his might and the cage tipped over hitting the ground.

Christian's grip was broken. He grabbed for the spear. Seeing this, Akash heaved the entire cage off of him with Christian inside. It landed twenty feet away and the frame cracked. The spear was gone, but Christian was able to kick the wooden floor out and run.

As Akash grabbed a dagger, Christian sprinted for the parked vehicles. He was wounded and still not as strong as Akash. He jumped into a pickup truck and punched his fist through the thin plastic that protected the ignition. With a twist of his wrist, he broke the lock and turned the ignition switch. The engine roared to life and he grabbed the gearshift.

Before he could move, Akash smashed in the driver side window. Glass went flying in all directions, and with a quick stabbing motion he speared Christian's shoulder.

Christian dodged another strike as the dagger impaled the seat. He turned and kicked the driver's door open, flinging Akash onto the sand.

Before Akash could get up, Christian slammed the transmission into drive and floored it.

Akash ran after him and jumped into the bed of the truck. He smashed the back window and started to climb into the cabin. Christian slammed on the brakes and Akash flew forward, off of the truck and out onto the sand. Even before Akash hit the ground, Christian was stomping on the gas again. The tires kicked up long tails of sand as the truck sped forward.

Akash looked up to see the truck barreling straight for him. He moved too late. The truck hit him, center of mass, but instead of getting ground underneath the tires, he held on and began punching his hands through the sheet metal trying to ruin the engine.

Christian spun the wheel to the left and then the right, skidding through the desert, trying to shake Akash off, until he saw what he needed. He turned hard to the right, kept the pedal floored and drove full speed into a rocky outcropping behind the tents.

The airbags in the truck went off along with the sound of crunching metal and breaking bones. Even the stone hard ribs of a demon couldn't survive that impact.

Christian was knocked out himself and came to amid a fog of white dust from the airbag's explosives. The pickup was smoldering and belching steam, the smell of gas, oil and other fluids permeated the air.

Christian pushed the deflating airbag off of him and stumbled out and onto the ground. He lay there in the dark, trying to recover from the bone shattering crash. When he finally gained the strength to stand, he found Akash pinned between the rock and the mangled piece of metal that use to be the truck's V-8 engine.

Incredibly, Akash was still alive and moving. Like a bug half-squashed under someone's foot, his arms and legs were failing around.

As Christian looked him over, Akash tried to speak, but nothing came out. Christian shook his head. He couldn't leave Akash like this, not even one as evil as he deserved a death that painful.

He looked for any type of object to put him out of his misery and then ripped a small metal rod out from the suspension. He walked over to the dying vampire, raised the piece of metal in the air, but held off as he listened to Akash began mumbling something to himself, over and over again.

Christian couldn't make out the words but he guessed what they meant. Akash was praying for mercy or life or forgiveness.

As he listened to the incoherent words, Christian thought back to what James Hecht had said. Hecht was right, Drake was the evil thread that all this misery came from. He'd found a damaged soul in Akash and twisted him further, turning him from a broken child into this murderous thing.

Everyone has to answer for their own choices, Christian reasoned, even one with a history as dreadful as Akash's, but Drake was the deceiver leading them down the dark path.

As the stream of incoherent words faded, Christian prepared to finish Akash off. Whatever God he was praying to, at the end, Christian hoped He heard him.

The Half Life

With a deep breath Christian thrust the lance forward. It hit home and instantly Akash erupted into flames.

Christian turned and walked away. He was sick of death and dying, but he knew that the war must go on. He was exhausted and battered, but he would continue because he had to. In the end, he was a soldier.

Chapter 42

Christian limped his way back to the camp and spotted movement in the tent. He found Fahad, trying desperately to load a rifle. His face was bloody; one eye was swollen and half closed. He held the rifle weakly in the crook of one arm.

"That won't do you much good," Christian said.

Fahad raised the weapon. "These men were my brothers," he spat, almost sobbing.

"I'm sorry for them," Christian said. "Trust me, I've lost more brothers than you could possibly imagine."

"I will not let you go," Fahad said, finally getting the magazine into the slot and pulling back the slide on the rifle.

Christian ignored Fahad and put his hand on the door of another vehicle.

"You will not leave!" Fahad shouted, stumbling forward and raising the rifle almost to Christian's face.

Christian turned and snatched the rifle from Fahad's hand before he could fire. He tossed it away.

"It is my task to protect the stone," Fahad said, falling back. "I must not fail."

It dawned on Christian that Fahad could become a powerful ally in this last leg of the race. Obviously, he knew the way to the ruins and the location of the Dark Star. But Christian was done taking on allies only to have them killed right in front of him.

He turned from the truck, and sat Fahad down. The man was bleeding from a pair of stab wounds in the side, he was bruised all over and probably suffering from a concussion.

"You're fortunate," Christian said. "The blood is bright red. It's not coming from your stomach or your liver."

"What are you doing?" Fahad asked.

"Saving your life."

With no anesthetic, Christian needed a way to numb Fahad's pain. He looked into his eyes, fought with Fahad for control, and then numbed his senses. In a trance-like state, Christian worked on his former captor. He used boiling water to clean the wound and then stitched up a layer of muscle and closed the skin.

As Fahad sat there, Christian probed his mind. He saw the way to ruins, a place the group called the House of the Sultan, though it was no house. He saw the entrance, discovered the booby traps, the maze and the flood waiting to happen. "Quite a set up," he mentioned.

When the wound was closed, Christian released Fahad from his trance, stood and washed the blood from his hands. Strangely, it had no effect on him. It was just blood, nothing mystical, nothing different than what he'd seen spilled all over the world his entire life.

"What shall I do now?" Fahad said, still disoriented from the trance.

Christian moved to the nearest SUV and pulled open the door. "Go home," he said. "And pray that I find this stone of power before the Akash's friends do, otherwise there'll be no hope for any of us."

Chapter 43

Christian pulled the SUV to a stop. He'd come upon fresh tracks in the lakebed - five, maybe six vehicles.

He followed the tracks to the far side of the dry lake. Detouring to hide the SUV, he then went on foot. He was close. He'd seen a canyon in Fahad's mind, though more than one ravine cut through the foothills.

Instead of walking in the valley, he took the high ground and noticed that the tracks continued forward. He could tell by the look of the stony walls around them that the convoy had gone in the wrong direction. They'd taken the wrong fork.

Good, he thought. Whoever it was they'd be lost for hours.

He was about to turn when he sensed something that surprised him.

Kate. Kate was with them.

* * *

John Wellington drove the lead vehicle as the lead team from the Righteous Fire came upon a ruined Bedouin camp in the desert.

"What happened here?" one of the men asked.

"Nothing good," Wellington replied, pulling a radio from the dashboard. "Stop the convoy," he said. "We need to check this out."

He pulled up to a shredded tent, parked and stepped out.

"Should we put our armor on?" one of the crew asked.

Panning his flashlight around, Wellington shook his head. "Whatever happened here, it's over. Fan out."

He stepped away from the truck, pistol in one hand, long knife resting in a sheath diagonally across his chest. He found one body in the sand, another just outside the tent.

As he poked around one of his men called out.

"What do you make of this?" The man was pointing to a collapsed cage, lying on the desert floor. A second cage just like it sat upright in the back of a truck.

Wellington wasn't sure. "A cage for animals maybe? Looks like one of them got out."

He stepped into the tent and found a dozen more bodies, slashed and ripped apart.

"Look at this," a shout came from outside.

John made his way out of the tent and found his men gathered around a wrecked vehicle a hundred yards away. The front end was crumpled where it'd been driven into a wall of boulders. But it was the pile of gray ash beneath the bumper and the engine block melted into sludge that confirmed what he'd guessed.

John put his hand in the ash, rubbing some of it between his fingers. "Still hot," he said, flicking the soot away as if it were filth. "Animals alright. One of *the Fallen* burned here."

The men looked at him. This was his first command.

"We need to get back on the road," he said, firmly.

"What about the bodies? Should we bury them?"

"No time," he said. "Radio Henrick. Give him our position and heading. Tell him the demons are ahead of us and we're moving forward. We'll do everything we can to catch them. But he'd better hurry or he's going to miss all the fun."

* * *

Upon sensing Kate's presence, Christian immediately dropped to the ground, hiding himself physically and mentally.

Through meditation and powerful concentration the Fallen could either reach out to other members of their kind—especially those they created or were created by—or they could do the opposite and mask their presence. Of the two it was harder to hide, the way absolute stillness was harder to prolong than continuous movement, but Christian had become a master at it. As had Drake and his clan.

Until they bumped into each other, or until either one of them wanted to be felt, they would be concealed from one another as if shrouded in invisible cloaks. But Kate was another story. She was still in the Half-Life. She barely understood what was happening to her. She was barely far enough along to grasp the powers she'd been given, let alone master them. As such, her presence was radiating like a beacon.

Christian focused in on her; he could tell she was in tremendous pain, physically as well as emotionally. She was dying and, worse, she wanted to die.

Just let me go. Just get it over with.

It seemed as if she was being threatened, but he could sense that the turmoil was in her mind. The demons she was fighting were inside. She'd been beaten severely, coerced and tortured, but what she felt now was fear, fear for her son.

Kate…

He allowed the thought to escape like a whisper.

Kate… I'm here.

Christian remained still. As if connected to her, he could feel her heart begin to race.

I'm here. And I can help you.

He hoped she could sense him clearly enough to reply. He hoped her mind was not too broken to focus.

Christian?

It was a thought. A hope against hope.

I'm here.

Her heart began to pound.

Hurry. They've left me here. I'm alone.

Christian was up like a shot and scrambling over the rocks. A minute later he came upon the parked vehicles of Drake's convoy. Far up ahead he could see movement in the canyon. The path had become too narrow for the vehicles. Drake had taken his force forward on foot.

Christian picked his way down the rock face will all possible speed. Kate was chained up. Palladium. And she wasn't quite alone. Sitting on the hood of one SUV was Tereza, the one who'd slashed Akash's face.

Her eyes went wide with surprise as she spotted Christian. She tried to shout a warning, but Christian locked her mind up in a violent mental attack, casting upon her all the anger he'd felt at losing friends over the past few days.

She tried to fend him off, but the attack was too fierce. Clutching her head she fell off the hood. Christian would have killed her, but the fire would have brought the others. Instead, he found a gauntlet, pulled the chains off of Kate and wrapped them around her. As he chained Tereza up, Kate swarmed in and began punching her. She slammed her fist into Tereza's face twice and kicked her in the stomach before Christian could block her.

"Stop," Christian shouted, pushing her away.

"You don't know what they did to me," Kate shouted, tears filling her eyes. Apparently she was still human enough to cry. "They took everything I believed in, everything I loved. They made me watch my husband die, over and over again."

As she spoke, Kate lunged forward again and grasped Tereza's throat as if she would rip it apart.

Christian pulled her hands loose and threw Kate to the ground.

"You want to kill her and bring them all running back here?" he said sharply. "Do you? I don't know about you, but I don't have enough left in the tank to fight them right now, so get it together. We don't have much time."

Kate calmed a bit, her eyes going from Tereza to Christian and then back again. Her chest was heaving, but she seemed to be regaining some control.

"Ready?" Christian said.

Kate stood slowly and calmly, and then she lunged forward and fired one more punch at Tereza, snapping her head back and knocking her cold.

"Okay," Kate said. "Now I'm ready."

Christian lifted Tereza from the ground and tossed her in the back of one of Drake's vehicles. He gagged her, covered her with a blanket and locked the doors. The palladium chains would sap her strength. The blanket would keep her from seeing which way they went even if she came to, but she'd wake up sooner or later and worm her way out or call for help.

Christian figured they had an hour at the most. Which was all the time until morning anyway. "Come on," he said. "It's not far now."

With Kate by his side, he made his way back to the fork in the canyon and followed the proper direction. As they moved down the canyon, the moon began to rise, painting the sands like snow in the wintertime.

"Are we leaving?" Kate asked.

"No," Christian said. "We're cutting to the front of the line. Drake's gone down the wrong path; no pun intended."

"He's evil," she said, shivering.

"I know."

"I tried to run," Kate said, almost apologetically, "but he caught me. A vampire named Artimous grabbed me..."

"It's not your fault."

Silence for a second and then, "Is Faust with you?"

"No," Christian said, sadly. "He's dead."

Kate's surprise suggested she hadn't seen into his mind yet. "I thought you got away?"

"We escaped the museum and made it to Rome," he said. "But the *Ignis Purgata* chased us. They shot him. Shot me actually, but the bullets went right through and killed him."

She looked at him strangely and then turned her eyes forward. For some reason this news seemed to make her numb. It was too much, he thought. He should have lied.

"Maybe you should have let me die," she said. "Back there in the bayou."

Christian understood that feeling. "No," he said. "I thought that once. But enough people have died. Too many. We're going to heal you. And we're going to get you back to your son. But to have any hope of success, we have to get to this weapon before Drake does. And to do that, you're going to need to stop talking and move faster."

They hustled on for a while in silence, but she didn't remain quiet for too long. "I've seen things I would never have wanted to see. I know things I never wanted to know. I saw my husband die."

"It's all an illusion Kate. Drake doesn't know how your husband died."

She looked at him strangely. "How would you know that?"

"Because he doesn't. He wasn't there. He just took what you knew and built a story around it, like those false psychics who ask a million questions and then run on with whatever you say to them. It's a ruse, a trick to break you. Whatever he showed you, don't trust it."

"You're sure he wasn't there?"

"Positive, Christian said. "Why would he be?"

She gave him another quizzical look, but he didn't have any more time to explain. They'd come to the ruins. "We're here," he said, stopping. "The House of the Sultan."

Chapter 44

*T*he ancients, Christian thought, *had chosen well.* The House of

the Sultan sat at the end of a box canyon on an oasis connected to an

aquifer. A trickle of water flowed through the canyon even now. Just

enough that scrub brush and desert grasses grew up in a narrow channel

on each side.

The main structure, the Great House of the Sultan itself, sat dark

and dilapidated, the wind making a hollow call as it blew through the

structure.

Christian stepped inside. The enormous doors had collapsed or

been destroyed many years ago.

"Which way?" Kate asked.

"Somewhere in the east wing is the entrance to the tunnels."

"How can you be so sure?"

"I know someone who's been here."

Navigating off of Fahad's memories, Christian found the entrance

to the stone staircase that led down into the labyrinth. Quickly down

the staircase they traveled. There were torches along the walls, but they

hadn't been lit in years. Christian grabbed one and put his lighter to it. The bone dry fibers of the torch lit up and the flames burst to life. He gave that one to Kate and then lit another one for himself.

Upon reaching the bottom, they entered a chamber with four pathways leading out into the abyss, but only one would take them to the Dark Star.

Kate moved to the path in the center.

"No!" Christian said. "That tunnel leads to a pit. One you can never climb out of, because the bottom is wider than the top."

He was looking around trying to match what he saw with the Guardian's memories. Suddenly it wasn't all that clear. Could it have been a trick Fahad played on him? He doubted it, just a long time since the man had been here.

And then he realized he didn't need Fahad's memories at all.

"It's the one on the far left."

"How do you know?" Kate asked.

"Because I can feel the power emanating from that tunnel."

Kate looked at him and then back. "But can you be sure? What about the second one?"

"The second one leads to a labyrinth which slowly changes. The stones move. Once you enter you can never again find your way out. The other two Fahad didn't elaborate on, but death in one form or another awaits all who enter them."

She looked unsure.

"Let yourself be still. You'll feel it too."

Kate held quiet for a moment and then nodded her head. The power source clearly reacted with the soul of the undead even more acutely than the living. It was like electricity coursing through the air to the Nosferatu.

"Let's go," she said.

Together they ventured inside, following the gradient of the rocky tunnel as it slowly pitched upwards. A small opening lay ahead.

This was it. He could feel it.

As they entered the chamber, the flaming torches they carried lit up the room. Part of the ceiling was like blocks of glass and it reflected and diffused the light.

The rest of the chamber was surprisingly sparse. Nothing in it was extravagant, except the golden chest that sat in the center, polished to a mirror-like shine.

Christian's eye lingered on that chest, not because of its simple golden beauty, but because of the power from within it. He could hear it, feel it, and taste it. It was like rain on the wind, like the throbbing of blood in the ears.

He took a step towards it, wondering how he could remove it without getting caught in the flood. Before he could decide what to do, something wrapped around his neck, pulled him back and whipped him off his feet.

The chain was palladium. He tried to shout, "Run… Kate run!" But only a raspy whisper came out.

He landed on the ground and looked back to see his attacker. Not the *Ignis Purgata*, not Drake or his minions or even Fahad and his

Guardians. It was Kate holding the ends tightly and strangling him with it.

She was yelling something at him, but he could hardly make it out.

"I saw you! I saw you kill him!" she shouted. "You bastard! You son of a bitch I saw you kill my husband!"

He tried to respond. "Not true!"

"Don't lie to me," she said. "I saw it with my own eyes!"

Drake had tricked her, bent her mind and left her for him to find.

She pulled a dagger out and stabbed down at him. He moved far enough to avoid a chest puncture, but it went into his arm. The dagger was made of palladium as well and Christian realized his second mistake. Kate was still half-human, the palladium would feel toxic to her, rough and charged electrically, but it wouldn't do to her what it was doing to him. He should have realized that when he found her. He should have realized it was a trap.

With his strength going, all he could do was weakly grab at her. "You've been tricked Kate," he gasped. "Drake lied to you."

"I saw it!"

"The vision was a lie."

"You said he wasn't there," Kate insisted. "You were so sure of it. Because you were there."

Christian twisted and squirmed, but she had him tight and her rage was giving her strength. "I had nothing to do with your husband's death. You know that." The words squeaked out. "I never met you until our paths crossed in New Orleans."

"Lies!" She twisted harder.

"Why… would… I…" he managed.

"I saw you," she shouted, crazed by the pain of the image. "You called out to him, and when he turned you stabbed him and cut his throat."

Christian managed to knock one of her hands from the chain, but only long enough to shout. "How could I call out to him? I don't know his name, even now I don't."

Kate looked confused for an instant.

"Search my mind—"

Whatever tiny window of reality had opened, it slammed shut with a great bang. She renewed her attack and began choking the life out of him. Christian began to blackout.

"Enough!" a voice called out.

The choking ended and the life was not strangled out of him, but he was weakened, bound and chained. Artimous and another vampire with whom he was unfamiliar came in. This new arrival wore African clothes and took the chains from Kate, holding them in unprotected hands like she had. He must have been in the Half-Life as well. Beyond these two he saw Tereza with her battered face, and their master, his old friend and enemy, Drakos the Deceiver.

"You've done well Katherine," Drake said. "You will avenge your husband yet."

Chapter 45

In Drake's presence Kate went still; she seemed almost catatonic. She sidled over to Tereza as if the two had bonded and she was some kind of pet. Christian could see the truth now. They'd broken her mind after all, found her greatest pain and used it against her. She wouldn't even look at him.

Drake, on the other hand, studied him with great curiosity, examining the stab wounds, the grime of the desert, the burned hands. "You look worse and worse every time I see you."

Christian couldn't deny that, nor could he deny that Drake looked better, stronger than he'd been in Amsterdam. Almost back to his old dominant self.

"I gave you a choice on the oil platform," Drake continued. "Rejoin me or die. You chose death, and that will be your fate today."

Christian was almost too weak to reply, but he spoke anyway. "It won't make you whole, Drake. Even if you burn all the churches of the world to the ground, you'll still be empty. You and I both know that."

"I beg to differ," Drake said, turning his attention to the golden chest on the altar. "Can you feel it? The power in this room? It abounds. And soon it shall abound in me. I will be… filled."

Christian could feel it. It was enough to distract him when he'd stepped into the room, enough to make him slightly dizzy even before Kate had attacked. He only hoped it was having the same effect on Drake. If it were enough to cloud his judgment, to trigger the synapses of avarice that burned so brightly in Drake's mind, then perhaps Drake would take it, release the flood and drown them all.

Drake broke the lock on the chest and eased the top upward. Then he stood, gazing down into the chest.

Christian could see the reflection in Drake's mind. A polished obsidian rock. It had the appearance of crystal, but midnight black in color. It was attached to a great, dark chain. The grip was made of ivory and had an inscription carved on it.

Take it… Christian willed.

Drake began to reach for it, stretching his fingers forward, trembling at the power he was about to receive.

Take it, it's yours…

Suddenly, Drake stopped. He pulled his hand back, got control of himself and realized the danger.

"Bring him here," he said pointing to Christian.

Artimous dragged Christian over to the podium.

"I should like to kill you," Drake said, "to give you a soldier's death. You deserve that much at least. But if I do, you'll burn to ashes and I won't have anything left to keep the weight on this podium after I remove the sphere. So instead, I'll leave you here trapped and buried. You will eventually die, of course, as the palladium slowly burns through your skin, but that cannot be helped."

He turned to Artimous. "Lift him."

Artimous heaved Christian's bound form up into the air as if he was a feather, and as Drake pulled the chest free, Artimous shoved Christian onto the altar-like platform.

The chest clanged to the ground, and Artimous wrapped the chains that bound Christian around a set of small hooks on the altar.

Even as he did, a strange sound echoed through the chamber like stone sliding across stone. A trickle of water began to flow from openings in the wall, coming in from all sides. But as the echo died, the water dwindled and then ceased altogether.

"Success," Drake said, grinning in the dark.

He reached into the open chest and gripped the weapon. He lifted it by the handle and the thick chain unfurled link by ominous link. The energy funneled like effervescent fire from the sphere to Drake and back again. Drake opened his mouth as if in pain or pleasure as the power flowed around and through him.

"Are you alright?" Artimous asked.

Drake shuddered for a moment as if it were too much, as if it would bring him to his knees, but he stayed upright and then stiffened again. When he looked at Christian, Drake's eyes were darker than ever. To Christian's surprise, his mind was strangely closed off. Not a thought, not a feeling, it was just blank.

"Now we go," Drake said to his disciples. Even his voice was altered, deeper and raspy.

They filed out one by one, with Kate and Tereza leaving at the last. Christian was left alone in the dark, chained to the rock and slowly dying. It would take days, but the palladium chains would burn through him like salt on slug. It would be a painful, excruciating death.

No, he thought. *No!*

With all the strength left in his body, Christian began to squirm and twist. The chains burned him anew with each movement, but he didn't stop.

No! Not like this!

He flopped about like a fish on the dock, throwing himself this way and that, until one of the chains slipped from the hook and he tumbled off the platform.

As he landed on the stone floor, the podium rose up and the floodgates in the ceiling opened. Water came pouring through; funneling toward him from eight different openings, thousands of gallons, crashing around him like heavy surf on the beach

White foam swirled across the walls and shot up around the altar like a geyser, before dropping back down again. Christian was swung around by the force of the water. He banged against the side of the stone pedestal, but was held fast as he was still attached to the second hook with the chains tangled around him.

The doors began to shut, but Christian managed to kick the golden chest and wedge it into the gap. The door, and whatever mechanism moved it, began to bend and crush the soft metal box, but with every inch of closure the mangled chest was jammed more permanently into the space.

The doors ground to a stop, leaving a two foot gap. The water swirled up and over the obstruction, pouring down the tunnel like a sluiceway in the heart of some great dam.

The sound of the floodgates opening had echoed down the passageway with an odd resonance. When Drake and his followers turned back, the rush of water caught them by surprise.

Because of the slope of the walkway and the narrowness of the tunnel, the flood came at them with swift vengeance. It hit hard, knocking all of them off their feet and sweeping them forward.

They were dumped out into the anteroom and tossed against the stairs. The water surged around them, foamy and white, and began draining through grates in the corners of the room, but it kept coming like a river.

Drake was up first, climbing onto the stairs.

Artimous was next. "Christian must have broken free. Gotten off the pedestal."

"Thank you for stating the obvious," Tereza grumbled. "You should have chained him better."

"We should go back and finish him," Artimous said.

"Can you wade uphill against a raging river?" she asked.

Artimous looked at the gushing water pouring out of the tunnel. He shook his head.

"Let him drown," Tereza replied. "We'll be rid of him just the same."

Drake said nothing. Their conversations were beneath him now. He was already moving up the stairs, striding with newfound purpose in his mind and the weapon in his right hand. He no longer cared about Christian, it was time to find the Angel, to destroy the abomination, to set right the balance of power and bring all those under his sway back into line.

Chapter 46

Drake walked toward the grand foyer of the Sultan's House with his mind set on destruction. The angel would be first and then the Church that had vexed him for two thousand years. Zwana, Tereza, Artimous and Kate were with him. A group of guardian Drones waited for them. But soon his entire army would gather and the moments of doubt in their minds would be erased by the power he now held, which all of them would feel.

He stepped through the doors out into the night and was hit with a wave of blue and purple light that blinded him instantly. He dropped to one knee, raising an arm over his eyes.

Artimous, Zwana and Kate were subdued seconds later. There was no sound except for a strange high pitched whirring and the audible cries of the four members of the Fallen.

The pain was intense. It seemed to come from the inside out. Drake had felt it before: daylight, but it was the middle of the night.

Tereza had come out last and unnoticed. She tried to run, but was hit in the back with some kind of barbed arrow connected to a line of high strength rope.

Drake heard her scream and saw her being dragged backward like a spear-fisherman's catch. She caught fire on the sand. Out in the canyon, he saw a dozen additional fires. More Drones killed and burning.

"Drakos, King of the Demons," an English voice shouted. "This is your end!"

A crossbow fired, the bolt flying directly for Drake's heart. Without thinking, he swung the Dark Star and knocked the bolt from the sky. A second bolt was deflected as well.

In a wave of anger beyond anything he'd ever felt, Drake stood and brought the Dark Star down in a crashing motion. The flail impacted the ground and sent out a shock wave that launched everyone in its path flying backwards.

The hunters landed on their backs.

"Get the Nova rifles back on him," the English voice yelled. "All of them on, Drakos!"

Three of the light weapons converged on him instantly. Two more came his way and then all of them. They burned for a second as the king of the dead stood in the combined beam of ten million candle power, but then the pain vanished and Drake seemed to be glowing darkly, gripping the Dark Star.

He raised the flail above his head, whirled it around twice and slammed it into the ground again. This time the shockwave not only knocked the men down, it blew the weapons of light apart in their hands and raised a cloud of dust between them.

Two of the closest hunters abandoned their rifles and charged, leading with the short serrated swords they so loved to use. They were clad in armor, looking more like machines or even the knights of medieval times whom Drake had fought seven hundred years ago.

Armor hadn't availed them much then, and it would be no different now. He swung the Dark Star and caught the first man in the chest. The blow crushed the armor, breaking the man, caving his ribs in with a single swing and snapping his spine. It sent his folded body flying through the air, out into the canyon beyond. The second man fared no better as Drake's return swing took off his helmeted skull.

By now some of the others had gotten their Nova rifles restarted. They aimed them Drake's way, but the light bent towards the Dark Star, where it was absorbed and extinguished.

With no thought in his mind except devastation, Drake waded into their lines and unleashed his wrath. They had no idea what they were facing. They simply couldn't comprehend the amount of power Drake now held.

He smashed through them in rapid succession, an unstoppable killing machine. Some of them used knives and spears while others resorted to the traditional guns they carried, firing entire magazines of palladium tipped bullets in vain.

Another crossbow bolt glanced off the handle of the weapon, and Drake got the feeling the Dark Star almost had a will of its own, a consciousness that was now joined with him. As if finally freed from its prison the weapon was unwilling to go back and would protect him from everything that came his way.

In a moment Drake had broken their ranks. The screams of the wounded and the dying flowed through the canyon. Some began to flee, but Drake chased them down. Smashing their helmeted heads into unrecognizable pulp, crushing their titanium armored bodies as easily as one steps on a small insect.

The Englishman was the last. He stood with his own sword, unwilling to flee. He even pulled off his helmet and charged. Drake smashed both his legs with a single blow, snapping them like matchsticks. With the man on the ground, Drake knocked the sword from his weakening hand and then brought the Dark Star down upon his skull.

It was over. Never in history had the *Ignis Purgata* caught him with such a force, and never had he crushed them so easily.

Drake turned to those behind him. "Follow me."

And without a word, or even a thought, they did just that.

Chapter 47

Back in the hidden chamber, Christian tried to squirm loose from the chains. They weren't locked but merely wrapped around him like a spider's thread. Still they proved too heavy to shirk off and too tightly wrapped to slip out of. The water rose slowly to a depth of several feet, but there it reached a point of equilibrium with as much flowing out through the door as there was coming in from above.

Unfortunately the equilibrium wouldn't last. He could see the flow of water wiggling the chest and the force of the doors continued to crush and tear at the soft gold. A section of it broke loose, the doors crushed the rest and the water began to rise once again.

Still in a sitting position, Christian tried to wedge himself upward. Pressing against the altar and leveraging himself to his feet, he'd almost reached a standing position when the swirling current pulled down.

He plunged beneath the churning surface, and gazed from one direction to another, looking for anything he could find that would help him break free.

He saw nothing.

With the buoyancy of the water buffeting him he tried once again to stand. He made it to his feet and popped his head out of the water. He inhaled a deep breath, managed to roll himself onto the altar and climb to his knees.

He stood, but with nothing to lean against he was at the mercy of the swirling current and as it reached above his waist, he became unstable and was knocked from his perch.

Hitting the water again and plunging deeper now, he drifted into the lower section of the room. He tried once more to get to the surface, but it was no use. His squirming soon became less frantic and he sank back to the bottom, exhausted. He hit the stone floor with a peaceful *bump*.

As he lay there, the rushing water no longer sounded like death; it was soothing, like a distant waterfall. Like the fountains in his garden in Rome.

He thought of Elsa. He hoped against hope that he would see her on the other side, but guessed that the boatman would be taking him to hell where he belonged. After all, he'd failed.

A calm feeling seemed to settle down on him. *At least it was over, one last meeting to have with his Maker and it was done.*

He began blacking out. Thinking of home. *It was time to go...*

He was so far gone, that he didn't notice the sudden change in the pull of the current, like a riptide or an undertow. He was swept along the floor, pulled violently through the widening gap of the doors and down the long tunnel.

He slid along it, bumping and banging the walls until he was spat out into the anteroom.

The water drained away to all corners of the room and when it was gone, Christian lay there on his side, coughing, sputtering and spitting out water.

The darkness was so complete and his body so exhausted by the fight that he couldn't see through it. Nor could he speak, even as the chains were unwrapped. Some unseen hand pulled them free and tossed them away. They rattled down the grate in one corner of the room and fell into the dark. Muted echoes reached them as they landed some distance below.

"Can you breathe?" a voice asked. "Are you alive?"

A light flashed on. A waterproof flashlight. Christian saw the face of a Bedouin. He wore a sad smile. It was Fahad.

"You *are* alive," Fahad said to him, helping Christian to sit.

Christian didn't have the energy to explain. Between the chains, the battle, the flooding waters and the despair, he was probably feeling the closest to death he'd felt in years. "What are you doing here, Fahad? I told you to go home."

"You also told me to pray that the evil ones wouldn't find the Sphere of Power. That you would find it and protect it. And with every prayer I offered, the same answer came back to me: *That's your job Fahad.*"

"You're too late," Christian said. "It's gone."

"I know," Fahad said. "I saw who took it and the destruction he brings. And my heart is filled with more fear than I can say."

"What do you mean?"

"Some men tried to stop him," Fahad said. "Westerners, Europeans. Twenty or so, with swords and guns and weapons of light. He destroyed them all. It was horrifying. He showed no mercy."

The Ignis Purgata, Christian thought. If ever he'd wished for the Righteous Fire to succeed it was then. But like him, they'd failed.

"Help me to my feet and then leave me," Christian said.

"I will help you." Fahad said. "But I will not leave."

"I'm going after Drake," Christian said. "I'm going after the stone."

Fahad nodded. "Yes, I would guess that. You want to retrieve it, but it's my task more than yours."

"You don't understand," Christian said.

"No," Fahad said, "it's you who fails to understand. Protecting the stone is *my reason for existing*, my reason for not taking my own life after this failure, after my father was killed days ago, and after my brothers and family were slaughtered. I will not rest, lest I disgrace their valiant sacrifice."

"That might be the *only* thing I do understand," Christian said. "Help me up."

With Fahad's help Christian stood, and together they made their way to the surface.

Out into the dark of the night, they found nothing but carnage. They passed beyond the ashes of Tereza and the Drones, beyond the bloody obliteration of the Righteous Fire's brave vanguard. They climbed up to the highest point on the wall of the canyon. In the distance, Christian saw the lights of Drake's convoy tracking across the sand with the stone and Kate still in their clutches.

Even in his battered, exhausted state, he considered going after Drake again. But with the weapon Drake now held it would be suicide.

Drake had done it, Christian thought. He'd found and taken the one thing on earth that might allow him to wrestle with God and his angels and somehow prevail. With the Dark Star in his hand, Drake would destroy the Angel of Redemption, obliterate hope from existence and crush any group that stood before him; including Christian, the *Ignis Purgata* and the Church itself. Drakos the Deceiver had become all but invincible.

"Now what?" Fahad said. "What will you do from here?"

"I need a weapon that can overcome the one Drake now holds."

"Does such a thing exist?" Fahad asked.

Christian wasn't sure. "There's a sword I was told about once," he said, thinking back to Simon and his fatal gamble in New Orleans. "A blade the Church calls the Sword of God. If there's anything on this earth that can counter the power of the Dark Star, that sword is it."

"How do we get our hands on it," Fahad asked.

That question was more apropos than Fahad could imagine. Even if Christian could find it—even if he could steal it from the very people who considered him the enemy of all mankind—it was highly possible that he'd be unable to wield such a weapon. *Unable even to touch it.* The Staff of Constantine had almost been too much.

"I don't know," he said, answering the question on both levels. "But we have to try. Otherwise humanity will fall into a dark age the likes of which has never been seen."

PULSE-POUNDING FICTION FROM

GRAHAM BROWN
and
SPENCER J. ANDREWS

The world stands on the brink of ruin...

A HIGH-TECH DETECTIVE IN
A FUTURE THAT NOBODY WANTED...

WHITE-HOT SUBMARINE WARFARE BY

JOHN R. MONTEITH

www.StealthBooks.Com

MAN AND MACHINE. SOLDIER AND DRONE.
WHERE DOES ONE END AND THE OTHER BEGIN?

THOMAS A. MAYS

War is hell, even if you're not pulling the trigger...

www.ingramcontent.com/pod-product-compliance
Lightning Source LLC
Chambersburg PA
CBHW051332250626
47155CB00007B/2566